catching Liam

Geneva Lee

🏛 IVY ESTATE

Ivy Estate Press P.O. Box 255 Keyport, WA 98345

Print ISBN-13: 978-1-945163-08-1

Cover Illustration © 2017 LuckyStep48/BigStockPhoto.

Cover Design © 2017 Date Book Designs.

catching Liam

Geneva Lee

🏛 IVY ESTATE

Also by Geneva Lee

THE ROYALS SAGA

Command Me

Conquer Me

Crown Me

Crave Me

Covet Me

Capture Me

Complete Me

THE GOOD GIRLS DON'T SERIES

Novels

Catching Liam

Teaching Roman

Novellas

Unwrapping Liam

STANDALONES AND NOVELLAS

The Sins That Bind Us

Two Week Turnaround

To E, G, & N,
for all the stories.

Prologue

Monday was boy catching night. A fact we'd established about two weeks into our freshman year. And this Monday was the first boy catching night of the season, following the start of fall classes at Olympic State, but tonight I was alone, putting on my best coral lipstick in a shade called Trouble, and silently cursing Cassie, who had already called to beg out, making up an excuse about a communications paper. I knew that meant Trevor wanted her to stay in. I'd written it off, because going boy catching with someone who was already caught was no fun. It still sucked though.

I pushed aside my disappointment as I wiggled my feet into my most impractical three-inch wedges. This was the closest I came to commitment—my shoes. Once they were chosen, I was married to them. It was one of our rules. We wouldn't be those girls who walked home barefoot from the bar. Because *gross*. I'd seen enough freshman puking on the sidewalks and guys taking a leak in alleys near Pine Street to know exactly what I'd be walking through. It was still warm in coastal Washington, so I shrugged on a slip of a dress and silently dared Jessica to cancel on me.

Tonight was going to be epic—no matter what.

I had no idea how right I was.

Chapter One

The scent of vanilla woke me up, which was pretty impossible because I owned nothing vanilla—no candles, no lotions, and certainly no extract. What junior does? Jess's and my galley kitchen barely had room for more than a pot and some Dixie cups, and then there was the fact that I was in bed. Jessica had begged out early from our usual Monday night plans to meet up with Brett, which meant I should be alone in the apartment.

I rolled over to discover the other side of my bed mussed up from its previous occupant. I sifted through memories of last night until I found him. Cute, but otherwise nondescript, although that could be a result of too many drinks and too little thinking. Although as more flashes of last night's activities replayed, I remembered that he had a truly stunning six-pack. If beer tasted like those abs looked, I would be a lifelong drinker.

An off-key rendition of a Mumford & Sons song further explained the smell wafting through my room.

This was not happening.

Struggling out of bed, I grabbed for a wadded t-shirt and pulled it over my head. I tied my hair into a messy pile on top of my head and decided to skip the bathroom and head straight to investigate the shenanigans occurring in my kitchen.

As I rounded the corner of our small two bedroom apartment, I froze in my tracks. Standing stark-ass naked in the middle of my kitchen was six feet of smoking hotness. I remembered he was cute, and he was. He had a good face. It wasn't the kind that would grace any movie posters, but it was symmetrical with a well-defined nose and a strong jawline. His eyes were a sky-blue and his dark blondish hair was untidy enough to look a little sexy. But his body was another story, right down to his absolutely perfect, carved-by-the-gods-themselves calves.

"Hello, beautiful." He had an accent. How had I forgotten that he had an accent? Mercifully, his name popped into my head as soon as he spoke. Liam. I guess that explained the accent. Even if I hadn't been looking to catch a boy last night, I wouldn't have been able to resist that trace of Scotland on his tongue.

I propped myself against the bar, leaning over to discover every dish in my kitchen strewn across the counter.

"That's a meat tenderizer," I said, reaching for the strange contraption my mother had *gifted* me for my apartment. It was one of my mom's particular talents to give me all the home goods she'd never used and make me feel obliged to keep them.

"Sorry, I'll clean up. But these will be worth it," he said as he held up a mixing bowl.

"You know it's common decency to just sneak out the door in the morning without destroying a girl's entire house."

"My mother raised me to be polite."

"This is polite?" I asked him.

"Making a beautiful woman breakfast after a night of debauchery is the definition of polite."

"You really don't have to," I started and then groaned as he pulled a carton of eggs from the fridge. This was my fault, I really should know better than to bring a boy home to a full fridge. I made a mental note to make sure it was empty before next week.

"You should never make waffles without eggs," he advised me as he cracked one into the bowl.

"Wait? We have a waffle-maker?" I asked. I looked around my kitchen, not entirely sure I was in the right house anymore. It seemed like my kitchen, down to the crocheted dish towels from my MeMa that skirted the hipster line well enough to look cool. It wasn't until my gaze landed on a carton of Chiclets that I relaxed.

"Technically you have two waffle-makers," he said, nodding to the stainless steel bowl in front of him, its gleaming surface reflecting back a tight set of abs.

"How very meta of you." I desperately hoped he hadn't caught me staring at his muscles on the mixing bowl. The quick cheep of a timer finally distracted me from them, er, him, but it wasn't the sound of the oven going off.

Liam noticed at the same time. "I have no clue what that is. It's been beeping for an hour or so."

"Shit!" I yelled as I scrambled toward the cabinet doing math in my head. One hour late equals—

Liam's arms interrupted my calculation and admittedly the sight of his very naked body distracted me as he pulled me to him. So what was another five minutes late at this point? Or ten, I thought, as his lips trailed along my throat. The scruff of his five o'clock shadow scratched softly against my skin, sending slight trembles of anticipation rippling along my neck. It was way too soon, yet way too long, before his mouth closed over mine, but when it did, I crushed my body into his, letting our hips lock together as eagerly as our lips. Liam's hands stole down my back and gripped my hips for a moment. They were strong and hot against my bare flesh and then they slid down further, cupping my ass and lifting me off the ground. I wrapped my legs around his waist as he set me against the counter.

Right onto the meat tenderizer.

"Ouch!" I yelped, throwing myself against him and away from the offending gadget. He caught me, stumbling back against the kitchen pantry as we collapsed in laughter.

"Maybe the kitchen isn't the best place for...." He wiggled his eyebrows—a clear invitation for a follow-up in the bedroom.

"The waffles," I reminded him.

"What waffles?" a sleepy voice called from the hall. "You made waffles?"

Liam's eyes widened and we both looked down at *all his glory*.

"Crap, Jess is home," I said, pushing back against the giggle bubbling up my throat.

"I can't wait to meet her," Liam said.

"Good, because you're about to." I tossed him one of MeMa's dishtowels. "Here! Cover up."

Liam covered himself, but given our very recent close encounter with the counter, it looked like he had pitched a small crocheted tent over his lower extremities.

"That's not going to work," he said, grinning at me. My stomach flip-flopped as he grabbed my hand and pulled me in front of him. Not three seconds later, Jess stumbled into the living room, rubbing her eyes which got large when they landed on me acting as Liam's fig leaf.

"Good morning!" she said brightly.

"I thought you were at Brett's," I said, trying hard to not get distracted by the naked Scottish boy behind me or by thoughts of poor MeMa's kitchen towel.

"Nope." She smiled wickedly at us. I'd somehow managed to prevent a boy from sleeping over for years. My freshman year boyfriend was probably the last, and that had only gone on for two or three weeks. Clearly, Jess was enjoying this a bit too much, especially because I had recently walked in on her and Brett on the couch. They weren't studying.

"I never heard you come in," I said in a weak voice. She wasn't going to be nice and excuse herself, which meant I was going to have to find a way to get her out of the room so Liam could get dressed.

And hopefully go home.

"I imagine you didn't," she said knowingly. "You seemed rather absorbed in your...activity."

"Jess—" I started, prepared to tell her to leave, even if she would pout about it the rest of the week.

"Would you like some breakfast?" Liam piped up, cutting me off. "I'm making waffles."

"I would *love* waffles," she said, her eyes fixed on mine. They glimmered with the kind of *I'm-dragging-this-out-as-long-as-possible* amusement that only a best friend can muster.

"Fan-tastic," I said. "The toilet is leaking again. Can you help me with it?"

It was the lamest excuse ever, and all three of us knew it. But Jess gestured for me to meet her in the bathroom, and I hurried after her, turning once to mouth a quick "sorry" to Liam. He waved it off, but I stopped in my bedroom, found his jeans and threw them into the living room before I followed Jess into the bathroom.

Jess crossed her thin arms over her chest and waited while I checked myself out in the mirror. It was totally unfair that Jess's blonde hair hung so perfectly straight first thing in the morning while my unruly dark waves looked like they had been through a hurricane. Everything about my best friend was precise and well-behaved down to her size six waist and her med school prospects. Meanwhile my curves were as out of control as my hair and my grades weren't much better.

"I hate my hair," I complained.

"You look fabulous," Jess said. "Your hair is so untamed, it's sexy, and you have that just-screwed glow about you."

I winked at her in the mirror, glad she'd noticed.

"Just tell me that just-screwed glow is not courtesy of the kitchen counter," she begged.

I lifted my shirt to show her the patterned dents on my butt cheek. "Saved by the meat tenderizer."

"Oh! Is that what you're supposed to do with it?" We both giggled, and I grabbed for a brush to run through my hair. My hands went momentarily limp, and I dropped it, cursing. The familiar frustration I felt with my body crept through me, turning my skin hot with anger and leaving blotches across my chest.

"It's okay," Jess said in a quiet voice. She picked up the brush and started to sweep it through my tangles, but I pulled away from her.

"Can you get rid of him?" I asked, and she nodded. No questions asked. Jess always understood.

"Make sure you take—"

"I know," I cut her off. "The more important thing right now is that there is a naked Scottish dude in our kitchen."

"Making waffles," she reminded me.

I rolled my eyes at her to show that I didn't care about Liam or his waffles or the feeling of his breath on my neck or wrapping my legs around his tight waist. No, I didn't care one bit.

"Fine," Jess said. "I'll get rid of him, but for the record, he seemed nice."

"You say that about all the boys."

"That is not true!" Jess whirled back toward me. "Most of them are—"

I pushed her out into the hallway and shut the door in her face. I didn't need one of Jess's lectures today. I already knew she was right about boys and school and everything else, because Jess had her shit together. She had a future. But Jess couldn't see the gray space my life occupied, even if she tried harder than anyone else. Although, she was wrong about one thing: a nice guy wasn't going to fix me.

Besides, I wasn't interested in catching for keeps, but when I thought of Liam's lopsided grin and unearthly body, I almost changed my mind.

Chapter Two

※☆※

Jess was sitting at the bar when I bounded down the hallway a few minutes later. I'd successfully tamed my hair, but I was still undressed, unmedicated, and unfed. Unfortunately, there was a shirtless Scot handing Jess a plate of waffles. I glared from across the room, focusing all my energy on getting her to turn and look at me.

"I'm here on a student visa. It's only for the year, but I wouldn't mind staying longer," he told her.

"And you're from Edinburgh?" Jess asked him, but he laughed. "I'm butchering that name, right?"

"It's Ed-in-burr-oh," he said, pronouncing it slowly for emphasis. "It's the capitol of Scotland. We have the best artists and businesses."

"Except for America?" Jess teased.

"Anyone ever tell you Americans have a superiority complex?" he asked, but his damn accent made it sound sexy instead of insulting. Liam pushed himself up to sit on the counter. He must have put the meat tenderizer away.

"You said the best," she pointed out.

"I meant they're good. I'm not used to this American competitiveness." Liam winked at her, as in he actually winked like the charming love interest in a bad romantic comedy.

I shook my head to clear it of the dizzying effect his accent had on me. I didn't want pronunciation and geography lessons from Liam, I wanted him to leave. But the more Jess talked to him, the less likely he was going to.

Traitor. Traitor. Traitor. I hurled the word psychically as though she might be able to hear it in her head since I couldn't say it out loud.

But she didn't turn around, so I was forced to join them. I plastered a scowl across my face so she would know exactly how much trouble she was in.

"Hi, hen." Liam winked again, but since this time it was directed at me, I found it significantly less annoying.

"Did you just call me a chicken?" I asked.

Liam gave me a sheepish grin. "Sorry. It's like what you Americans say—baby?"

I clucked twice at him. "Keep digging the hole."

"Let me make you a plate," he said.

"I really shouldn't," I called, trying to stop him, but he was already pulling a fresh waffle from the mysterious waffle iron he'd discovered somewhere in the depths of our kitchen. "I have class in an hour."

"There's plenty of time," he said. "And a growing girl needs breakfast."

Jess's hand shot out and squeezed mine, reminding me to stay calm.

"Growing?" I repeated. Once you hit twenty, you only grew one direction.

"Shite. I keep putting my foot in my mouth, don't I?"

I could think of a few other places for him to put it. Thoughts like this are what Jess calls "putting up barriers to healthy relationships." She was an expert on such things after two semesters of psych class.

"Please, sit down," Liam begged. His eyes softened until he looked like a sad puppy.

I groaned but I pulled the stool out.

"Sorry," she mouthed as I sat down.

I ignored her. If I couldn't count on her to help me with pest control, I might have to revoke her best friend card. It's not like I put her in this situation a lot. I usually have a pretty good eye for the clingy types—the ones who want to take you out to dinner or actually talk about your major. I never brought those types home. I'd honestly thought Liam was looking for an American conquest, and why wouldn't I want to bag a Scot for my own bragging rights?

The buzz of a text message forced me to look over at her. I angled my head to see who she was texting, but the counter blocked my view. I reached over and made a play for the phone.

"Hey!" Jess elbowed me, but I caught her arm and

used my other hand to tickle her neck. It worked like a charm. Jess dropped the phone just like I knew she would, and I lunged for it. Liam was oblivious, too busy searching for a clean fork.

CASSIE: OMG, AND HE'S MAKING BREAK-FAST?!?! DON'T LET HER FUCK IT UP.

Above the text there was a fuzzy pic of Liam snapped when he wasn't looking. I waved the phone at her and stuck it in my pocket. I might want Liam to leave but I wasn't going to reveal that my crazy room-mate, and soon-to-be-former best friend, was taking pictures of him half-naked in my kitchen.

"Give it back," Jess whined.

"If you're good," I said, settling back onto my bar stool.

Liam placed a waffle in front of me. It looked suspiciously like there was butter and syrup on it.

"Did you buy groceries?" I asked Jess.

"I ran to the market," Liam said with a wave of the hand. "You didn't have any food in your flat."

"Because we don't cook," I said. Not only had he not run off this morning, he had come back, and with groceries, no less!

"We cook, Jills," Jess said, but I shot her a look that warned her not to encourage him.

I cut into the waffle and took a bite. Butter. Syrup. Vanilla. Despite myself, I moaned.

"Somebody likes your waffles," Jess said, smirking at me.

"I have a high proficiency in moan-inducing," Liam said without missing a beat.

Jess's eyes grew wide, and I swatted her across the back. "Don't choke."

"That's what she said," they both teased on cue.

The game of wit was interrupted by Taylor Swift belting out a song about breaking up. Liam snatched my phone up from the counter. "It says Tara."

"My mom. Ignore it. I'll call her back later," I said, grabbing it and hitting the ignore button. The last thing I needed right now was a chat with Tara.

"Jillian." Jess's voice held a familiar warning edge. She knew not taking a call from Tara was tantamount to raising the national security level. Of course, Jess had been there when the campus police knocked on my door sophomore year to check on a report of a missing person only to discover the missing person was at home, ignoring her mother's phone calls. My mom could be a tad too dramatic.

"I will call her later," I repeated. I turned my gaze on my friend and flashed her my phone. "Don't you need to get going?"

"Crap." Jess shoveled her last bite in her mouth and scrambled off her chair. "It was lovely to meet you, Liam. Feel free to come back and feed us anytime."

"I'd be happy to." Liam's lips curved into a crooked smile.

Damn, he was really cute.

As soon as Jess made for her bedroom, I grabbed my plate and dared entry into the kitchen.

"Are you sure you don't want seconds?" Liam asked. From his tone, I couldn't tell if we were talking about waffles or something else.

"The thing is that I don't go back for seconds," I said, putting my plate into the sink.

"Not even another waffle?" Liam asked. "I hear they're delicious."

"If your student visa runs out, you should get a job at the waffle house," I said.

"High praise from the snow queen!" he cried, scooping a waffle off the iron and buttering it.

"I am not a snow queen." Liam had known me all of five minutes. Apparently having sex with someone unlocked their innermost secrets now. "Why are you still here?"

"Not done with breakfast."

"And then you'll leave?" I asked.

"I have other plans after breakfast." He abandoned the slightly burned waffle and lunged for me. I stepped back, and he planted his hands on either side of the counter, trapping me between him and freedom. He was close enough to touch but he hovered just inches away.

"And they are?" I breathed.

"Warm up the snow queen."

"I'm not the snow—"

His lips were over mine before I finished the sentence. It didn't matter anyway as his arms circled around me, and I dissolved against him, momentarily too distracted by his mouth to think logically. Only my thin t-shirt lay between me and his coiled muscles, and when I ran my fingers down them, I could feel each rigidly cut ab. This was what people meant when they said washboard.

"What were you saying about seconds?" he whispered in my ear, nipping at it with his teeth.

"I never go back for them."

"Sure about that?" he asked.

His stubble tickled just behind my earlobe, raising goosebumps along my arms. I wrapped them around his neck and brushed my lips against his. "I guess there's a first time for everything."

But before he could kiss me back, I ducked out from his embrace.

"That's not fair," Liam said.

"Sorry." I tossed his wadded up t-shirt at him. "I have class."

I watched as he pulled the shirt over his head, admiring the way it tousled his light hair. I imagined running my fingers through it and skin and sweat and...

Class, I thought firmly.

"Why don't you skip today?" he suggested as he leaned against the counter. The tight knit of his shirt showcased his chiseled upper body. It didn't seem possible, but he might look even better with a shirt on. "We have to work off those waffles, and if you behave, I'll show you how I make a naked lunch."

"That's a book," I said automatically, forcing myself to look at his face and change the subject.

"I know."

God, I hoped he wasn't going to try to talk about it with me. I'd used an online study guide to squeak by on the test.

"I've never read it," he admitted, grinning sheepishly.

There was something insanely sexy about his confession. I'd encountered enough guys on campus who waxed philosophical to try to get into my pants. Liam, on the other hand, seemed smart without being pretentious, which made me want to jump him more.

A warning bell went off in my head.

"What do you say?"

I shook my head. "I can't."

"Forget about the work-out. We can just hang out."

It was a sweet offer, and I could tell by the way his blue eyes grew wide with hope that he was being sincere. Nothing sounded better than staying in bed with him for one last hurrah before I avoided him for the rest of the academic year, but this time I was telling the truth. I couldn't skip class. "It's not that. I have to maintain a certain grade point average or I'm outta here."

"Scholarship?" he asked. He sounded too interested.

"Something like that." I skirted around the question to avoid the twenty more questions it would raise. I'd learned a long time ago that it was easier to let people think I was dependent on financial aid than to explain the strange deal I had struck with my mother. "Look, I'm going to be late and I hate being late."

"I'll get out of your hair."

He leaned over and gave me a chaste kiss on the cheek, which I took as a sign that I'd finally won. I practically strutted over to the front door to let him out. At the last second, he turned to say something, but I cut him off with a firm "good-bye" and closed the door in his face.

As I locked it behind him, I couldn't help but wonder what he was about to tell me. Probably something cheesy like "thank you" or worse yet—"I'll call you." He might have even meant it.

For now.

"You don't have class for three hours," Jess said, startling me from my thoughts.

"He doesn't know that," I said as I pushed past her towards my bedroom.

"He's nice." Jess followed me, despite the fact that she did actually have a nine o'clock lab. Unlike my reduced schedule, Jess was taking more classes than two sane people combined.

"That's exactly why I wanted him to go," I said. He was nice. *Too nice.*

Jess opened her mouth and shut it again. She'd learned a long time ago this was one point I wouldn't budge on. Getting attached at the hip just meant heartbreak. It was better to get attached at the groin once and call it a good night.

"Call your mom," she finally said. "I've got to get to Anatomy."

"Enjoy!" I called. Jess didn't respond, so I knew she

was pissed at me, even though she'd dropped the issue. Later tonight, I would swipe her textbook and put naughty Post-It notes in it, labeling all the bodily organs with dirty words. She had enough stress in her life without me adding to it, but nothing cheered a girl up like a well-placed series of the-birds-and-the-bees inspired commentary in your Anatomy text.

When the front door locked, I picked up my phone and did the last thing I felt like doing. I called my mother. I figured I may as well get all the crappy stuff out of the way before 9 a.m. Besides, maybe she had more useless kitchen gadgets for me.

Chapter Three

✵

I got to my first Interpersonal Communications class in time to slide into a seat in the back. It was the perfect spot to guarantee that the professor wouldn't call on me to answer questions on chapters I wasn't going to read. I unpacked my laptop and popped onto Facebook. Jess had recommended the class, but Cassie, who was majoring in Public Relations, was the one who had assured me it would be cake and that I would have plenty of time to screw around online. I was well into checking status updates from my friends, many of whom I hadn't seen since summer vacation ended, when the professor walked in.

"Good afternoon, or should I say good morning? I'm Professor Markson," he said as he pulled a stack of stapled papers from his messenger bag. He was in his late twenties but wore a sweater vest in a bid to gain the respect of students that weren't much his junior and probably to hide the fact that he was otherwise gorgeous. Maybe Hispanic, I couldn't be sure with the distraction of the horrible sweater. Regardless, I could guess why Jess found the class so interesting.

There was a smattering of appreciative laughs throughout the room. It was well-established on the Olympic State campus that you shouldn't plan a Thursday morning class. Everyone went out on Wednesday nights, so the earliest acceptable class time was after noon, preferably later if you were someone like me. But this semester, I couldn't do any better than twelve, so I went with it.

"I'm sure a lot of you are hoping for an easy A this semester, and I'm happy to grant you that," the professor continued. I perked up. This was very good news.

"But—"

Crap, there was always a but. This didn't bode well.

"I'm going to make you work for that A while you are in class." He smiled as several people groaned. "First of all, they've given us a really big classroom, so I'm going to ask all of you who snuck into the back to move up and join the rest of us."

This time I was the one who groaned, but I grabbed my laptop and bag and found a seat near the front of the room.

"You'll be working with partners this semester, so take a look to your left or right and find your new best friend."

I did as I was told, but as I turned my head I found

myself face to face with Liam. He was grinning, his arms folded behind his head, looking rather triumphant. He'd tamed his hair, but a few pieces stuck up, and I liked to think I'd given him a case of unbreakable bedhead.

"Hey, chicken," he said.

I immediately looked to the other side of me and found the chair empty.

"My name is Jillian," I reminded him, turning back to him.

"I know. Sorry, I won't call you chicken anymore." He looked a little hurt, which made him look a little sexy. Fantastic.

I immediately began to think of all the ways I was going to murder Jess for suggesting this class. Strangling? Too nice. Hit and run? Too much work. I finally landed on spoon just as a syllabus slid onto the desk in front of me.

"You two will be partners," Markson said.

I wanted to thank him for the reminder, but I was too busy trying to avoid eye contact with Liam.

"As you can see, there are a variety of exercises you will work through with your partner in class. If you're lucky, you will each have landed with someone who actually does the reading, but the statistics aren't in your favor. So may I suggest you do the readings just in case?"

I scanned the syllabus and realized with horror that the final wasn't going to be a test but a conversation in front of the whole class with my partner. I was sure they'd be thrilled to listen in on Liam and I debating our one-night stand. I imagined how it would go down. In my head, the entire argument came down to the meat tenderizer. Or maybe the mysterious waffle iron.

"This doesn't look bad," Liam said, scooting his desk a bit closer to mine.

"I'm dropping this class," I announced.

"You'd go that far to avoid talking to me, huh?" Liam asked. "You're going to give me a complex. Am I that bad in bed?"

The answer was definitely not, so I kept it to myself.

"I was told this class was easy," I said. I didn't actually want to hurt his feelings, but I didn't want to encourage them either.

"It looks easy. We'll learn to communicate better."

"I can talk already. Thanks," I said.

"But if you talked to me, I could convince you that waking up to my waffles is a good life decision," Liam said.

A figure coughed, and we looked up to see Professor Markson watching us.

"Yes?" I asked. If I was going to drop the class, I didn't feel the need to be polite. After all, he had screwed up my chance at a nice easy class this semester. The rest of my schedule looked tough, and I was already getting flak for having no declared major. Not that it mattered.

"I had some notes for you on your interaction," he

said to us. "It seems that she isn't very open to your overtures."

I almost choked on my own spit by gasping so hard at his boldness. By now the whole class had turned to stare at us.

"Actually, mate, she's not," Liam said with a grin. "I'd love some pointers."

"You keep using YOU statements when you try to convince her to give you a chance," Markson pointed out. "I noticed you saying things like 'you should.'"

"So?" I asked him. I couldn't believe he was actually meddling with my love life in front of twenty other students.

"It's making you defensive. Look how you're reacting to my critique," he said to me.

"You're embarrassing me," I said. "That's why I'm reacting to your critique."

"That's another YOU statement."

"What exactly is a YOU statement?" Liam asked. He leaned forward, and I got a glimpse of his glorious arms. I wondered if his ego was half as big as his biceps.

"Instead of couching a statement in how you feel, you make an assumption about what the other person is doing or why. Often, it's when you accuse someone of acting a certain way."

"So like when I accused you of being totally up in my business?" I asked.

Professor Markson laughed nervously, adjusting his petite bow tie. "Fair enough. But I'm trying to use you as an example."

"I'm a student. Not a lab rat," I muttered.

"When you communicate how someone's actions are affecting you, say 'I feel like you're embarrassing me in front of the class.' It sounds less accusative, yes? And you—" he gestured to Liam— "might say 'I feel like you're avoiding talking to me.' This opens up a direct line of conversation through which you can more effectively communicate and resolve issues."

He really wasn't going to drop this. I spotted more than a few of my classmates covering their smiles behind their syllabi. Fine, two could play this game.

"Okay, I think I get it," I said. "I feel like this is pointless."

Markson tipped his head to the side. "Do you? That's a shame. It will be essential for your careers and domestic life to be able to communicate your needs."

Liam raised his hand. "I would like to state that I feel I would like to communicate effectively with Jillian."

"Then why don't you try again?" Markson suggested.

I hid my face in my hands as Liam swiveled to face me in his seat. I could feel the eyes of everyone in the class on us.

"I feel like I'd like to make you waffles in the morning and maybe the morning after, too. I feel strongly I could be convinced to make you waffles for a very long stretch of the foreseeable future," he said.

The class broke out in a fit of applause. More than a few people whooped their approval of his "I" statements. One girl even yelled, "You can make me waffles anytime!"

"Now how do you want to respond, Miss...?" Markson trailed off.

"Nichols," I said. "Okay. I feel like I'm dropping this class." I scooped up my things and made a beeline for the door. This drew some boos, although a few kind souls yelled for me to come back.

No way was I going to stay there to be humiliated in the name of Interpersonal Communication. I slammed through the doors at the end of the hall and found myself in the building's entrance when my phone rang. I fished it out of my pocket and, when I saw Tara on the caller ID, decided I was properly worked up to handle a conversation with my mother.

"Hi, Tara," I said as I answered the call. I could almost hear the wince on the other end when I called her by her first name.

"Jillian," my mother said, extending my name as though it was a drawn out thought. I often wondered if she was actually puzzling out why she was on the phone with me when she started a conversation this way. "How is the first day?"

"Fan-fucking-tastic," I snapped.

"Language, Jillian."

I had to disappoint her at least four times every phone call, so I ticked off one mentally.

I'm not sure why she would care how my day was. Tara had no interest in seeing me graduate from college, and she'd made her feelings on the matter known on multiple occasions.

She didn't notice the annoyance I had *so carefully*displayed in my answer. She never did. Instead, she immediately switched to business mode. "Your father received the bill for tuition. You're only taking twelve credit hours."

"For someone who keeps advising me to drop out, I would think you would be thrilled I'm taking a lighter course load this semester," I said as I wedged the phone so I could shove my laptop back in my bag.

"Your father and I want to know that this isn't a waste of time," she said.

"You want to know it isn't a waste of money," I corrected her.

"You know what they say about time and money," she said. This was my mother's idea of a joke but neither of us laughed.

"If you want, I'll just get loans," I said. This wasn't really about money, because my parents were loaded. It was just another instance of Tara attempting to control my life.

"Don't be dramatic," she said in a flat voice.

"You're the one who called me on my first day of classes to criticize me!" I was really getting it on all sides right now. I could imagine Markson would have a lot to say about my mother's and my interpersonal communication.

"I want to know you are taking care of yourself. If

you feel you can only handle twelve credit hours, maybe you should consider—"

"Mom," I cut her off. "I have to get to class. I'll email you later."

"Fine." The call ended without an *I love you* or a *talk to you later*. Just like every other conversation I'd ever had with Tara.

Someone tapped me on the shoulder, and I jerked around to discover Liam standing behind me.

"I'm sorry for what happened back there," he said. "I promise if you come back to class that I will defend your honor and tell Markson to bugger off."

Despite my foul mood, his proficient use of UK slang made me smile. It went well with his accent.

"A smile!" His face lit up all the way to his bright blue eyes. "Does that mean you accept my apology?"

"Don't push it," I muttered.

"If you don't come back to class, I will be forced to work with Markson on my communication skills," he warned.

"That would be a fitting punishment for going along with him," I said as I slung my bag over my shoulder.

"Or worse yet," Liam said, "I could remain partner-less and be forced to cultivate multiple personalities to effectively learn to communicate and then I would wind up alone and talking to myself."

"I'm sure one of the other girls will save you from that fate worse than death," I said. "Listen, there's no way I'm going back in there. It was humiliating."

I hated to admit this to him, but it was the truth and since I wasn't going to see him after today, it didn't matter if I told him. I didn't bother to add that I'd had my fair share of embarrassing experiences in the classrooms of Olympic State. I really didn't need my professor to tack on any additional indignities for the sake of higher learning.

"You made your point. I think you shamed poor Markson. He barely finished going over the syllabus before he let us go," Liam said.

Good, I thought. At the same time, I gave Liam a defiant shake of my head. "No deal."

"Okay, let's compromise," Liam said. "I won't ask you out again if you come back. It will be strictly academic."

I took one look at his crooked grin and wondered if he could keep his own promise.

"I'll think about it," I said.

Liam leaned in to whisper in my ear. "Here's the catch. If you don't come back to class, I will be forced to sing at your window and write you bad poetry until you do."

I glanced at his face and realized he was serious.

"You really do need to work on your communication," I said. "If you're going to threaten me with bad poetry to get me to talk to you."

"Every girl's nightmare?" he asked.

I'm guessing it was more than a few girls' fantasy. Not mine though.

"I'll see you on Thursday," I said finally.

If seeing Liam two days a week would cement him firmly into the friend category, I was willing to put up with Markson.

"Oh, piece of advice?" he called as I pushed open the exit. "Use more 'I' statements with your mom."

I tossed my hair over my shoulder, deciding to ignore him, but I couldn't help but throw one last look at him as I backed through the door. All he did was wink.

Chapter Four

Tuesday nights at Garrett's were dead except for people dropping in for dinner. The pizzas were from a box, but the food was cheap and we'd gotten into the habit of going every week since we were freshman. The pub boasted a dance floor and a deejay on busy nights. A few people filtered in and out, but we had the place mostly to ourselves.

Cassie and Jess were busy comparing notes for their courses. Since Cassie was a Public Relations major, she was freaking out over her last required core science course, while Jess promised to help her. As they discussed labs and tests, I thought about my mom and her threat earlier today. Once again, Tara was hinting that she wanted me to drop out and come home. I wasn't sure it was worth telling them, though. Jess would worry about it, and then she would become unbearable if I was so much as ten minutes late to class.

I sat wedged into the corner booth, not saying a word for fifteen minutes before they noticed. Between the scene in Interpersonal Communications and my less than pleasant conversation with my mother, I didn't feel like talking.

"How was your communications class?" Cassie finally asked. Whereas I had slipped into pajama pants before heading out with them, Cassie was perfectly polished. Her black hair was tucked in a neat bun. Her outfit looked like a fashion tutorial from Pinterest, complete with chic suede boots and chunky, handmade jewelry. She looked like she had walked off a runway, not out of a classroom at Olympic State.

I shook my head. "I'm dropping it."

"You only have a 12 hour load," Jess reminded me.

"I can't stay in the class. The professor humiliated me."

"Shit, I thought you were taking that with Markson. I heard he was a goddamn cakewalk." Cassie cursed like it was art form. She had managed to make it a required syntactical component.

I shrugged at her while Jess stayed silent. She had recommended the class after she took it last semester, and now I couldn't help but wonder if she was trying to tell me something.

Frank, Garrett's longest running bartender, slid a combo pizza in front of us. "That's hot," he warned us.

On cue, we all busted out, "That's what she said."

"You girls staying out of trouble this year?" he

asked. Frank was old enough to be our grandfather, and he took the role seriously.

"It's too early in the year to determine that," I said to him with a sly smile. He shook his head, muttering under his breath as he headed back to the bar.

"How did he humiliate you?" Jess asked, grabbing for a slice of pizza.

"It was just Markson," I admitted, ignoring my own food.

"Intriguing," Cassie said.

"Liam was there."

"Wait, *Liam*, Liam?" Cassie asked with a squeal.

"You have not even met Liam," I pointed out. She had no business being this wildly excited by a bad camera pic.

"Well," Jess said, "she's about to."

I followed Jess's gaze behind us to spot Liam walking into the bar with a few other guys. He was still in a t-shirt and jeans, and I couldn't help but admire how they hung off his hips. I knew what was under those jeans. My pulse increased just thinking about it, and I could feel heat creeping onto my cheeks. I wasn't sure why I was so embarrassed. It was hardly the first time I'd run into a guy I had slept with casually.

"Great Scot! Liam's hot!" Cassie said in a low voice.

"Cassie, darling, you're rhyming." But I could see how his body would have that effect on her. Liam looked every bit the Scottish Highlander fantasy at the moment—rugged and well-built, but without the kilt or long hair.

"Call him over," Cassie begged.

"No freakin' way," I said in a warning tone. "You have a boyfriend."

"You don't," Jess said.

I shot her my best withering stare. Ever since Cassie and Jess started seeing their boyfriends, they'd been sneaking plenty of hints about hooking me up with someone. The wicked gleam in Jess's eyes suggested that she wanted to make this dream a reality. "Markson made an example of us in class today. I don't need to give Liam any more false hope."

"False hope?" Jess said, and her eyes sparkled as she spoke. "Don't you think you've gone a little too far to not expect him to be hopeful?"

"I swear to God, if every guy I screw is going to expect a relationship, I'm going to have to start an application process," I muttered.

Cassie's and Jess's eyes grew wide, and my heart sunk into my stomach.

"He's right behind me, isn't he?" I asked.

They both nodded, discomfort written across their faces.

"Jess," Liam said in a cool voice.

I couldn't bring myself to turn and face him. He had definitely heard what I just said. I considered crawling under the table, but Garrett's wasn't the cleanest establishment and I would probably contract some type of STD.

"It's nice to see you," Jess said as she tried to smile. It came out looking more like a grimace.

Liam didn't say anything else, and, a minute later, Cassie and Jess both collapsed against each other, signaling he was safely out of earshot.

"Ohmigod, awkward!" Cassie exclaimed against Jess's shoulder.

"You should have been in class," I said with a groan. I picked up my pizza and then set it right back down. I suddenly wasn't very hungry.

"What exactly happened?" Jess asked, widening her eyes in concern. The ones that made her look like Bambi; they were impossible to resist.

I related the events of the class with Professor Markson, pausing occasionally to allow them to express their horror. But by the end of my story, I could tell they were both holding back smirks.

"You two are unbelievable. Show a little moral support, why don't you?" I said. I hadn't bothered to fill them in on my phone call with my mother or how Liam had heard half of it. I didn't like to expose that side of myself to them. Jess worried more than my mother, although her heart was in a much better place.

"It's just that we kind of agree with Markson," Jess admitted.

I picked a piece of sausage off my slice and threw it at her.

"No food fights!" Frank yelled from the bar.

"Nothing gets past him," Cassie said. She smiled sweetly at him and called out an apology. No one could resist Cassie's charm, not even nosy old Frank. But

Cassie's easy-going nature also made it hard to get her to take anything seriously. Jess and Cassie were the perfect foils for one another. They both cared, but they displayed it from opposite ends of the friend spectrum.

"I don't need my professor getting involved with my love life," I said.

"What fucking love life?" Cassie asked and froze. It was a totally un-Cassie-like thing to say, and it stung.

"I don't need a boy to feel complete," I said. "Unlike some."

Jess held her hand up. "That is totally unfair. We never make you feel bad for not wanting a boyfriend. You shouldn't make us feel bad for dating."

"You made me feel bad this morning," I reminded her. I reached for my purse and pulled it over my head. "You made me feel bad five minutes ago." I stood up so quickly that I knocked my chair over. I couldn't even bend over to pick it up, I was shaking so bad.

"Dammit, Jills," Cassie said. "Don't do this. Calm down. It's not good for—"

"Stop," I commanded her. "Just stop. I'm going home."

"Jills, you need to take—" Jess began, but I shot her a look that shut her up.

I turned on my heel and started toward the door. Unfortunately, going by the door meant that I would have to go by Liam. I hesitated a minute before I lifted my chin and took a deep breath. Olympic State was a small school, and I was bound to run into him, even if I dropped the class. I focused on the door, walking a straight line toward it with quick, purposeful steps. My hands were trembling, and I clenched and unclenched them, trying to control it like I'd been taught in physical therapy.

"Bye, hen," Liam called, the farewell coated in an especially thick Scottish brogue. I knew he was doing it to get a rise out of me. He probably wanted to get back at me for what I'd said earlier, but I hadn't been talking to him then, so he had no right to be mad now.

I rounded on him and held up one shaky finger. "I am not a chicken. I am not your chicken. So take your cock somewhere else."

One of Liam's friends smacked him on the shoulder, laughing, until he realized that neither Liam or I were joking.

"Tastes like chicken," another quipped beside him, but Liam and I were frozen in a mutual glare.

I pushed open the door and stepped into the night air. It was already cool in the September evenings in the Pacific Northwest, and the cold air hit my eyes, stinging them as tears began to pool. I'd known Jess and Cassie wanted to set me up when they started dropping hints last school year. Of course, they had been more subtle about it then.

"Jillian," Liam called, following me outside. "I promise that I'm not interested in applying to be your fling. I'm on a student visa, and I'm afraid I'm not allowed to work full-time jobs."

His words were cold and hard, containing none of the charm and silliness he'd shown me this morning or after class. I swallowed hard and nodded, walking away from him. He continued after me, catching up to walk beside me.

"You might think—" he began before he cut himself off.

I tried to hide my face, so he wouldn't see my tears. I couldn't think of anyone else I wanted to see me cry less. Especially because I didn't want Liam to think that these were tears over him. These were about much, much more than our stupid one-night stand.

"I didn't mean to make you cry," he said quietly.

"I'm not crying over you," I screamed at him, which only made me cry harder. "I'm crying because my best friends think I'm a loser, and my mom wants me to drop out of college, and I can't afford to pay my own tuition if her and my dad decide they won't pay anymore."

Liam didn't say anything, so I kept going, unable to control the trembling in my hands. It spread up from my wrists until tremors rolled through my arms. "Which, by the way, means that my parents think I'm a loser, too. And Professor Markson thinks I'm so broken that I should be a class project, and you—" I pointed at him "—keep calling me chicken."

The tears fell in fat drops down my cheeks, but my hands shook so badly that I couldn't even wipe them away.

"Are you cold?" Liam asked. The anger had melted from his voice.

"I'm fine." I didn't want his sympathy, not after I'd been such a bitch to him earlier.

"You're shaking," he accused.

I might have just vomited all my problems onto him, but this was one subject I wasn't going to touch. Instead, I quickened my pace in the hope that he would give up and leave me alone.

Liam reached out and caught my hand, which hurt, given the attack I was having. It forced me to stop and shake him off. But he took the opportunity to pull me into his arms, wrapping his arms tightly around me. I wanted to push him away, but my hands were too weak, so I settled against his chest, slowly feeling my body relax back to normal. Our breathing shifted, each inhale and exhale coming at the same time.

"Let me take you home," Liam suggested in a soft voice.

I shook my head and pulled out of his arms. "I'm okay. It's not that far. Go back to your friends. I was just upset."

"I won't call you hen anymore," he promised.

It was such a little thing, but it made me want to cry more. It felt like forever since someone had listened to one simple request of mine. Jess, my mom—they were all too busy telling me what to do or treating me like I was still a little kid.

"Do they really call girls hens in Scotland?" I asked him.

His mouth crept into a grin. "Only the cute ones."

"So I'm cute then?" I bet I looked hot right now with my blotchy eyes and red nose.

Liam laughed and turned back toward the bar, but before I could start heading home, he called out to me. "No, Jillian. You're beautiful."

Chapter Five

The following Thursday found me perched nervously in Professor Markson's class. Somehow I had been so freaked out that I'd wound up getting there five minutes early. I hadn't been early to a single moment in my life so far. I checked my notebook. Opened it. Closed it. Clicked my pen. My iPhone vibrated, and I pulled it out of my bag.

JESS: GOOD LUCK ;)

I wasn't sure how she had convinced me to come back, and I wasn't about to admit to her that Liam's concern the other night at Garrett's did more to make the decision for me than her lecture. Letting Jess know that would have been akin to showing her my entire hand at poker. She would know she won. It was safer to keep bluffing.

"Hey, Ch-Jillian," Liam corrected himself as he dropped his messenger bag on the floor between us. He looked tired, like he had been out all night.

That wouldn't be a surprise. Yesterday was the first Wednesday night out that I had skipped in two years at Olympic State, except for when I had the flu or my period. If I had to get serious about my grades to keep my parents footing my tuition bill, I was going to have to slow down.

"Out late?" I asked him.

"We went to Garrett's. I thought I might see you there."

I almost asked him who "we" was. It was probably the guys I'd seen him with on Tuesday night. "I'm trying to party less."

"I didn't get the impression that you were the party less type." Liam pulled out his MacBook, flipping it open.

"I am not giving it up," I told him. There was no chance of that, but I figured if I went out every other week, my grades were sure to improve. It was simple math. Fifty percent less partying, fifty percent improvement in my GPA. Of course, I hated math, so it might be a flawed equation.

Markson strode into the room and grabbed a piece of chalk. I winced as it squeaked across the chalkboard. He stepped back and revealed today's topic: Getting to Know You. Markson tugged on his vest and cleared his throat over the buzz of a dozen conversations.

"I'm glad to see we haven't lost anyone yet," he said, and his gaze landed on me.

I kept my face impassive. He better watch it. It was still early enough to pull out of this class.

"Today you'll be doing one of your most important interpersonal activities with your partner. You're going to get to know them. I want each of you to find out ten things about your partner," he instructed.

That sounded easy enough. I was certain I already knew ten things about Liam. He makes waffles. He could be totally obnoxious. I doubted Markson wanted a length estimate. Though, I could provide that too.

"But there are rules!" Markson called out. Several partners had already started chatting quietly. "Listen up. You may not tell me anything about clothes. I don't care how phat their pants are."

There was a collective groan at his use of "phat."

"Do you guys say wicked?" he asked.

"Sick!" someone yelled from the back of the room.

"Okay, I don't care how sick their pants are. You may also not give me a rundown of their class schedule. I want you to get to know them. By the end of this class, you should feel like you've been on a really great first date."

I frowned. The last thing I wanted was to feel like I had been on a date with Liam.

"Write it down on a sheet of paper. I can't wait to learn all sorts of interesting and terrifying things about each of you."

Liam scooted his desk so that he faced me as I tore out a sheet from my notebook. He was humming something under his breath. The melody sounded vaguely familiar.

"What is that?" I asked him.

"It's 'Getting to Know You' from *The King and I*—the musical." He said it without a hint of embarrassment. Further proof that he wasn't your typical American male.

"Okay, Liam likes musicals," I said as I scrawled it on the paper. One down, nine to go.

"You sounded a little judgmental, Jillian."

A cough interrupted us. Markson was watching us and he mouthed, "I statements."

"Sorry," Liam said. "I feel like you're judging me."

"I'm just getting to know you," I reminded him. "Do you like musicals?"

"I do," he admitted, folding his hands behind his head, revealing his rather impressive biceps and triceps and several smaller, but well-defined "ceps" of some sort. "I have five sisters."

"You have five sisters?" I repeated in disbelief.

"And I'm not gay."

I rolled my eyes. I knew that much about him. I jotted down the bit about five sisters.

"What about you? Brothers? Sisters?" Liam had his own pen poised to take notes.

I shook my head. "Just me. My parents decided it was better to break the mold, which was a benefit to all humanity."

"Well, now I know you're self-deprecating." Thankfully, he didn't write that down.

"I don't really get along with my mom," I said. "You heard us on the phone the other day."

"I can't imagine not having my sisters," Liam said in

a thoughtful voice. His words were sad and distant, as though he was stuck halfway between here and Scotland.

"You miss them," I said.

"I do. They taught me everything I know about women and waffles."

"I suppose I owe them a note or something." I wrote *Liam makes good waffles* on my paper alongside *five sisters*.

"A thank-you note?" Liam wiggled his eyebrows.

Or a reprimand. "Something like that."

"It feels like cheating to put down that you're from Scotland, because I already knew that," I said, reading over my notes. So far I had discovered two new things about Liam.

"I only have one thing about you," he pointed out. "What's your major?"

I supposed that didn't fall into the no-course-schedule rule, but I dreaded answering the question. It was one thing to admit to being undeclared when I was a freshman, but the weird, pitying looks had started last year.

"I don't have one yet. I'm still deciding."

Liam didn't even blink as he wrote it on his sheet. "Okay, so you're undeclared."

"I have one," I said, thinking of the guys he was with the other night. "Where do you live? I mean, do you go home to Scotland for breaks?"

"Can't afford it. I saved up for two years so that I could study over here. One of the biology professors it sponsoring me. He has a son in the Alpha Lambda fraternity," he told me as I scribbled several things on my paper.

That explained the guys he was with. "So you came here specifically to study?"

"I'm going into oceanography," he said. "I volunteer at the aquarium, so I can get acquainted with the local aquatic life."

"The one on Pine Street?" It was only a few blocks down from Garrett's, which explained why I kept running into him there.

"That's the one," he said. Liam leaned forward in his chair and turned the full force of his blue eyes on me. "Are you going to visit me?"

My breath hitched in my throat, but I shook my head. "Not really my thing."

"But you're undeclared, maybe it would inspire you."

"I love the ocean," I admitted, "but swimming in it terrifies me."

"Yeah, you can't be scared of the ocean as an oceanographer."

"Do you dive?" I asked him. I had seen guys in wet suits at the local beach. I thought they looked crazy, but I wouldn't mind seeing Liam in a wet suit.

"Yeah, you want to come with me?"

"Not a swimmer, remember?"

"I won't let you drown." His words were thick. Possibly because of his accent, but maybe because he was staring at me so intensely.

"Okay." I focused on my paper. "So you're a budding oceanographer with five sisters who makes waffles and lives with a professor." I wasn't too bad at this assignment, and I'd managed to mostly avoid flirting with him so far.

"And you're an undeclared major with no siblings. That's not enough. I need to know more about you," he said as he tapped his pen on his paper.

I don't think I was imagining how he emphasized the word *need*.

"I live with my best friend, Jess. You met her," I said.

"When did you meet her?" he asked.

"We were assigned as roommates freshman year when I lived in the dorms."

"Good. That's three things. Who was the other girl you were with at Garrett's?" he asked.

"Cassie. She lived across the hall. She's actually still in the dorms. Her scholarship covers her living expenses." Cassie was ridiculously smart, which most people didn't realize given her sailor-in-training vocabulary. But I wouldn't trade places with her if it meant I had to keep living in the dorms.

"Favorite food?" He was reaching for things now.

"Tacos," I said. "Although it's impossible to get good Mexican food here. It's easier in California."

Liam looked fascinated by this information. Almost as if he was hanging off my every word. Maybe this assignment was more dangerous than I thought. Now he could build up an image of me to go with the night we spent together. I needed a way to remind him that I was only interested in being friends or class partners. But his next question surprised me.

"Have you been to Disneyland?"

I blinked and laughed a little by his boyish interest. "Of course. It was my parents go-to vacation idea."

"I'm so jealous." Liam smacked the table with his hand. "I've always wanted to go to Disneyland."

I grinned and wrote this down. "It's not that great. Bad animatronics and old rides. Disneyworld is much cooler."

"Stop," he said, holding a hand up. "We don't have anything like that in Scotland. I keep hoping I'll get a chance to go while I'm here."

"Maybe you can come home with me for a break." The suggestion was out of my mouth before I could swallow it back. Had I just invited him to my house? Was I trying to encourage him?

Liam gave me a wicked smile. "Maybe I will."

The memory of our bodies pressed together, sweaty and naked, flashed through my mind, and I tried to shake it out. I wasn't about to wind up back in bed with him. The suggestion was a polite invitation. I didn't have to follow through on it.

In the front of the room, Markson called the class to attention, asking us to leave our papers for his perusal over the weekend. I looked over to see if Liam had been able to get all ten things about me. To my surprise, the sheet was full. I didn't feel like I had told him that much. My own paper was missing one thing, so I scrawled one final thing I knew about him on the bottom of the page.

Markson stood by the door, collecting our papers, but he paused when I handed him mine.

"I'm sorry if I embarrassed you the other day. I'm glad you came back." Up close he was younger than I thought. His closely cropped hair and preppy clothes hid his real age. He probably wasn't even a real professor, but one of the grad students who taught the more generalized courses for the department. I even thought I spotted a tattoo creeping out of his button-down shirt.

"No big deal," I said with a shrug. Even though it was a really big deal to me. But if he had the balls to apologize, then he probably would back off for the rest of the course. If not, I could always get my revenge when we filled out feedback forms during finals.

Liam followed me out the door, walking closely by my side as we excited Taylor Hall. I tried to shake him, but he seemed content to tail me.

"Listen, Jillian, do you want to grab coffee?" he asked me in a hopeful voice, adding, "As friends?"

I wanted to tell him no, but instead a "maybe" slipped out.

"Maybe next week?" he suggested. "I wouldn't mind knowing more than ten things about you."

Before I could react, he grabbed my iPhone from me and tapped in a number.

"Sure," I said, adding another "maybe" to the end of it.

"I hope I see you out this weekend." Liam slung his

bag over his shoulder as his lips curved into a pleased grin.

Thanks to this class, he officially knew more about me than any guy I'd known since high school. I slid the lock on my phone and went to delete his number, but I couldn't bring myself to do it when I saw it listed under Waffle-maker.

Chapter Six

It only took one more well-meaning phone call from Tara to send me spiraling into despair. She must have known that calling on Friday would effectively ruin my weekend, but I was determined not to let her get me down. It took a considerable amount of coaxing, but I managed to convince Cassie and Jess to go out. As I sat across from them and their boyfriends, I wondered if it was really worth it.

Trevor, who had an obsessive need for our approval, was buying all our drinks, so it wasn't all that bad. At least he actually tried to talk to us, unlike Brett who sat like a sad statue next to Jess.

Garrett's had decided to make the bar into a more club-like atmosphere on the weekends, so the place was packed. They'd also introduced two burly bouncers, which were totally unnecessary in Olympic Falls, population 9,200.

A waitress popped by our table. "Can I get you another round?"

"Yes, you can." Trevor flashed her a Cheshire cat smile, and Cassie snuggled into him, giving him a peck on the cheek. Trevor liked to show off his money as much as possible, and Cassie didn't seem to mind. Of course, I couldn't help but notice how his gaze followed the waitress's ass as she headed toward the bar.

The music pulsed into something electronic, which was very un-Garrett's, but the crowd didn't seem to mind. Jess leaned over to Brett, but he shook his head, so she grabbed my hand. We pushed our way onto the dance floor and started shaking with the beat. Dancing with Jess was always a laugh, because she totally let loose. For a minute, as I watched her fling her blonde hair wildly, I remembered the carefree girl I'd been assigned to live with my first year at Olympic State. Now that she was serious about her MCATs and getting into the right med school, she'd chilled considerably. It was nice to see her having some fun.

Cassie joined us, and we all pressed close together, waving our hands over our heads. It didn't take long for Trevor to sneak in, which attracted a few more guys to our party. Apparently Trevor's presence was like a homing beacon for horny dudes. One of them grinded against me as I scanned the crowd, but I didn't recognize anyone. I barely noticed how the guy's hands were creeping up my stomach until Jess pulled me closer to her and out of his grasp. I mouthed a *thank you*. The danger of the new Garrett's was that I was too comfortable here, which meant I wound up not realizing that I was falling victim to loose change. We'd coined the term our freshman year for the sleazy types who acted like they were in the opening scenes of some bad porno flick.

Jess put her arms around my waist and danced close to me, preventing any guys from getting too close to us, although more than a few stopped to admire the spectacle. They all looked like jerks, and I couldn't help but think that it was sad that two girls dancing together was such an asshole magnet.

The music changed to something slower and we turned into one another and pretended to waltz. This was what I missed, being silly with my best friends. Cassie was tangled up with Trevor, her eyes glued to his as his hands groped down her back. Jess made a gagging face, but then her eyes swept over to Brett. I pushed her toward him.

"No," she called over the loud music.

"It's cool. I need to go to the bathroom."

Jess looked torn, but she headed back to Brett. I watched as she looped her arms around his neck, and a wave of jealousy rolled through me. I couldn't help but feel like the fifth wheel with the guys around.

In the bathroom, a freshman was puking in the toilet, and I stopped to pull her hair back.

"Thanks," she moaned before she retched again.

It was the unwritten rule of Garrett's that you held hair for girls in the bathroom. Cassie, Jess and I had all done our time over the toilet here, and there was nothing worse than being sick alone on the dirty bar floor.

But suddenly the whole atmosphere felt less than glamourous. Once I was sure she was okay, if a bit gutted, I headed back to our table. A mess of blonde hair caught my attention, and I slowed down, but when the guy turned around, I didn't recognize him and my heart sank. Was I actually looking for Liam? Had I gotten that pathetic? I wiggled through the crowd. Brett and Jess had progressed to a full-blown make-out session, and Cassie was nowhere to be seen. Jess broke away as soon as I plopped down on the stool.

"Cass headed home with Trevor," she told me.

I spotted Brett's hand rubbing her thigh.

"I think I'm going to head home too," I said, giving her the out to go home with Brett and have boring, quiet sex. At least, someone would get laid tonight.

"It's early though." There was hesitation in her voice, and I knew she was only sticking around for me.

"I'm tired," I lied. I was wide awake, but a night watching Netflix was sounding better and better. It was that or staying here to watch Jess and Brett's foreplay. I grabbed my wallet and pecked Jess on the cheek.

"You want us to walk you home?"

"I'm fine. It's only ten," I reminded her.

"I'll see you in the morning. Get some rest." It was an order. Sometimes she sounded like she'd already taken her Hippocratic Oath.

"Yes, Dr. Stone." I gave her a salute.

The air outside Garrett's was chilly. It was only the

beginning of September, but it didn't take long for the Washington nights to turn cool. I fumbled with my iPhone as I headed home, lingering over the newest entry in my contact list, before I hit the sleep button and shoved it in my pocket.

Did I really want to wind up like Jess and Cassie running home early on Friday nights with their boyfriends? Sure, they had access to on-demand sex, but I had on-demand movies waiting for me. A night at home would be fun. I couldn't remember the last time I'd just been alone. Wouldn't it be a drag to have to share that with a boyfriend?

I ignored the little voice in my head that whispered "no."

Chapter Seven

M arkson skated into class five minutes late, narrowly avoiding the ten minute rule every student at Olympic Falls lived by. We were only five more minutes away from walking out of the classroom. His vest was wrinkled and he ran his hands through his tangled black hair, trying to smooth it into place. He had the distinct look of someone who had just woken up.

"Sorry," he called, waving a stack of papers. "Copier jammed."

"Alarm didn't work?" I asked.

"I wish," he said as he handed sheets of paper to each row. "More like no rest for the wicked."

There was a devilish gleam in his eyes as he said it. Apparently, Markson had a life outside of his office, and that life kept him out late. Maybe we had more in common than I previously thought. I watched as he continued through the classroom. In his disheveled attire, he looked like a frat guy who had just rolled out of bed.

"Should I be jealous?" Liam whispered.

"I don't do jealous friends," I said in an effort to remind him of where he stood with me. It was also a real warning. I couldn't stand when my friends got pushy and jealous, and that went even more for guys. The last boy I'd bothered to date was possessive, which irritated me to no end. Although it did end—and quickly at that.

Liam leaned against his chair and whistled as he read his assignment paper. "This should be fun."

That didn't sound good. Scanning the paper, my stomach turned over. It was a project to be completed with our partner outside of class.

But that wasn't the fun part.

"Now," Markson said, pushing himself onto the front desk, "before you all freak out. I realize that this sounds a lot like a date. It is not a date!"

I reread the paper. It sounded like a date to me.

"I'm not complaining," Liam said, his mouth splitting into a grin.

"Thank you for the validation, Mr. McAvoy."

Liam gave him a very masculine-code-of-conduct nod. *Boys.*

"The purpose of this assignment is to teach you to consider the various needs of your partner..."

"I like this assignment," Liam whispered to me.

"You would."

Meanwhile, Markson continued his explanation,

although he shot us a warning glance to stop talking. "We all act within certain societal constructs, so the roles we engage in are based on our experiences. If you will, a person who grew up with a lot of money, for instance, might act differently on a date than someone who grew up poor."

"I thought you said this *wasn't* a date," someone said from the back row.

"It was an example." Markson held up his hands as if to say don't shoot the messenger.

"I'm in favor of calling it a date," Liam said.

From across the classroom someone hummed a few bars of "Matchmaker, Matchmaker."

"As much as I'd love to see you all get married, have babies, and name them for your venerable professor, I'm fairly certain most of you aren't interested in dating each other, save for Mr. McAvoy."

There were a few catcalls and Liam gave a half-bow from his seat.

"All this project asks you to do is spend an afternoon or evening with your partner, trying to engage in the behavior you anticipate *they* would normally assume if you spent recreational time together. Ideally, you will base this on the information you've garnered from getting to know them in class, but you can also fall back on more stereotypical models. Girls, hold open the doors and pay the tabs. Boys, ask her to pick you up."

"That's not really how it works. Guys don't hold open doors, and I don't expect people to pick me up," I complained. Markson was way too young to have such a '50s attitude toward dating.

"Chivalry is dead," a girl said in agreement.

"'Cause feminism killed it," her partner said.

"Because we never needed it in the first place," I shot back.

"We still have chivalry in Scotland," Liam said to me. "Let me show you sometime."

"Once again, examples! You can choose whatever takes you out of your comfort zone and forces you to consider how to meet the expectations of your partner while communicating your own. It's called walking a mile in someone else's shoes."

I glanced around the classroom. Two guys shifted uncomfortably in their seats, looking at each other. What I wouldn't give to see what they would come up with. For a brief second, I imagined the two of them getting pedicures at Tough as Nails down the street. Not that I was going to do it myself. Markson couldn't force me to go out with Liam. If it wasn't completely crazy, I might have asked if Liam had put him up to it.

"And for those of you who are thinking, he can't make me do this," Markson said as if he were reading my thoughts. "You are right. However, please note this is your mid-term assignment. I'm giving you ample time to complete this, and it's worth 40% of your final grade."

I groaned, checking my sheet to see that I had to complete the assignment by mid-term, which was only two weeks away. I cursed the unusually short semesters that ran all of three and a half months at Olympic State.

"You each need to write up a five to seven page paper on the experience, which will be turned in separately from your partner."

This time everyone in the class groaned along with me. Why did every professor at the college think they taught the only class we were taking? There was nothing like getting hit with an unexpected paper two weeks before mid-term exams, especially when it required such uncomfortable research.

"Please write your paper independently from your partner. I want your insight into the experiment, not what your partner wants you to say." I wasn't dreaming that he looked right at me as he added the last part of the assignment.

So all I had to do was go on a not-a-date with Liam, who thought it was a date, and then pretend to be him, and write a paper about the experience.

"And to show you that I am not heartless, you are free to go for the day once you've worked out the details of your project with your partner," Markson said to a smattering of applause. He beamed at us, but I wanted to wipe the smug grin from his face. I should have dropped this class when I had the chance for a tuition refund. Jess hadn't mentioned any of these torturous assignments when she took this class. Had she been going out on not-a-dates last semester without me realizing it? Of course, with the number of study groups she attended each week, it wasn't unthinkable.

"So—" Liam turned to me "—what works for your schedule?"

"Whatever. Maybe next week. We have two weeks to get it in," I said with a shrug of my shoulders. I was simultaneously eager to get it over with while wanting to put it off forever. Liam had that effect on me.

"If it's okay, I have a lot of big tests coming up the week this is due. I'd rather get it over with."

Get it over with? How his tune had changed in a matter of minutes.

"Fine," I agreed. It would be like a Band-Aid, much easier to rip off immediately rather than take too much time thinking about it. Waiting nearly two more weeks would only result in a slow, painful reminder of my impending doom.

"Tonight?"

I hesitated. "I have plans with my friend Jess."

"Sorry, I'm being rash." He reached over and grabbed my notebook, scribbling a number across a sheet. "I'm guessing you deleted my number."

I hadn't but I wasn't about to admit it to him. Besides, there was something so delightfully old-school about the move that I reconsidered. "I'll be done by eight. How about I call you?"

Liam raised an eyebrow.

"I'm adopting a traditional male role for this one," I told him.

"Will I feel like I'm on an episode of *Mad Men*?" he asked me.

"Yes, I plan to speak down to you, and I expect you

to bring me cocktails at the door," I said in a flat voice. "I'm taking the initiative here. That's what guys are supposed to do, right?"

"I'm not complaining," Liam said. "But, and I hate to break it to you, in my experience, you usually take the initiative."

I flushed scarlet as his words, unable to ignore the thought of his skin on my skin. Even the memory sizzled.

"Then maybe I should be the one who waits around for you? That's definitely not like me." It was a challenge.

Liam shook his head. "How about we use the things we learned from that first assignment? Forget the *Mad Men* remake."

I tried to remember all the items Liam had listed about me, or the things I had learned about him. "Okay."

"You don't sound sure."

"I'm not, but since you're always so sure, I guess I'm trying that on for size."

"I like the way you think." Liam dropped his pen into his bag and stood. "See you tonight, Jillian."

I tried to tell myself that the brief thrill that shivered through me was all part of the experience. I was clearly channeling Liam's enthusiasm for this project, because racing hearts and date nights so weren't my scene.

Chapter Eight

I was ten minutes late to meet Jess at Garrett's for pizza night, which was nothing new. Save for the weird incident in Markson's class a few weeks ago, I hadn't been on time since I'd gotten out from under Tara's roof. It was probably some form of subconscious rebellion at the near-military precision with which she ran the family schedule. But being late meant that Jess was probably buried under a mountain of books, and when I found her in the side booth, she was poring over anatomy notes.

"Sorry," I said breathlessly.

Jess waved off my apology but didn't bother to look up. This was why I needed to be on time when I met up with her. Cassie had texted to say she couldn't make it, which meant it was my lone responsibility to get Jess to think about something besides blood types and autoimmune diseases for the next hour. It wasn't going to be easy.

"Did you order?" I asked her, and she shook her head.

Waving at Frank who was wiping down the bar, I held up two fingers. "The usual!"

I folded my arms on the table and rested my chin on them, so I could stare her down. "Can you tell me what a penis is?"

Jess barely cracked a smile. This was an old game, and she'd built up a little bit of an immunity to my shenanigans in the last year. I racked my head for any number of the ridiculous questions Jess had shared from her anatomy class. Since most students thought anatomy was simple memorization, pre-med types like Jess were always getting stuck in there with slackers who wanted to avoid Biology.

"Do girls have testicles?" I asked her. That was my favorite one. I still didn't know if a boy or a girl had asked the question. I didn't have the heart to ask.

"You better have a big old set if you keep interrupting me," Jess said, but she was definitely grinning.

"How do girls pee when they're on their periods?"

Jess slammed the book shut and laughed. "You win. I'll stop."

"That was only three questions," I said, puffing my chest out. "I think that's a record."

"I need a break from studying. I'm actually dreaming that I'm reading my textbooks. With my luck, I'm going to answer one of my midterms with something from one of them."

"In your dreams, do girls have balls?" I asked her. Frank slapped two beers down on our table.

"I'm not going to ask you girls what you're talking about," he said, throwing a bar towel over his shoulder and shaking his head as he left.

"No, but the other day, I woke up convinced that I'd dissected a deer."

I gagged on my beer and scowled at her. "Why the hell would you do that?"

"It was a dream," she reminded me. "I didn't actually do it, but the dream was so real that I thought I did. My professor was there and my labmate. When I woke up, I was almost sick over it."

"You do know what you'll have to do when you're a doctor, right?" Dead bodies were pretty par for the course in her field.

"Of course, I know that. But the lab is different than seeing deer guts when I close my eyes." Despite our conversation, Jess grabbed for a slice of pizza as soon as Frank slid the tray onto the table.

"Hot!" he warned.

"Jess has an unnatural ability to withstand heat," I assured him.

"I don't have time to wait for things to cool down." That was the understatement of the century. Jess could pack away more food in five minutes than most teenage boys I'd met in my lifetime.

"It's like you were biologically programmed to be a doctor," I said as I watched her down half of a steaming slice. I couldn't even pick a piece up without burning my fingers.

"Thanks!"

"So you won't believe what Markson is making me do." I told her about the project he assigned to us today.

"I did that one," Jess said. "Of course, I was partnered with a girl, and I hadn't slept with her."

"Exactly! And it's painfully obvious that we've done it," I said to her. "Liam has spilled enough in front of Markson that he has to know."

"Roman won't care." Jess reached for another piece.

"Roman?" I asked with a raised eyebrow.

"Professor Markson." She almost managed to hide her blush, but not quite.

"Now I see why you liked the class."

"That's not it," she said, but her words were defensive.

"What did you do on your date...um, your project?" I asked her. After her shenanigans with Liam, she didn't deserve a free pass over Markson, but I gave her one anyway.

"I can't remember exactly, although she planned most of it because, you know, I'm a control freak."

I nodded, and Jess kicked me under the table.

"Hey! I was just being supportive," I said, leaning down to rub the affected area. "Shit, Jess, are you wearing steel-toed boots?"

"I think we went to a football game, actually. Sara and I had a lot in common, so it was kinda hard for us."

"That's what I'm worried about. I need enough

material to warrant 40% of my grade." I screwed my face up. I didn't relish the idea of analyzing Liam for two hours. It felt too much like a real date. Although I would be trying to figure out how to meet his *interpersonal needs* instead of wondering if he liked me. I wasn't sure what the difference was exactly.

"It'll be fun. You can always make stuff up," Jess suggested.

"Is that what you do? Do humans now have opposable toes?" I made a grab for her textbook like I was going to check.

"Get it done early in case you need to meet up later and come up with more stuff for the paper."

"I think we're meeting tonight," I said in a soft voice. I wasn't sure I wanted Jess to hear where I was going after this.

"*Oh really.* You two kids be safe." She winked at me as she wiped pizza sauce off her fingers.

"Not a date! There will be no funny business," I said.

"You forget that I've seen Liam. If you can keep your hands off him, then you're a better person than I am." Jess stood and gathered her books while I finished my last few bites. Our dinners always ended like this: with me shoveling food in my mouth because she had to be somewhere. Just once, I wanted to be the one with somewhere to rush off to. Maybe if I picked out a major that would happen.

"Isn't this whole project a chance to get out of my

comfort zone? I would be much more comfortable taking him to bed than going out in public with him."

"I'm sure that's what every guy wants to hear," Jess said.

We both paused and then met each other's eyes. I was the one who said it, "Actually, it probably is. Yet another reason I'm not going to bed with him."

"It's cool." Jess checked her phone screen. "It's too early anyway."

"What do you mean?" I asked her, and then it dawned on me in horrifying clarity. "Do you have bets on when I'll go to bed with him again?"

"No!" Jess answered too quickly, and I grabbed for her phone. "Okay! Maybe!"

"You disgust me," I said, trying hard to sound serious.

"If you can hold out another week, I'll split the pot with you."

"What do I win?" I asked her.

"A latte at Coffee & Cream."

"Wow. Big money." Still winning was winning. "Deal. *If* I go back to bed with him, I'll hold out."

"Excellent," Jess chirped. "A week! Don't forget!"

"Got it," I promised absent-mindedly, too caught up in texting Liam that I was ready. All the while thinking that this was one bet both of them were going to lose.

Chapter Nine

Liam had a plan of action by the time I reached him, which was excellent since I didn't have any ideas. I was to pick him up at his host family's house, and he would take it over from there. It wasn't exactly a ground-breaking reversal of gender roles but it felt like a nice give and take. His host family's house sat on the edge of campus in an old neighborhood that was an eclectic blend of bungalows, stone Tudors and small mansions. Nearly all the houses were occupied by professors, except one lonely street that boasted Greek housing.

Stars peppered the night sky and a thumbnail moon peeked from behind the clouds when I got to the address he provided. The perfectly restored Queen Anne wasn't the biggest house on the block, but it was close. I hesitated for a moment, tugging at my sweater, before I finally found the courage to ring the doorbell.

A petite redhead threw open the door and grabbed

my hands. The hair around her temples was graying, which, other than a few light lines around her eyes, was the only indication of her age. "You must be Jillian. Liam is expecting you."

"Vivian!" Liam's voice called from somewhere in the depths of the house.

"He's worried I'll embarrass him." Vivian draped an arm around my shoulder and walked me down the hall. The house was tastefully decorated with expensive antiques and Persian rugs, and I felt more out of place than ever as I treaded on them in my worn-out TOMS. "But I've promised to stay out of your hair. I'm just thrilled he's brought a girl over. He's quite the catch, don't you think?"

I managed not to grimace at the thought. "Liam and I are class partners."

"Oh, I know. He told me, but I've heard a lot about you, too."

I suddenly wished a large sinkhole would open in the floor and suck me through it. How much had Liam told this woman about our relationship? I wasn't sure I wanted to know, but it was clear that she viewed me as a romantic possibility.

"You two sound...close," I said, choosing my words carefully. "Are you related?"

"Heavens no! My husband helped to arrange Liam's year in the States. He's a biology professor at Olympic State. Dr. Kemp?" She waited as if expecting me to know the name.

"I haven't taken many science classes," I admitted.

"Neither did I," Vivian whispered, as though we were part of some conspiracy. "I'm more artsy." She pointed to a large canvas hanging on the wall. I recognized the sweeping expanse of Olympic Bay carefully captured in soft brushstrokes.

"It's lovely," I said as she steered me out of the hall and into the kitchen. Liam was busily stirring a pot over the stove, but he looked up and shot me a grin.

"What's this?" I asked.

"I am making you dinner," he said.

"Why?" I couldn't contain the question even though it came out more rudely than I had intended.

Vivian, perhaps sensing the tension in the air between Liam and I, clutched my hand one last time, disappearing into the hallway with a "it was so nice to meet you" before I could respond.

"As as I see it, cooking dinner for a woman upends gender expectations. But cooking dinner for you is the perfect way to tend to your needs," he said, holding up a spoon.

I slurped the sauce off it cautiously, nodding my approval, even though I didn't see how this met my needs at all. I needed to write a paper, not go on a date, and cooking dinner for me felt very much like a date. "I'm not sure I follow your logic."

"You don't have to," he said with a shrug. "I'm the one who has to write the paper."

He had a point, but that didn't help me with my paper. How was I supposed to get material for my own paper with Liam babying me all night? I watched as he pulled bread from the oven and considered what he needed from me at the moment. Markson's whole point for this assignment was to force me to consider what the other person needed based on what I knew about him.

I thought back to the first activity we did together. Liam came from a large family, full of women, and apparently he spent a lot of time in the kitchen.

"How can I help you?" I asked him, seizing on the most productive way to deal with the situation.

"You can set the table," he suggested.

As he finished cooking the pasta, I opened cabinets and drawers looking for plates and utensils. It was a relief that he hadn't gone over-the-top and presented me with a fancy, laid out dinner. There was something easy and natural about being in the kitchen with him like this. We moved like clockwork around each other as I pulled forks from the drawer, and he grabbed a salad from the fridge. When we sat down a few minutes later, I dug into the pasta, surprised by how well-cooked it was. It seemed Liam's talents were not confined to waffle-making.

"This is really good," I said as I tore off a hunk of bread and sopped up some of the sauce with it.

"You sound surprised." Liam poured wine into two glasses and brought them over to us.

"I thought the waffles might be a hat trick," I said. "You know, that one thing you can do to impress girls."

Liam smirked as he took a sip of wine. "I'd like to think I have many ways to impress girls."

He leaned back in his chair, watching me eat, with more than casual interest. Meanwhile, I tried to ignore the strip of exposed skin right over his stomach where his fitted shirt had ridden up.

"So Vivian seems nice," I said in an attempt to change the subject.

"She's great," he said. "Housing cost almost prevented me from coming this year, but she and Dr. Kemp offered to let me stay here. Their son started grad school this fall, so I think they like having me around. She was very chuffed that you were coming tonight."

"I'm an only child, and my parents wouldn't even let me have sleepovers. I'm always surprised that there are people that like having me around," I admitted, immediately wishing I could take it back. The confession made me even more vulnerable to him, and I didn't like it.

"Your parents sound like real pieces of work. I can't even imagine my parents making me feel that way."

"Obviously, you have like twenty sisters, right?" It was one of the things I remembered from our earlier class assignment.

"Five," he said with a laugh. "But sometimes it feels like twenty."

"I hope you have more than one bathroom in your house."

"We have two. Why do you think I came to the States?" he asked, brushing his arm against mine as he reached for the garlic bread.

The small gesture did funny things to my stomach,

and I laid my fork down, not sure I could eat another bite.

"Done?" he asked, his hand reaching out to grab my plate.

"Yes. It was delicious, just as good as your waffles."

"I don't know about that." Liam stood and moved to the sink. He rinsed the plate and bent over the dishwasher, revealing his tight ass. I couldn't look away even as Jess's words flashed through my mind: *Remember! A week!*

Except I wasn't going to sleep with him. That would send him the wrong message, and between our conversations in class and tonight's dinner, I was increasingly convinced that Liam was a relationship kind of guy. I stacked the rest of the dishes from the table and carried them to him in a bid to distract myself from staring at his ass any longer.

"Thanks," he said, taking them from me. "I got this."

"I'll help," I offered, but when I reached for a glass, it tumbled from my hand, shattering across the floor. I cursed and bent to start collecting the pieces.

"Let me," he said, retrieving a broom from the pantry.

"I'm really sorry. I'm so clumsy." I didn't add that I wasn't just a helpless clutz. I had a real reason for my clumsiness, but that was one thing I didn't want to wind up in his paper.

"It's just a glass, Jillian. Sit down so you don't get glass in your shoes."

I looked down at my TOMS and realized he had a point, so I watched as he swept up my accident. As soon as he was done, I jumped up and turned on the faucet, filling the sink with soapy water for the pots.

"You don't listen, do you?" he asked.

I pointed to the pasta pot, and he passed it to me. "I don't like feeling useless."

I left it at that, not bothering to explain that my body made me feel useless on a near daily basis. It was only going to get worse, too, so I might as well do as much as I could now before I became dependent on other people to do things for me.

"You are practically writing this paper for me." He moved next to me and took the washed pot from me to rinse.

"Am I that full of neurosis?" I asked him, reaching for the next pan.

"It's not a psych class."

"It might as well be. We're supposed to spend all of our time analyzing each other," I pointed out.

"And what have you discovered about me?" he asked.

I bit my lip, unsure how to answer. Despite how worried I'd been about spending the night analyzing Liam, I hadn't done much of it. I'd been too obsessed with what he was thinking about me, but that didn't mean I couldn't come up with something. "You love your family, and you have a lot of respect for women."

"You got all that from spaghetti?" he asked, bumping his elbow into my side.

"You cook and you help do dishes. I'm not sure my Dad knows how to turn on the dishwasher," I said.

"Perhaps I'm trying to lure an unsuspecting woman to my bed by pretending I like to do dishes," he suggested.

I splashed some water at him. "One: I don't buy that. I think you like to do dishes. Two: I suspect your motives deeply, so your plan is foiled."

"Curses." Liam snapped his fingers. "It's not such a bad thing to make something that's dirty clean again."

I burst into laughter, barely able to stay upright.

"I know, I know. That's what she said."

"You sound like an evangelical minister," I teased him when I could speak again.

"I would do the sign of the cross, but, you know, blasphemy," he said in a serious tone.

"Are you Catholic?" The question jumped out of me.

"I think you know better than to ask me that," he said, shaking his head. "I'm not really religious."

"Me either."

We finished the dishes, and I lingered at the edge of the sink, unsure if I should stay or go.

"Another glass of wine?" he offered.

"No," I said. It didn't seem like a good idea to stay for another drink. "I should get home."

"Early class?"

"Yeah." It was a lie. I never scheduled classes before noon if I could help it, but sticking around with Liam would almost certainly result in Cassie winning the bet, especially if more wine was involved.

"Can I walk you home?" he offered.

"I'm fine. I'm only a block away." Of course, Liam already knew that. I wanted to avoid the awkward parting at my door, and it wasn't late enough to warrant an escort home.

Liam followed me to the door, pausing as he opened it for me. "We should do this again sometime."

"I don't think Markson will ask us to go on any more dates. I mean, do more projects," I backpedalled. *This was not a date*, I reminded myself as I ducked through the open door.

"That's a shame. I like seeing you outside of class," he said, stepping out behind me.

The awkward pause came anyway, despite refusing his offer to walk me home. Neither of us seemed to know what to say. If I told him I liked seeing him outside of class too, he would certainly make an effort to make it happen again. But I had a bigger problem than that. I liked the idea of seeing him again. His dinner invitation tempted me too much. That's why I had to get out of here.

"Thank you for dinner," I said, turning to face him.

He hesitated and then reached out and ran a finger down my face. "I will make you dinner any time. Breakfast, if you'll let me."

My breath caught in my throat as I struggled for something to say in response to this. I should put a stop to whatever was shifting between us right now, but I couldn't bring myself to do it. Instead, I murmured a good-bye and flew down the sidewalk, safely out of his reach. I wasn't sure how I felt about Liam McAvoy any more. I only knew I should stay away from him, even as I realized that I didn't want to.

Chapter Ten

The beat of the latest Macklemore single pumped through the bar. Sweaty bodies pushed around me, calling out drink orders, while I sipped on a gin and tonic. I searched the crowd for Jess or Cassie, not sure I would even see them when they finally made an appearance. It felt good to be at Garrett's, like I'd rediscovered my equilibrium after a week of flirtations with Liam. He hadn't asked me out again, but it was pretty clear from our interactions in Markson's class that the offer stood. Here at Garrett's, I was reminded of who I was: a girl who didn't need a boy. It was fun to bring them home once in a while, but I wasn't about to get into anything serious, especially with a guy on a temporary student visa.

A hand grabbed my body, and I shoved the guy next to me.

"Sorry," he slurred. "Lost my balance."

"Try grabbing for the bar next time," I barked.

So far I'd spotted no likely candidates for an adventure this evening. There was a table of frat guys looking at me, but I avoided eye contact with them. I'd learned early on in my college career that they were more trouble than they were worth. I'd slept with one guy freshman year only to have his entire fraternity label me as an easy target.

I might be a little easy, but I wasn't anyone's target.

The music slowed to a steady pulse and the deejay took the mic. "I hope you've had enough to drink because it's karaoke time," he announced. "And whether you have the balls to get up here and sing, or you have to listen to all the *American Idol* wannabes, you're going to need liquor."

His proclamation elicited a chorus of shouts. I raised my glass.

"Does this mean you're going to sing?" a voice next to me asked.

I didn't bother to turn towards Liam. "I don't sing."

"Not enough booze?" he guessed.

"There is not enough booze in the world to make me get up there and sing," I said, not taking my eyes of the swarm of co-eds.

A girl named Stacey stumbled to the stage and grabbed the mic as the opening beats of a vintage No Doubt song began. Stacey could not sing, although she'd drank enough to think she could.

"This is unfortunate," Liam said.

I couldn't help but giggle. Stacey sounded a bit like a drowned cat although she was gyrating her hips like she was Gwen Stefani.

"This is why I don't sing," I told him as I finally turned to face him.

"Because you sound like someone is murdering you?" he asked.

"Definitely."

Liam grabbed my free hand. "Dance with me?"

He tipped his head toward the dance floor and tugged me along, but I planted my feet in place and shook my head. "I'm not dancing to that."

Was this his idea of being romantic?

"Come on. It will be ironic," he pleaded. The bar's pulsing lights landed in shadows and highlights on his smooth face, accenting his strong jawline. For a minute, I imagined licking it. But that would break rule #1: Don't bring the same guy home twice. Of course, I was the only one still abiding by that code these days. Then there was the fact that we had committed to being friends and class partners. Nothing more.

"I'm waiting for Jess," I told him. It was as good of an excuse as any to get rid of him.

Just then the drunk guy from earlier careened into me, nearly knocking me off my feet. The guy caught me around the waist and gave me a boozy smile. "Hello, beautiful."

I pulled at his hands, trying to pry him off me. Every year I spent more and more time peeling the lightweights off of me. But the guy just pressed closer to me. I think he was trying to dance with me, which felt a lot more like getting humped than any type of rhythm.

"Let me go," I demanded in a firm voice.

"Don't be that way," he said. His mouth was so close to my face that I felt like I could get contact drunk.

Liam appeared behind us and placed a hand on the guy's shoulder. "The lady asked you to let her go."

"She can tell me that," he said, shrugging out of Liam's grip but not letting me go.

"I did tell you that." I shimmied out of his grasp, but he lunged for me.

Liam caught him by the shirt, allowing me enough time to escape. "Walk away, mate."

"Mate?" the guy said in a mocking voice. "Are you some sissy Brit?"

Liam actually grinned at this when he shook his head. "I'm from Scotland, and no one has ever accused the Scots of being sissies."

"Shouldn't you be wearing a skirt?" the guy asked.

I gulped. Liam might the most laid-back man I knew, but if he was feeling half as angry as I was, this wasn't going to be good.

As if to prove me right, Liam's fist cracked into the guy's face, knocking him flat on the floor. He never stood a chance against those biceps even if he hadn't been drinking. Liam peered over him and leaned down while a group of gawkers gathered around us.

"We call them kilts, and we wear them so we can let our enormous cocks breathe."

I didn't usually go in for the alpha male types, and maybe if I didn't know Liam so well, I wouldn't feel the need to screw him on the spot.

An overweight bouncer I'd never seen before waddled over and grabbed Liam's arm. "You're out of here."

"He was defending me," I said. I couldn't let him get kicked out for helping me get rid of that piece of dirt.

"You can leave, too, if you like," the bouncer growled at me.

I balked. I'd been coming to Garrett's for three years, since I was a wee thing with a fresh, new fake ID. They knew me here. I looked around for Frank but he was nowhere in sight. My sense of injustice flared in my chest, and I set my jaw, marching past the bouncer and out the door. The cool night air was my first reminder that I had no Plan B. Jess and Cassie would be looking for me. I didn't have a ride home, and I was wearing completely impractical shoes. I shuffled down the sidewalk, hoping to prolong the onset of blisters from the mile walk back to my apartment as I texted Cassie and Jess that there was a change of plans.

"Hey," Liam called, catching up to me. "You didn't have to leave."

"It's the principle of the matter," I said, not bothering to look up from my cell phone.

"I shouldn't have lost my cool like that. I'm not usually the bar fight type." He fell into step beside me.

"I thought the Scots were famous for their fighting."

"We are," he said with a grin. "We usually save it for the battlefield though."

I thought of the number of unprovoked advances I'd endured over the years and the amount of time I'd spent planning tactical strategies with my friends. From tag-teaming a hottie to escaping the handsy jerks, we'd developed our game plan over the years. "The bar is the modern battlefield."

"If every time you go out it's like that, you might have a point," he said.

We'd reached the corner and I still had no reply from either of my friends, so I pocketed my phone. "I'm heading home. I'll catch you on Tuesday."

"No way," Liam said. "I can't let you walk home alone."

"You've done your time. Defended my honor. I've got it from here." It was only a few blocks and well-lit. I'd walked it a dozen times in my time at Olympic State.

"I think I'm honor-bound to see you home after you left the bar for me."

"I left the bar because that was totally unfair," I said. "That guy was about three drinks shy of becoming a date rapist, but they kicked you out."

"See?" he said, his lips curving up. "You defended my honor."

"And you defended mine. That makes us even."

"I would rather be in your debt," Liam admitted.

I started to protest when the tell-tale first drop of a Pacific Northwest storm splatted on my forehead. This was why I always had a plan for getting home from the bar. It was way too inconvenient to carry a slicker and wellies with me everywhere, and now I was trapped in the start of an epic thunderstorm.

Liam quickened his pace, waving for me to run with him. I bounded a few steps before my ankle twisted under me.

"Shit!" I yelped as I got my balance back.

"You okay?" he asked, wrapping an arm around me like he was going to help me stagger home.

"I'm fine, but there's no way I can run in these."

The rain picked up in intensity, pelting us with fat, cold drops. A splinter of lightening cut across the sky. It was going to be one of those rare storms that was more intense than long-lasting. I shook the rain off my face and wiped it from my eyelashes, opening my eyes to see Liam squatting in front of me.

"What are you doing?" I called over a blast of thunder.

"Jump on," he said.

"You can't be serious."

"I generally don't joke around when I'm in the middle of drowning. Let me carry you."

I took a deep breath and hoisted myself onto his back. His hands found my knees and locked onto them. I couldn't resist the urge to bury my face into the back of his neck. I told myself it was to avoid being assaulted by more water, but that didn't explain why I enjoyed his soap-clean scent and the hint of cologne I found there.

"Now I'm in your debt," I told him as he began jogging toward my apartment complex.

"I'll think of a way for you to pay me back."

"So is that really why you wear kilts?" I asked him. My mind was already concocting a variety of ways to repay him for what seemed like a feat of god-like proportions.

"Pants are a modern oppression on men," he said. "I would wear a kilt every day."

I'd seen Liam's calves before and couldn't help but think if anyone could rock a kilt, he could.

He managed to get us into the complex's stairwell within five minutes, and despite running the whole way with me on his back, he wasn't even winded. His stamina was certainly impressive. I wondered briefly if I should test it further. Once we were out of the rain, I shimmied off his back and glanced at my locked apartment door.

"It's late," I said, feeling awkward suddenly. I was used to bringing guys home, but not many had carried me there.

"I should get going while I'm still wet," he said as he twisted his t-shirt, wringing out some of the rain.

"No way. I'm in your debt, remember?" I said. "This storm won't last long, and I have a dryer."

My hands shook a little as I unlocked my door and flipped on the light switch. I made a beeline for the cabinet and grabbed for my pill bottle. I had it down before he'd managed to tug his soaked shoes off.

"What's that?" he called.

I stuffed the bottle back behind the plates and grabbed my Chiclets box, popping a few in my mouth. "The greatest gum on Earth."

"And you're not going to offer me any?"

"My bad." I offered him the box and watched as he poured a few into his hands.

"Amazing," he said as he chewed.

"I know."

"No, it's amazing that it's just like chewing little rubber balls."

I smacked him on the shoulder. "I want my Chiclets back."

Before I could even consider what I'd said, his mouth was on mine. I opened my mouth, allowing his tongue to glide across my tongue. Our skin was slick with rain, and I could make out the contours of his muscles as I slid my fingers over his clinging t-shirt. His hands seized my ass, pulling me up and around him as he pressed me against the door to my apartment. Every movement, every slight change in his body mirrored mine in natural, graceful precision. His lips traced secrets down my neck coming to rest at the top of my breasts.

"We should get out of these wet clothes," I breathed into his ear.

Liam set me down on the floor and pulled off his

shirt. Without his lips to distract me, I realized the amount of gum in my mouth had doubled.

"Did you just pass off your Chiclets to me?" I asked, popping my shoes off my feet.

"You said you wanted them back." He grinned as he unbuttoned the fly of his jeans.

"If you can't appreciate a thing of beauty..." I yanked my sweater over my head. Liam's eyes drooped lustily to my breasts.

"Believe me, I appreciate beauty."

I dropped the rest of my clothes in a wet pile by the door and raised an eyebrow at Liam. He met my challenge by dropping his jeans, revealing the swell of his cock in his tight, gray boxer briefs.

"It's true what they say about Scots," I said.

Liam reached for me, and I met him with urgency as we stumbled down the hall to my bedroom. His hands wandered like a traveler exploring a new and foreign country—excited and hesitant at the same time. When we tumbled onto my bed, I pulled my lips from his.

"We can stop," he said, but even as he extended the invitation I knew neither of us could go back.

"I feel scared," I admitted through panting breaths.

"Look at you using 'I' terms," he whispered. "Professor Markson would be proud."

"Clearly, I deserve an A in that class." I giggled nervously as his hand trailed along my bare stomach, tracing the outline of my belly button and igniting a ring of fiery longing deep within my core.

"What are you scared of?" he asked.

I nuzzled my face into his neck and held my breath for a moment before I answered. "I'm no good at this. At relationships."

"I think you're wrong about that." His hand stroked my hair from my face.

"I fuck them up. I don't know how to be a good girl."

"Exactly what is a good girl?" he asked. "Because you're smart and passionate and funny, which lands you squarely in good girl territory for me."

"No." I shook my head. "I'm mean. You have no idea what you're getting into."

"I've heard you talking about Jess and Cassie," he reminded me. "You are good at relationships."

Except for all the times I'd pushed them away or yelled at them for trying to help me. Liam had no idea how big of a bitch I could be.

"I don't fuck Jess and Cassie," I pointed out.

"I need you to understand something, Jillian," Liam said in a low voice, his words warm against my hair. "You don't fuck me either. Not anymore. We make love."

I bit back a laugh at this. "That's something that I'm definitely not any good at."

"Lucky for you, I'm an excellent teacher." He pushed my hair aside and gripped my chin, bringing my lips to meet his. The kiss was soft and deep, slipping into something serious. His hands didn't waver. Instead, he held my face and my belly with gentle strength, forcing me to focus on the press of our lips. His tongue brushed the back of my teeth, and I nipped at it, causing him to growl lowly and shift his body, but he didn't bring it into closer contact with mine. Our tongues massaged into one another's, and he sucked mine tenderly, sending a thrill pulsing between my legs. I could feel myself growing hotter as my body squirmed trying to get closer to him. But he didn't relent on the kiss, and I found myself falling deeper into a haze of lust and longing, eager for his hands to explore my body, ready to press my skin against his.

Liam's mouth trailed down my jawline, and he lingered at the hollow of my neck, breathing life into my chest and setting my heart to racing with the anticipation of his trek downwards. But he didn't continue. Instead, he hooked his hand around my head and pulled me gently up to meet his lips, his other hand cradling my back and pulling me against his firm chest. My breasts brushed against his pectorals and a tremor raced down my spine. I needed him like I needed to breathe. He sat up and brought me up to meet him, guiding my legs around his waist. I felt his dick swelling against my thigh, making my body ache with emptiness. I pushed against his length, causing my core to stir and pulse with desire.

"Do you—?" he let the question fade away as I reached to my nightstand and pulled a condom from the drawer.

There was no need for more words. A moment later, he slid into me and the ache was replaced with mounting energy. His arms hooked under my shoulders and gripped my back, holding me steady as we moved together rhythmically. Liam's lips found my breasts, and he circled my right nipple with his tongue, loosing a moan from me as I threw my head back so he could have better access and bit my lip as he sucked each peak with slow, but eager hunger. Drawing me back to him, the cadence of our movements became faster. He pushed deep inside me and I met each thrust with force, wanting him, all of him, as much of him, as I could have.

My body trembled, each muscle contracting, growing tight with anticipated release. I squeezed my eyes shut resting my head against his, our sweat mingling together, my breath stolen from his own.

"I think you're amazing," he whispered, the words tickling my earlobe and shivering down my swollen nerves. My body burst into flames, pleasure splintering through me in great, tremulous surges as he held me, pumping deep inside of me. I felt his muscles tense against me, and he groaned as he came in furious thrusts.

I melted against him, wrapping my arms around his neck and counting the beats of his heart as they thumped against my skin. Our breathing slowed and he brought his lips to mine as he withdrew from me, lessening the exquisite agony of emptiness I felt between my legs. He laid me back across the bed and brought his body close, cocooning me in his arms. He hummed something soft in my ear as I felt sleep taking over my body. I wanted to ask him to stay. I wanted him to be there in the morning, but I didn't know what to say. I'd spent all my energy for the last few weeks pushing him away. Why would he choose to stay now?

"Liam—"

"Shhh," he hushed me, kissing the nape of my neck. "Get some sleep. In the morning, I'm making waffles."

I settled into my dreams still smiling.

Chapter Eleven

❦

I woke to a familiar vanilla scent wafting through my house. I rolled over in my otherwise empty bed and stretched my arms wide to shake off the sleep still lingering in my limbs. And then I realized something.

Liam had stayed. He was making me breakfast. When I got up and walked into the kitchen, he would be there and that didn't scare me. It made me happy. Really and truly happy. I wasn't sure what had shifted overnight to allow that, but then again, if I was being honest, things had been evolving with Liam for a while now. I had tried to ignore that fact, but I couldn't any more.

My bedspread was MIA and pillows were scattered on the floor, so I grabbed the loose top sheet and wrapped it around me. It felt like a very movie star thing to do. Wrap a sheet around my naked body and go out to my boyfriend.

The heady feeling evaporated immediately.

Boyfriend? Had I really just mind-bombed myself with that? Liam was many things to me. Friend, classmate, adorably vulgar Scottish boy. But was he my boyfriend? He had used the term making love last night, and I knew he was all in then. That was perfectly obvious since the first day I couldn't get him out of my kitchen.

I didn't know how I felt about it though. I'd managed to avoid boyfriends for years. Not only did they require a lot of maintenance, but it was nearly impossible to keep them from finding out about my condition. And then came the questions, followed by the concern and the nagging, and finally it always ended with:

"I'm not sure I can handle this."

I could barely handle it myself, but some guy who has known me a few weeks wasn't sure how he could handle it? As Cassie would say, *fuck you very much*. Being unattached was easier, but then again, Liam came with an expiration date himself. He had to be back In Edinburgh in June. Maybe if I looked at the whole relationship like a short-term lease or a really long vacation, it wouldn't be so bad. In June we could return back to our normal lives.

No harm done. That's what I told myself as I shuffled toward the bathroom as quickly as possible. I brushed my teeth, repeating my doctor's mantra in my head. Today is normal. Today I am strong. Glancing in the mirror, I couldn't help but feel sexy, wrapped in a sheet with a just-fucked glow on my face. *Don't get cocky*, I thought and headed for the kitchen. Liam's face split into a smile when he saw me. His hair was messy and uncombed, and I could almost see where my fingers had clutched it the night before. I admired his bare chest and how his muscles flexed ever so slightly as he grabbed a whisk or reached for the fridge door. He had on jeans, which was a shame, but he wore no belt so they hung low on his hips, displaying the chiseled v that screamed *this way down*.

I was suddenly very hungry.

"Morning, chicken," he said.

I pretended to glower at him, not quite ready to admit I'd liked how comfortable the nickname sounded coming from his lips, wrapped up in his accent, after last night.

"That smells good." I scooted around him in the kitchen and stealthily grabbed my medication. He opened the fridge and grabbed a carton of eggs, meeting my eyes as I swallowed it with a dry gulp. He didn't say anything, but he turned around and caught me around the waist.

"Good morning," I murmured as his lips brushed over mine, sending a spark of electricity through my body.

"I used your toothbrush," he said. "I hope you don't mind."

I rolled my eyes at him. "I stuck my tongue in your mouth repeatedly last night. I hope you don't mind."

"I do actually, but only because that was last night." Our lips crushed together, our tongues tangling greedily. Liam guided me back toward the fridge, and I grabbed his face, pulling him hard against me and crushing the carton of eggs he was still holding into my back.

"We should not make out in the kitchen," he said, his eyes full of laughter.

"It's too dangerous." I took a step forward. "How bad is it?"

"They haven't started to fry yet, but if we keep them on that ass much longer, they won't be able to withstand the heat." I groaned as he tugged at my sheet and gently wiped the broken eggs from my backside.

"And now I'm the one naked in my kitchen," I said.

"Let's hope Jess doesn't come home," he said, tipping his head toward the locked front door.

"Jess has seen me naked before."

Liam cocked his head and nodded. "Tell me more."

"Perv," I said, swatting his shoulder.

"I can't help it. You're standing here naked. I can not be held accountable for my actions." He took a step toward me, a wicked grin creeping over his face, and stepped onto an egg.

I laughed so hard that I snorted.

"That's funny, eh?" Liam reached toward the counter and a moment later a puff of flour blasted over my breasts.

"This is war," I said, but I didn't just grab a handful of flour, I dumped the bag of it over his head. It settled over him like a layer of ash and he wiped his face as he laughed.

"You're cleaning up breakfast," he said.

"We haven't even eaten yet," I said.

He pinned my arms to my sides and kissed me slowly. His lips burning into mine before he pushed open my mouth with his tongue. I sucked it with gentle pressure, and he yanked my body against his. I could feel his erection through his jeans, and I slipped my hand down his loose waistline, gripping it firmly.

"Should we go to the bedroom?" he whispered, but I shook my head as I dropped to my knees, barely noticing the egg shells I landed on.

"Jess texted. She's at Brett's. We have the place to ourselves." I wrenched his zipper down. He wasn't wearing any boxers, so he sprang out of the loose confines of his pants at full attention.

"What did you, uh, have in mind?" he asked.

"I thought we should expand our study of communications," I said, pushing him backwards so that his hands gripped the counter behind him.

"That sounds practical. Where should we start?" He looked down at me, and I could see the slight quickness to his breath as he anticipated my move. I let my fingers trace the V cutting across his hips and he moaned.

"I was thinking Oral Communications." I slid one hand over his thickness and brought his cock to my mouth. Popping my lips over its crown, I took his length deep into my throat. I held myself steady, one arm wrapped around his hip and the other jerking in rhythm with each suck and plunge. I could feel him struggling to stay still as his breathing became more labored.

"Fuck, Jillian. You are so beautiful." I kept my eyes focused up on him as I blew him. When I saw his eyes shut, I urged him with my free hand to grind against my mouth as wet heat hit the back of my throat. I swallowed eagerly, pretty sure that I'd left a lasting impression.

A moment later he pulled me to my feet. "Seconds or you want breakfast?"

"I'm starving," I admitted.

"Shite. The waffles!" He turned around and pulled the charred remains of breakfast from the waffle maker. "Let me try that again."

"It's cool. I'm going to throw something on," I said, heading toward my bedroom.

"That is a tragedy," he called after me.

When I came back, a waffle was sitting on the bar. I sat down and started cutting it up while Liam put more batter on the waffle iron.

"So what are your plans today?" he asked.

"I was thinking of doing something novel, like homework."

"You're getting wild this weekend," he said, sliding onto the stool next to me with his plate.

"I know." I forked another piece, but my hands shook as I brought it to my mouth, and I dropped it onto my lap.

"Careful there." He laughed, not noticing my embarrassment. "Here."

Liam grabbed the fork and brought the bite to my mouth. I pulled it off with my teeth and chewed it with mock ecstasy. When I opened my eyes, his own mouth was open.

"I could watch you eat waffles all day."

"If you're making them," I said.

"I will make you waffles anytime." There was a promise in his words, and I swallowed hard on the bite in my mouth. I took my fork back and focused on finishing my plate.

"So today?"

I knew he was asking me a question, but I didn't know how to answer.

"I'm meeting Jess later," I lied. Well, it wasn't exactly a lie. I would almost certainly see her today. After all, we lived together.

"What if I told you I had a hot tip on a Chiclets stash?" he teased.

"I would want to know how a fine, young Scottish man happened upon such valuable information." I grinned despite myself. He knew me so well already, which is exactly what scared me.

"Tonight then?"

I regarded him for a second and turned my attention to my last few bites. Would it be so bad to say yes? To make plans?

"What did you have in mind?" I asked him.

"Rob a liquor store, hold up a bank, you name it."

"That will certainly get your student visa revoked," I said.

"Only if we get caught," he said. "A movie. I thought we could see a movie."

I almost never went to movies. My budget was too tight to allow much spending money, and I tended to save it for going out.

"I don't know," I hesitated.

"My treat," he said.

"I don't even know what's out."

"Doesn't matter. I say we find the worst sounding movie and then sit in the back and make out."

This plan had potential. I hadn't made out in a movie theater since I was a teenager back when I dated steady guys, one at a time. There were a lot of things I hadn't done since then, and despite all my new and interesting experiences, part of me longed for the idea of something simple like a date at the movies.

"Deal," I said.

"I'll text you the times and you pick the one you want to see the most," he said. He stood and gathered my dish. "Do you want seconds?"

"Not this time," I said.

He raised his eyebrows.

"Maybe next time," I added.

Liam leaned down and gave me a swift kiss on the lips. It lingered like fire there, and I wanted to pull him down to me, but I didn't trust myself to stop, and I needed space. If I kissed him again, I'd find myself back in bed with him, which was a very tempting proposition, but I needed to think, and I couldn't do that with him there.

We washed the dishes together, blowing bubbles at each other and nearly breaking half the plates fooling around. When I finally pushed him out the door an hour later, I slumped against it.

I wasn't sure what I was getting into with him. Somewhere deep inside me a voice chastised me. This was an epically bad idea. I was only going to get worse, but a second voice piped up, reminding me that I wasn't just risking my own heart. I was risking his.

The problem was that I already knew I didn't have the strength to stay away from him. I had tried that, but Liam pulled me to him like a magnet. The more I resisted, the harder it became. That was the real issue. I knew in the end whether he wound up back in Scotland or if he found out the truth, we were both heading for heartbreak. But for the first time in a long time, I wanted the moments that would happen between this day and the one that was inevitably coming, because I knew they would be worth it.

What I didn't know was whether or not I could survive losing my heart to him, but thinking of his lips and his hands holding me close to him as we made love, I couldn't bring myself to care.

Chapter Twelve

"You will not fucking believe who I ran into!" The f-bomb heralded Cassie's arrival at the apartment before I could pop my head out of my room to see who was there.

"Do tell," I called as I threw a thin sweater over a low-cut tank top. It was sexy enough without looking like I was going out on a hot date.

Even though I totally was.

"Do you remember Ryan?" she asked.

We plopped onto the couch, and she grabbed for our remote while I searched my brain for any memory of a Ryan. "Wait, the metrosexual wannabe farmer?"

"Yes, him! He's from New York City—"

"And he wants to be an organic farmer," I finished for her. "What's up with him?"

"He's goddamned gorgeous. Busy playing in dirt," she said. She flipped through channels, showing no interest in any shows.

"Should Trevor be jealous?" I asked.

Cassie's big brown eyes rolled up. "No way. I can still appreciate something beautiful though, can't I?"

"Of course." Ryan was almost too pretty, but he rocked a body that made him look like a male model. It seemed a shame to waste it, or his fashion sense, out on a farm.

"How was last night?" Cassie asked.

I froze, confused as to how she knew what had finally happened with me and Liam. Then I realized she was referring to my absence at Garrett's. I'd discovered a dozen texts sent last night when she and Jess tried to find me. Each text more panicked than the last and all unanswered.

"There was a fight at the bar, and I got mixed up with it, so they kicked me out," I said, conveniently leaving out Liam's role in the evening's events. But even as I innocently recounted them to Cassie, I felt overheated, and I was sure she would notice.

"No shit?" Cassie turned, eager for more details, but interest immediately turned to concern when she saw I was flustered. "Are you feeling okay? Do you need me to grab something for you?"

"I'm fine." I shook off her concern. It was at once reassuring that she didn't realize I was flushed from excitement and annoying that she immediately turned into a mother hen.

Hen.

I smiled.

"Now you're just acting strangely," she said. She

watched me with narrowed eyes, trying to decipher what was going on with me.

"More strangely than normal?" Jess asked, lumbering into the room with a stack of ten or so text-books cradled in her arms.

I stuck my tongue out at both of them and grabbed for the remote, switching the channel to a *Bachelor* marathon.

"She got kicked out of the fucking bar," Cassie told Jess. "Did you know that?"

Jess shook her head as she slammed the books onto the counter. "How did you get kicked out?"

"She got in the middle of a fight," Cassie said. She clicked her nails together like she always did when we were gossiping.

Except I didn't like being the center of the gossip. "I didn't say I was in the fight. There was a mix-up."

"You know, I heard about a fight when we got there." Jess perched on the barstool and shot a mischievous smile my way.

Oh shit.

"You did?" I asked weakly.

"It was the talk of the bar."

"It was?" Cassie asked, sounding confused.

"You were too busy sexting Trevor," Jess reminded her.

"Guilty." Cassie blew her a kiss.

"So everyone was talking about this Scottish guy just laying some asshole out flat. Apparently, he insulted a girl." Jess paused and waited for me to respond.

I took a deep breath then groaned loudly. "It was not about me."

"What was it then?" Cassie and Jess asked at the same time.

"This guy sort of drunk-dived me and then he wouldn't let go, so Liam stepped in. He was just trying to be nice."

"His version of nice sounds a little violent." There was disapproval in Jess's voice.

"Was it totally hot?" Cassie asked me. As usual, she was more interested in the dirty details than judgment.

"He didn't hit the guy because of me. The jerk called him a sissy Brit and asked him where his skirt was."

Cassie covered her laughter with her hand, and even Jess smiled.

"And?" Cassie prompted.

"So Liam punched him and then he sort of said something like 'they're called kilts and we wear them because of our enormous cocks.'"

Jess fell off the stool, and Cassie's head dropped into my lap as they both shook with laughter.

"He really said that?" Jess asked, panting.

"He really said that," I confirmed.

"The more important question is does Liam need to wear a kilt?" Cassie asked. She wiggled her eyebrows up at me.

"I am a lady," I said.

"Since when?"

"Not fair," I said with a pouty frown.

"So you got kicked out because Liam hit someone? That's what's not cool." Jess arranged herself cross-legged on the rug.

I hesitated, knowing they were going to blow this little tidbit out of proportion. "No, they kicked him out, so I left in protest."

"Wait." Jess said as she held up a hand. "You left with Liam?"

"We left the bar together." I wanted to drop it at that. At this point I wasn't lying to them, but I wasn't exactly telling them the truth, which suited me fine.

"And that sweet Scottish boy didn't walk you home?" It was moments like this that I cursed whatever remnants of Southern propriety Cassie still carried with her. The girl could curse and drink like a sailor, but she still expected chivalry.

I clamped my mouth shut, deciding that exercising my fifth amendment right was safer than actually telling them that he had, in fact, walked me home. There was no way I'd be able to stop their questions then, and no way I could hide my shifting feelings for Liam.

"Oh, come on, Jills," Jess begged. "I have to go to my study group soon."

"Skip your study group. We'll wait her out," Cassie advised.

I checked the time on my iPhone. If I could get

them both out of here within fifteen minutes I didn't
have to worry about them crossing paths with Liam.

"Omigod, are you texting him?" Cassie squealed,
swiping the phone from me.

"Is she?" Jess asked from the floor.

"No." Cassie sounded disappointed.

"You would think we were on an episode of *The
Bachelor* with all your imagined drama," I complained.
"It's not like I got into a fight at the bar. Chill out."

"You are keeping something from us," Cassie said.
She poked an accusatory finger into my side.

"There was something white all over the counter
this morning," Jess said, eying me suspiciously.

"It was probably dust," I said. "It's not like we
ever clean."

"It was not dust. It was flour!" Jess jumped onto her
feet and proceeding to dance around the living room.

"No one has ever been this excited over flour
before," I said, crossing my arms over my chest.

"You're dressed up," Cassie noticed.

This was exactly why I didn't tell them anything.
If I wasn't careful, they were going to insist on taking
photos of us when he came to pick me up. It would
be one horrible high school prom flashback after
another.

"He's coming over, isn't he?" Jess asked.

"Don't you need to head out for your study group?"
It was nearly eight already. Liam was going to be here
any minute.

"They can wait," she said, grinning at me.

"Guys," I pleaded, but Cassie and Jess grabbed each other and pretended to embrace passionately.

"Liam!" Jess cried.

"Jillian!" Cassie pulled her close like they were going to kiss.

A knock at the door startled them apart, and they turned to me with wide, expectant eyes.

"I'm revoking your friend cards," I said.

"By the way, you lose, Jess. The next latte is on you," Cassie crowed. She might as well have yelled nah-nah-nah-boo-boo.

"That could have been our latte," Jess said to me in a pouty voice.

"Sorry, it was worth it." I grinned at her just as there was another knock at the door.

"Open it," Jess said, but when I refused to budge, she ran to the door herself.

The door swung open to reveal Liam in his low-slung jeans and a black button-down shirt. Against his fair skin, he looked like he'd walked out of a teenage vampire novel. I gulped and forced myself up.

"Come in, Liam." Jess opened the door wider, allowing him to step inside our apartment.

Liam's hand was behind his back, and he gave us a crooked grin.

"Jess, it's nice to see you," he greeted her.

Cassie jumped forward, hand outstretched. "I'm Cassie."

"I've heard a lot about you from Jillian," he said, taking her hand. "I feel like I already know you."

"You know," Cassie said, "I feel the same way."

Probably because Jess had live-texted our first morning-after to her. I could only pray she didn't mention that to him now, but knowing Cassie, she probably would. Hell, she might even pull out her phone and show him the pic Jess snapped of him making waffles that morning.

"We have to get going," I said, grabbing his arm and attempting to haul him out the door before they could embarrass me any more.

His hand swept around to reveal a box of Chiclets. "I was going to get you flowers, but I didn't know what you liked. Well, other than poor chewing gum and waffles."

"Oh, she loves your waffles," Cassie said in a devilish voice.

I was going to get them back for this. One day, it was going to be a boy on the other side of the door looking for *them*. I made a mental note to ask their moms for old baby photos.

"I love making her waffles." Liam was enjoying their attention a little too much. I couldn't let him spill the beans.

"We have homework to do," I lied.

"Is that anatomy homework?" Cassie's eyes traveled down the length of Liam as obviously as possible.

"We're going to see a movie," Liam said. He took my hand, and then he leaned in and planted a full, hard kiss on my lips. I melted on the spot, my free hand absently reaching up to clutch his shirt.

"Whoa! Save that for after the date," Jess said. We broke apart, and I looked sheepishly at my best friends. There was no hiding any of this from them now.

"If she's lucky," Liam said with a smile.

"I'll expect waffles in the morning." Jess winked at me.

I pulled Liam out the open door, pausing when I realized I didn't have my wallet. "Hold on."

I walked back in, keeping my head down and reached for my wallet on the bar, but Jess grabbed my arm and gave me a peck on the cheek.

"He's a catch," she whispered in my ear.

That's exactly what I was afraid of.

Chapter Thirteen

I chose a horror movie, because it seemed like the right choice for our first date. I couldn't think of anything worse than winding up at a sappy romantic comedy full of awkward moments. Those inevitably feature Happily Ever Afters, which was a bit presumptuous on a first date, if you asked me. Liam bought the tickets and held open the door for me, and every once in a while as we stood in line for popcorn, he'd lean over and kiss my forehead, sending flutters tumbling through my stomach.

"A large popcorn and chocolate-covered raisins," Liam ordered. "Do you want candy?"

"You eat chocolate-covered raisins?" I asked.

"Says the girl obsessed with Chiclets." His hand pressed against the small of my back, hot and strong, as he teased me.

The teenage cashier coughed politely, and I shook myself out of my daze.

"Those chocolate mint thingys," I said to the kid.

"Is that the technical term?"

I stuck my tongue out at him, but he just grinned wider and slid his hand down to hook his thumb into the waistline of my jeans.

Liam paid and we grabbed our snacks. The theater lights had already dimmed by the time we made it into the very last row. As we tucked ourselves into the corner seats, I considered putting the armrest up between our seats or placing my hand on his leg or laying my head on his shoulder, but I couldn't make myself move. I had forgotten how to be on a date. I had forgotten how horrible those in-between moments were when you first started going out with someone. Always waiting for a sign to make a move. The constant bumping together of hands like each person is daring the other to finally reach out and hold hands. I tugged at my shirt and adjusted my sweater, suddenly feeling warm and cold and confused at the same time.

Then Liam slung an arm over my shoulder and pulled me closer to him.

"Hold on," he said, pushing the armrest up between the seats. "That's better."

I snuggled down next to him, watching the previews, feeling relieved. I wasn't used to being the girl who didn't know how to make a move. Kiss a boy? Sure. Flirt? I could totally handle it. But apparently seeing a movie was way out of my wheelhouse, and I didn't like it. I slid my hand onto his thigh, close enough to his groin to feel a slight twinge of lust. Liam lifted my hand and put it back in my lap.

So that was how this date was going to go? Two could play that game. I sat up straighter, putting space between the two of us, but letting his arm dangle casually over my shoulder. Liam offered me the popcorn tub, but I shook my head, my eyes glued to the screen and a lump in my throat.

He leaned over and put his lips so close to my ear that his breath tickled my neck. "Don't be mad, chicken."

"I'm not mad," I said too loudly, which elicited a shush from someone a couple rows away.

He pulled me back towards him, his strong arm wrapping possessively around my shoulders as his other hand turned my chin. As soon as our eyes met, I felt silly.

"It'll be more fun this way," he whispered. "I promise."

"What will be more fun?" I asked in a low voice, narrowing my eyes and trying to still look put out by his rejection.

He answered me with his lips. His kiss was hard and demanding, and despite my every intention to play hard to get, my fingers reached for his chest. I trailed my hands down, my fingertips practically vibrating over his washboard abs, but when I got to his jeans, he reached down, his mouth still over mine, and brought my arms up to his neck. I forgot the slight instantly as his teeth caught my tongue ever so lightly. I moaned, and he drew me closer, pressing our mouths harder together, to stifle the noise. His lips trailed away from my mouth, sketching across my jawline and finding my ear. He nibbled at it, and I had to clamp my mouth shut. It would set a bad precedent if we got kicked out of every place we went to together.

"Like secondary school, remember?" he breathed to me.

I couldn't help but remember the torture that was a high school date. There was always plenty of kissing and tongues and a fair bit of awkward groping. I'd even gotten the courage up to go down on my boyfriend senior year in a theater not unlike this one, but for the most part, a high school date was like being pumped full of aphrodisiacs and then put in separate glass boxes. There were always too many clothes and zippers and buttons.

But there was also the fear—of getting caught, of going one step too far. The fear was nearly as all-consuming as the hormones, and the fear made every single nerve in my body tingle with nervous anticipation. And then there was the possibility. That this would be the time he slipped his hand down my pants and magically knew exactly what to do. I could act shocked afterwards.

Liam and I were already well past this stage. I'd barely known his name when we covered all the old bases.

"I wouldn't have had the guts to do this in high school," I whispered to him, running a hand quickly over his crotch. I could feel that he was rock hard under his jeans, but Liam pushed my hand away again.

"You don't want me to?" I asked.

"Oh, chicken, I want you to," he said in a husky voice. "But I'll be able to screw you six ways to Sunday if you keep your hands off me."

So that's what this was about. Suddenly I made contact with my inner, horny teenager. I'd been in these positions before, clenching my thighs together and kissing for so long that I almost ceased being able to breathe independently. Yes, it had been torture to hold back then, but I'd gotten pretty good at teasing myself. I reached for my box of chocolate mints and ripped open the top. On the screen, a girl was already running through the woods, inexplicably topless, but I didn't care. Next to me, Liam shifted around in his seat, and I knew he was uncomfortable. I tilted my head toward him and popped a mint in my mouth, sucking off the chocolate coating. Liam raised an eyebrow, and I smiled at him, leaning over to kiss him. I kept the soft mint muddled under my tongue and opened my mouth against his, blowing ever so slightly into his mouth, my breath cold and hot at the same time. Liam's hand clamped over my shoulder, but I tugged it down onto my breast. He might not let me touch him, but second base was clearly within high school make-out session territory. His fingers skimmed over it lightly, and then he flicked my nipple. It was an expert move. No boy I dated in high school would have had the skill to do that, which is why a loud moan slipped from my lips.

A head popped over the seat in front of us. "That is disgusting," the woman chastised us. "Don't you have any shame?"

"Ma'am," Liam said in a polite tone, "there is a man currently dismembering someone in the film you chose to see. I could ask you the same thing."

She gawked at him, her face frozen against the gruesome scene on the screen.

"Make love, not war," I added.

She turned back in her seat and began whispering furiously to her friend, but neither of them turned back around.

"Should we go?" I asked him.

He shook his head. "New rule: mouths only."

"I can do a lot of things with my mouth," I said with an anticipatory bite of my lip.

He held a hand up to his throat. "Here and above," he whispered.

"You're no fun."

"Believe me, this will be fun," he said.

As it turned out, there is a lot more ground to cover at the neck and above than I had previously thought. With an hour of available study time, I learned that Liam was ticklish—two inches to the right of his collarbone to be precise; that having the spot behind my earlobe bit, licked, sucked, kissed, or hell, breathed on, sent my toes curling in my shoes and my legs pressing together; and that I could actually kiss a boy so long and so deeply that I forgot about wanting to have sex. The kiss with his fingers clutching my hair or his hands warm on my face was enough. And when the movie ended and the credits rolled, I didn't want to leave our dark corner.

I just wanted to kiss him some more.

As the house lights came up, the woman in front of us turned to shoot us a dirty glance.

"I hope you two enjoyed your evening," she snapped, saddling her way through the seats toward the aisle.

"Oh, it's not over yet," I called after her. "He promised to screw me six ways to Sunday."

The women scurried out of the theater as Liam stood and pulled me up.

"My place?" I asked.

"Not yet," he said, kissing me softly. "Ice cream."

He grabbed my hand as we exited the theater. It was so easy and natural for him that all of my earlier paranoia seemed to vanish.

"So you like horror movies?" he asked.

"Not particularly," I admitted with a laugh.

"Then why did we see a horror movie?"

"I didn't think our plans including watching the movie." I knocked my hip against his good-naturedly.

"I did imply that."

"You not only implied it," I said. "You followed through."

Liam caught me with his free arm and swept me into his arms, spinning me around once before depositing me onto my feet.

It was the kind of thing that only happens in the

bad romantic comedies I'd avoided so carefully when I picked the movie. Now I was living in one. Of course, those movies never had any sex in them, so we already had them beat.

"It's quiet tonight." Liam urged me along, bringing me out of my thoughts and back to him.

"Sunday is truly a day of rest around here. Everyone is still recovering from Friday and Saturday," I said.

"I hope Coffee & Cream is still open," he said.

"No coffee shop would dare to close down before midnight in this town," I reassured him. I'd been shocked at the sheer number of coffee shops and shacks when I'd come here three years ago from California. I'd once seen two kids selling espresso shots at a makeshift coffee stand instead of lemonade. There was no way the premier—meaning closest to campus—Olympic Falls coffee shop would be closed.

We walked through downtown Olympic Falls under the glow of street lamps. Only restaurants and coffee shops were open this late on a Sunday night, so the streets were clear of the usual bar crowd. I'd never been out when it was this quiet, and between the softly lit shopfronts and the bay glistening with moonlight in the distance, there was magic in the air.

I stopped and lifted my eyes to the stars. "No matter where you stand in Olympic Falls, it always looks like you could reach right up and pluck one from the darkness."

"What would you do with it?" he asked.

"Make a wish," I said in a soft voice. I turned into him and wrapped my arms around his waist, pushing up on my tiptoes to kiss him. Liam's hand cradled my head as he held me to him. Our bodies didn't fight to get closer as we pressed our lips together. This kiss was nothing more than a wish.

Chapter Fourteen

❧✦❧

Coffee & Cream hummed with the energy of a dozen laptops but was fairly quiet otherwise. Sunday night was always little dead at the spots near campus. Monday and Tuesday were the most well-attended class days of the week, and people were busy catching up with the coursework they had put off over the weekend. The coffee shop was a mish-mash of couches and chairs. I imagined it had been decorated during the height of the *Friends* frenzy and not much had changed since then. A large chalkboard listed fifty different espresso drinks and today's available ice creams. We wandered up to the counter and peered into the glass case.

"Does anyone really eat green tea ice cream?" Liam asked me.

"Oh, I love it." I waved for the girl behind the counter to give us a sample. I held it up to Liam, and he opened his mouth apprehensively. As soon as it hit his tongue, he grimaced and swallowed it hard.

"You like that?" he asked.

"Don't your people eat haggis?" I tossed the sample spoon into a Dixie cup.

"Not if we can help it."

He ordered a dark Mexican chocolate, and I got the offending green tea—both to go. As we turned to head back to my apartment, we ran directly into Professor Markson.

"Miss Nichols. Mr. McAvoy. Have a nice week-end?" he asked. He was juggling a hefty-looking brief-case and a steaming mug of coffee, but there was a slight smirk on his face. He was probably enjoying catching us together after all the grief I'd given Liam so far this semester.

"It's not over yet, sir," Liam said, sliding an arm around my waist.

"I'll expect to see you both in class on Tuesday," Markson said, and I could almost swear he winked at Liam. "If you aren't too busy."

"I'm sure we can drag ourselves out of bed to be in class."

I smacked Liam's shoulder, my face on fire.

"Out of our beds. Plural. As in two. As in separate," Liam corrected. It only made me blush deeper.

Markson didn't bother to hide his smile. "I think you both still have a ways to go in your communication skills."

"We've learned a lot already. Haven't we, chicken?"

I wanted to melt into a puddle on the floor and seep through the tiles. Had he really just called me chicken in front of a professor that took an inordinate amount of joy in embarrassing me?

"I will see you both on Tuesday then," Markson said, scooching past us to an unoccupied couch.

"Can you not call me chicken in front of people set on making my life a living hell?" I asked Liam as he opened the shop's door for me.

"Are there a lot of people who make your life hell?"

"Let me rephrase that: can you not call me chicken in front of other people?" I was only just getting used to the nickname myself, and I could only imagine how horrible it would be to have Cassie and Jess pick up on the nickname. Or even worse, someone like my mother.

"'Kay, chicken." He sealed the deal with a quick brush of his lips over my forehead.

As soon as we got back to my apartment, I did a quick check for Jess, but she was still out at study group. That girl seriously needed to get a life. Maybe if she had found a boyfriend with a real personality, she wouldn't spend all of her time reading medical textbooks. I grabbed a ceramic frog from the cabinet and set it on the counter.

"Redecorating?" Liam asked as he pulled two spoons from the drawer.

"It's a secret code," I told him. Jess and I had established the ceramic frog as a way to communicate that one of us had a boy over. We hadn't used it much lately. Not because we weren't getting any action, even though I hadn't brought a boy home since Liam. We had just fallen into a comfortable routine, but I knew Jess would be dying for details of my date as soon as she got in. I didn't really want her to pop her head into my room tonight though.

I had plans.

"Like espionage?" Liam asked. He picked up the frog and studied it as though it would reveal its secrets if he looked long enough.

"I don't want her to, uh, interrupt us." I blushed again and was immediately annoyed with myself. Jillian Nichols didn't blush, and yet I'd been doing just that since I met him. What was it about Liam that brought out this giggly, flushed girly side of me?

I excused myself to the bathroom. After popping my meds and doing a few stretches, I stared into the mirror. I'd never consciously come into the bathroom knowing that the guy I was with would be here in the morning. If I was going to bed on a normal night, I would take off my makeup. Maybe I would throw my bra on the floor. But he was going to be here when I walked out the bathroom door, and I knew he would be there in the morning, maybe even making me breakfast, when I woke up. I grabbed my face wash and scrubbed off my makeup. I slathered some lotion on my face, a remnant from when Cassie lived across from us. She was obsessed with facial care.

The girl looking back at me from the mirror wasn't the usual vixen that brought home boys. There was no coral lipstick or carefully applied eyeliner, but she was fresh with slightly pink cheeks. I felt naked like this, more exposed than I'd ever really let a boy see me. I thought briefly about taking off my bra, but decided there was no need to get too comfortable.

Liam was in my bedroom when I came out. I sucked in a breath at the sight of him. He'd pulled off his shirt and was lounging on the bed in his jeans. Two spoons lay across his chiseled abs, and he held up a pint of ice cream. But when his eyes met mine, they widened and his lips parted slightly.

"You should never wear makeup," he told me.

I covered my face with my hands. He'd noticed that I'd taken it off.

"Don't," he said in a low voice. "You look so unbelievably sexy. I'm afraid we won't be getting any sleep tonight."

"I usually don't eat in bed," I said to him, suddenly feeling flustered.

"That's a shame, because I'm going to have to break that rule."

I put my hands on my hips. "You are, huh?"

"Do you wear pantyhose?" he asked me.

"This just took a strange turn," I said, not hiding my confusion.

"Or scarves?" he suggested.

"That I have." I dug into my closet and tossed him a few.

"Perfect," he said. He stood up, abandoning the scarves and the spoons and drew me roughly to him. His mouth settled over my neck, biting down lightly where it curved into my shoulder. I slid my arms around him and ran my hands over his tight back as shivers raced through my body. He pulled back and stared into my eyes, and I couldn't look away. The blue of his eyes was so deep that I thought I might drown in them. I felt like a swimmer at sea, being pulled under by the tide. I was losing myself in him, and I was helpless to stop it.

His fingers snaked under my shirt, my skin blazing where he touched me as he tugged off my sweater. Then he unsnapped my jeans and pushed them down to my ankles. I stepped out of them, never once looking away from him as his eyes burned into my own. But once I was down to my thong and bra, he took a step back. His eyes travelled down my body and I felt it. I'd never been studied this way before. His gaze lingered slowly as it journeyed all the way down to my calves.

I reached out to unbutton his pants, but his hand caught my wrist as he shook his head.

"I need you on the bed now." There was a hunger in his words that sent a quiver through my core. Liam nudged me gently toward the bed, and then he was on top of me, his lips covering mine possessively. He pinned my wrists over my head and then I felt a scarf wrap around one of them. My eyes flew open in surprise.

"What are you doing?" I asked. "Are we getting all Fifty Shades up in here?"

He shushed me. "Nothing that dangerous. You won't need a safe word."

"It's considered polite to ask a woman before you tie her up," I reminded him.

"Jillian, I would like to spend the next hour giving you the greatest sixty minutes of your life," he said softly.

My knees trembled at the thought as nearly every muscle in my body tensed with anticipation at his offer.

"Can I tie you up?" he asked me.

I wet my lips with my tongue and nodded.

"And I'd like to cover up those beautiful eyes," he added.

"I like to see you." The confession escaped my lips before I could hold it back.

"You will, chicken. I promise. But trust me, please." He brushed a strand of hair from my face and laid a soft kiss on my lips.

"Okay," I said with some apprehension. The thing about one-night stands was that they weren't all that creative when it came to foreplay. I'd never let a guy tie me up, let alone blindfold me. My stomach did a little flip as he wrapped a scarf around my hands. Once. Twice. Three times. I heard him slide the scarf around the bars of my cheap, IKEA headboard, and my hands hit the cold metal as he tied me to it. He lifted my head gently and placed a scarf under it.

"Wait," I said.

He paused, and I took in his face—the strong curve of his jaw, his messy hair, the slight crookedness of his nose—and his body, hovering like a perfect statue over

me. I arched my back, trying to raise my head to his for
a kiss.

"None of that, chicken," he whispered as he
brought his lips to mine. Our mouths crushed together,
leaving me breathless and panting. I was totally at his
mercy. He looked into my eyes as he drew the scarf
over them. He wrapped it around again, tying it off in a
soft knot behind my head.

"No safe word, Jillian, but if you want to stop, just
say so," he whispered into my ear.

Between being trapped under him and the hotness
of his lips against my ear, I was just ready to get started.
I felt a familiar frenzy pulsing between my legs as he
lingered over my body, barely touching me.

I couldn't see him, but I could sense him, and then I
felt his fingers pluck at the straps of my lacy, red bra.

"This is so, so sexy, chicken, but I want to see
them." He twisted the front closure, and I felt the air
hit my nipples as he opened my bra wide. I waited for
him to touch them. I wanted him to, but he moved
down instead, his body heat gliding over me. There was
no contact, and I squirmed against the scarves.

"Be patient," he whispered.

"You're not the one tied up," I told him, adding
silently, *and totally revved up.*

He chuckled lowly as he hooked his thumbs under
my thong and wrenched it over my knees and off me
entirely. I spread my legs a little, eager for him, but he
pushed them back together. The heat of his body disappeared entirely, and I felt cold and exposed.

"If this is a joke..." I warned him, but my threat was met with a harsh shush.

And then he was back over me, and my body tensed, ready, for his lips and his hands. Ice ricocheted through my nerves as something cold and wet dripped down between my breasts. I moaned and bucked up, but his hand held me down as more of the cold liquid drizzled over my nipples.

"What is that?" I murmured.

"Dessert, baby." And then heat burst against the chill as his tongue licked across the ice cream. He licked it up with long strokes, starting between my breasts and circling up in slow, even motions upward. His tongue flicked against my already hard left nipple, and then he brought his mouth over it, licking and sucking it against his teeth. I gasped as the throb between my legs ratcheted up a notch. He moved to the next one, and I pulled against the scarves. I wanted to wrap my arms around him. I wanted to force him between my legs, but Liam's bindings held.

"I'm not done," he warned me. I melted into a mix of anticipation and longing at his words.

The spoon drew a biting line down my stomach, circling around my navel, and Liam's tongue followed in a trail of fire with one extended stroke downwards. He lingered at my belly button as one of his hands pushed my legs apart. I waited, biting down on my lip. He had me panting now, but nothing happened.

And then his tongue plunged into me, cold and hot at the same time, sending the first waves of pleasure off like emissaries sent to bring back the full onslaught. As quickly as it started, it disappeared, and I was left feeling bare and unsatisfied.

"Don't stop," I begged.

"I won't," he promised. His lips kissed along the edge of my bikini line. If my hands were free, I would push him down and make him finish what he started, but I was at his mercy.

And Liam knew it.

"I feel like I could stay here all day, looking at you like this."

"Stop using 'I' statements," I snapped. "You're driving me crazy."

"Good." There was a smile in his voice. He was enjoying this. Not just seeing me spread before him but making me wait, like I made him wait so long for me.

"Please," I whimpered.

"Since you asked nicely." His mouth closed over my clit before he moved lower and forced me open to him. He stroked me deep and hard with his tongue, and I felt my muscles tightening. My hands gripped the headboard and I held on as he fucked me with his mouth.

"Do. Not. Stop!" I cried in one breath. His finger slipped inside my channel, thrusting me over the edge as he sucked me hungrily.

My body split and knit together as I bucked against his mouth. I couldn't reach out to stop him and the pressure built up, pleasure cascading in surges through my body. It was relentless, and I never wanted it to end.

But even as I held my body rigid, trying to linger in the moment, I shattered again as I called his name, my legs clamping him to me.

Liam pried my thighs from his head and rested it on my bare belly. He breathed in hot pants against my skin, and I wanted to reach down and pull him to me. Pull him into me.

I heard him get up and then water running in the bathroom. I didn't care that I was naked, tied up and covered in sticky ice cream. I cared that he was gone. But then he came back, climbing in over me. He tugged the knot of the blindfold and pulled it off. I blinked against the light.

"Are you going to untie me?" I asked him. I wanted the use of my hands so that I could rip his jeans off.

"I'm considering it," he said with a devilish smile.

"Less considering, more doing," I urged.

"But I like this. Jillian is caught," he murmured. He brought his wicked smile within centimeters of mine, but he didn't kiss me. I could smell mint on his breath. His body still hovered carefully over me, not letting us touch.

"Just take your damn pants off," I said.

"Lady's choice then," he said. He sat back on his heels and I watched as he unsnapped the fly of his jeans. He shoved them down to his knees and settled against me without entering me. I pulled my knees up, using my feet to push his jeans off him completely. I'd gotten a peek at his eight inch long prize and I was ready to claim it.

"It's only fair," I told him as I wrapped my legs around his tight glutes.

"Condom?" he asked.

I blinked against the heady feeling caused by his warm erection resting against my belly. "I'm on the pill."

"Jillian?" It was a question.

I'd never done this before. I'd always doubled up, but I thought I would go crazy if he moved away from me for even a moment.

"I'm clean, and I trust you." It was permission.

One of the perks of constant doctor visits and blood tests was that I knew everything that was wrong with me, and STDs were not on the list, thanks to always being careful.

He hesitated but our eyes met and my heart slammed against my chest, and I knew then that nothing would be the same with us after this. He brought his lips to mine, but he didn't enter me. It was a slow kiss, full of promises. I knew we'd never keep them, but I didn't care, because in this moment all I needed was him.

"Are you sure?" he asked one more time, drawing his head back to meet my eyes.

"Yes." It was more a breath than a word. I was asking him as much as he was asking me.

His hands reached up and loosened the scarves, allowing my hands to slip free. He caught my arm, planting kisses along it as he brought it up to his neck. We watched each other with tentative need. Liam moved down and eased inside of me without another word. I gasped as he thrust gently into me, and tears pooled at the edge of my eyes as an ache burst in my chest. He slowed, and I knew he saw them.

"Jillian, I—"

I brought his mouth to mine. I couldn't bear to hear what he was going to say in this moment. Not when I wanted so badly for him to say something I had never heard before. And not when I wanted so badly for him to never say it.

But it was on his lips, and I could taste it, and I knew it was on my own as well, so we clung to each other, pressed together and entwined.

Liam rocked leisurely against me until we were both moving in the same rhythm. He never left me, and I felt swollen and alive with him inside of me. He pulled back and looked into my eyes as the pressure built in my core. I held his gaze, even as my eyes tried to close as the first tremors rippled through me. He groaned as he came, murmuring my name in invocation, and I met his cry with my own as an orgasm swelled in me and burst. But our eyes stayed locked on each other. We never looked away.

Chapter Fifteen

The apartment was quiet and dark as we laid there, wrapped together. Liam's face nuzzled my neck, his arm resting casually across my stomach. We didn't sleep for a long time. It was a magical sort of solitude, being there with each other like we were the only two people in the world. I drifted into my dreams in his arms.

When sun broke through my window, I woke to find myself still cocooned in Liam's arms. We had barely shifted in our sleep. I let myself stare at him for a few minutes, trying to decipher the ache I felt through the core of my body. His eyes were closed, his dark blond lashes fluttering slightly as he slept. I moved my hand up to his chest and felt the steady beat of his heart. I counted them, each one more precious than the last, and I realized I was falling in love with him.

I swallowed hard on this realization and extricated myself carefully from his arms. I slipped out of bed and found his long t-shirt. When I pulled it over my head, I could smell the cologne lingering on it, mixing with detergent and something else. The scent—Liam's scent —made my pulse race. I needed to get out of here, so I opened the door quietly and headed toward the bath-room. Before I could reach it, Jess poked her out of her bedroom and smiled.

"It was quiet in here," she said. "But given the frog on the counter and that shirt, I'm guessing we have breakfast plans."

I shook my head, trying to clear it so I could answer her, but all I could manage was, "Liam's still sleeping."

She followed me into the bathroom and brushed her hair while I started the shower. I could tell she wanted details, but she wasn't going to ask for them, and I wasn't sure I was ready to share them.

Last night had been more intimate than any other night of my life. The memory of it was raw and new, and I wasn't sure I could spill something that personal, even with Jess. It felt like it belonged to Liam and me, as though sharing it would have broken some unspoken rule.

But still, I wanted to share it with her. I just didn't know what to say.

"Was your date nice?" she finally asked, turning to watch as I grabbed for a fresh towel in the linen closet.

I nodded, avoiding her gaze as I found the shampoo bottle. Why couldn't I tell Jess how I felt about him? Why couldn't I tell *him*?

"Are you going to talk to me?" she asked. She

leaned against the bathroom counter and crossed her arms.

"I don't know what to say," I admitted to her. "I can't quite explain what happened last night. It's too fresh."

"Shit, Jills, what did you two do?" Jess looked a little worried.

"I'm not ready to talk about it." That felt right. I wasn't ready. I needed to process. The shower would help me do that, and then I could talk to Jess about Liam later.

"You're scaring me," Jess said in a soft voice.

"I don't know how to say it. It sounds cheesy," I said.

"Jills!"

"We...made love."

Jess's eyebrows popped up in surprise, and I buried my face in my hands. I could not believe that actually came out of my mouth. It sounded like a line from a bad movie. One of the ones where the girl dies or the guy goes off to war. It so didn't fit my life...until now.

"Wow," she murmured.

"That's all you've got, huh?"

Jess looked like she was trying to decide what to say. I couldn't blame her. Love was a dirty word by my standards. It didn't fit into my personal catch and release philosophy.

"So you two are dating then?" she asked me.

I took a deep breath and blew it out, trying to

steady myself against the dizziness swimming in my head. "I guess so."

Jess lunged forward and gripped me in a tight hug.

"Geez. We're not getting married," I muttered as she clutched me.

Jess leaned back, gripping my shoulders and looked at me with wide, serious eyes. "This is amazing, Jills."

"I know." I willed myself to believe it.

"No," she stopped me. "I know you're confused, but I saw you this morning. You were smiling. He makes you happy."

Liam made me more than happy. He made me laugh. He made my toes curl in bed. But there was one problem. "He barely knows me," I reminded her. "I haven't told him."

"You will." Jess kissed my cheek. "And it's going to be all right. If you didn't scare him off before now, I don't think that will scare him off."

"Are you saying I was a bitch?" I asked her with a raised eyebrow.

"Yes," she said without hesitation. "But you already knew that."

I looked to the running shower. "I need to grab a shower. I'm a little sticky."

Jess's mouth fell open. "You really aren't going to tell me about last night?"

"Nope," I said, grinning despite myself.

"You're killing me, Jills," she pouted as I pushed her out the bathroom door.

I peeked through the door and whispered, "It was mind-blowing."

I shut the door as she yelled, "Tease!"

Adjusting the heat of the shower, I got in and reached for the soap. Remnants of chocolate ice-cream had tightened my skin, and I washed it off, letting my mind wander back to the evening before. I'd never been with a guy like that before. Not just in bed, but on our date. There was something about Liam that helped me relax. I'd shown him my weird side on more than one occasion now, and he kept coming back. I wanted to believe Jess when she said that nothing I could tell him would make that change. The shower stall slid open, and Liam slipped in beside me.

"Were you going to let me sleep all morning?" he asked as we pressed close together under the running water.

"You looked peaceful," I told him. "Sated and happy. I thought I'd let you sleep."

"Sated?" he said with a laugh.

"Weren't you?" I asked him.

"Until I woke up without you, chicken," he murmured, brushing his lips across my jaw. I brought my mouth to his, but he pulled back.

"Jillian, about last night," he began.

"I need you to know something," I interrupted, taking a deep breath. "I've never done that with anyone before."

"I know," he said softly.

"I didn't want you think I was a slut or something."

The words tumbled out of my mouth. I knew I was babbling, but I couldn't stop myself.

"I would never think that," he said.

"I brought you home the first night I met you," I reminded him.

"I came home with you the first night I met you. What's your point?" he asked.

He had me there.

"But," he continued. "Last night was amazing, and while I'm fairly certain I could spend the rest of my life in bed with you, I want to slow down."

I blinked at his words. "Slow down?"

"We jumped into bed together. I don't want you think I'm only after sex," he said in a quiet voice.

That had never occurred to me with Liam. I had known plenty of guys who were just after sex. He didn't strike me as the type. The problem was that I liked sex. I *loved* sex with him. I wasn't entirely sold on this slowing down idea or the reasoning behind it. "So you got into the shower with me to tell me you don't want to have sex with me?" I asked him. "Is this some type of psychological experiment?"

Liam took a step back. "Sorry."

"No, you're right," I said. The closer I got to Liam, the more I was sure I was falling for him. It was happening too fast. Maybe putting sex on hold for a while would help us figure things out with clearer heads.

"I'm not going anywhere," he said.

"You're going back to Scotland," I said softly. For

the first time, just thinking about this sent a twinge of panic through me.

"Not for a long time, chicken." He wrapped his arms around me, and I settled into his chest. I wished I could stay here like this, but Jess might want to use the bathroom again today.

"Hand me the shampoo?" I asked, pulling out of his arms.

Liam reached behind him and squirted some shampoo into his palm. "Lean back."

I tipped my hair back into the stream of water, soaking it through completely. I brought my head back up to meet Liam's eyes as his fingers combed into my hair, spreading the shampoo through it. I moaned a little as his hands massaged into my scalp.

"I had no idea this would get you so excited," he teased.

"I moan at the salon, too. Don't get cocky."

Liam guided my head back under the water and washed it out.

"Your turn," I said as I wiggled to the other side of him and grabbed the shampoo. I reached up and soaped his hair until it was foamy, forming it into a mohawk.

"Do I look cool?" he asked.

"Very rock star."

He leaned back and rinsed. There was an awkward pause, so I leaned forward to turn off the water, but Liam blocked me.

"I could use a few minutes more, if you don't mind." His grin was unusually sheepish, and I frowned.

"Are you sure?" I asked. Stepping forward, I kissed him softly, feeling him press into my stomach. "Oh."

"Yeah," Liam said.

"We could always start taking it slowly tomorrow or the day after or next week?" I offered.

"Get out of here," he said with a laugh, swatting me on the ass.

"Your loss."

"Don't I know it?" he said as I slipped out of the shower and wrapped a towel around myself. I hurried out of the bathroom to give him some privacy and because every inch of me wanted to climb back in with him. Jess's door was shut as I passed it and went into my room to get dressed. I dug through my closet, looking for the perfect outfit. It felt like the first day of school again, as though the semester had restarted over night. Everything was new and exciting, just waiting to be discovered.

And that scared me.

Chapter Sixteen

❧

The aquarium sat on the edge of the bay. At first glance, it was easy to mistake it for an ordinary cottage, which is one of the reasons I loved it. I'd gone there fairly often when I'd first come to Olympic Falls, but I hadn't been this year so far. The clouds were low on the water, sending drifts of fog across my path and up through the city's cozy downtown hamlet.

I felt giddy as I smoothed my ponytail and applied a little cherry lip balm. I was going to visit the guy who might be my boyfriend, a fact that had my stomach doing flips. Once upon a time, it would have been because I felt stupid, but this was exciting. I wasn't sure how to feel about it, but when I pushed open the door, a familiar grin greeted me from across the building. My heart lurched from its steady beat as a pang shot through my chest. I had it bad.

The girl sitting behind the information desk looked

me up and down, scowling. "We're closed. We have a school group coming in."

Liam rushed over and grabbed my hand. "Kate, this is my girlfriend, Jillian. I asked her to come down."

My heart jumped. Liam had called me his girl-friend. It shouldn't surprise me, even though it did. But maybe more surprising was how much I liked hearing it.

"Okay." Kate said the word slowly like she was searching for an excuse to get me to leave. I wondered if she had a crush on Liam, but then I checked out his lean muscular form and thought of his rough, thick accent. Of course she did, and I didn't blame her one bit.

"There's about twenty first graders on their way. I'm doing a lesson on local tide pool life," Liam explained as he led me past the various tanks. He pulled me behind a large jellyfish exhibit and wrapped his arms around me. The kiss was slow and lingering, lacking the urgency he usually gave off when we were together. His lips were soft as they moved slowly over mine as though he was tasting me for the first time. His hand slipped up my neck and tangled into my hair, loosening my tight ponytail. He clutched my hair and deepened the kiss, crushing his mouth to mine as our hips locked against one another's. The sound of twenty unruly kids broke us apart, both of us panting as I adjusted my hair and tried to calm my ragged breathing.

Liam wanted to slow down now that we were dating. I wasn't so sure that was going to be possible.

He stepped out from behind the tank, throwing a wink my way, and called out a welcome to the class. I came out slowly, feeling a little shy given how flushed I felt, but the kids didn't seem to notice. They swarmed around us, already asking questions and trying to reach into the hands-on exhibits to touch the various anemones and starfish exhibited there. A little girl seized my hand and stared up at me with big eyes. I wasn't sure if I should shake her off or not. She looked a little scared, but I was the last person who should be entrusted with small children. I would probably say something that would scar her for life. I could just see myself dropping the f-bomb and poor Liam having to apologize to a mob of angry parents. Why hadn't this occurred to him when he invited me yesterday?

Leaning over, I whispered to him, "You could have told me there were going to be kids here."

"Why is she here? Is she our teacher?" a boy asked, whacking me in the belly. I shot him a dirty look before I remembered that he was like seven and likely had less impulse control then I did, which was saying something.

"Miss Nichols is my assistant today. Do you know what an assistant is?" Liam asked the group. They quieted and stared at him with confused faces.

"You talk funny," one yelled.

"Aye, I'm from Scotland, bonnie lass," he said, overemphasizing his native tongue. Most of the kids giggled at him.

"An assistant," a boy piped up, "is someone who helps because they don't know anything."

I bit back a laugh at this nugget of wisdom, even though in this case he was right. I knew about as much as they did about tide pools. Unless, of course, they had been studying them in class before today, in which case I knew less.

"Today, we're going to learn about the sea life you might find in a tide pool. We're going to start by watching this video," he explained as the teacher guided the students into a semi-circle on the floor. The video started, explaining how pockets of water were left in the wake of the tide. It was oddly absorbing, but Liam snuck up behind me midway through.

"I'm sorry I didn't tell you about the class. I forgot they were coming this morning," he admitted, following his confession with the crooked grin I was beginning to love.

"It's fine, but I should go. I'll just be in the way."

"Nonsense," he whispered. "Maybe you'll find your true calling amongst the anemones."

I doubted that. Even though I'd spent my whole life living near the ocean, I wasn't keen on touching something that looked like it might suck my fingers off.

As it turned out, Liam was gifted at holding the attention of seven-year-olds. Something I sure I would suck at. They hung off every word he said as he explained the correct way to touch the various creatures in the tide pool tanks. The class split into groups, and the little girl tugged my hand to come with her. Her name tag read "Sarah," and I reluctantly followed her, but stood back, amazed by how fearless the kids were as they used one finger to gently feel each animal.

"Come on, Miss Nichols," Liam said, grabbing my elbow and dragging me closer to the tank. "It's your turn."

I held back and shook my head as I peered into the water.

"What are those?" I asked as I pointed to a worm-like creature with warts covering its body.

"Sea cucumbers!" Sarah told me.

I made a face at Liam. "Do you eat them?"

"It's considered a delicacy in Asia," he said, laughing a little at my reaction.

"Remind me to steer clear of Asia." I dipped a finger into the tank and braced myself, but the sea cucumber felt like a squishy leather tube.

"That wasn't so bad, was it?" Liam said. "Let's all give a round of applause for Miss Nichols being brave." He clapped his hands in a huge circle, and the kids mimicked him enthusiastically. A few weeks ago, I would have pegged him as the world's biggest dork, but I had to admit that he actually looked pretty sexy. This was the guy that made waffles naked in my kitchen, after all. Embarrassment wasn't likely to hold him back.

By the end of the hour, I'd gotten brave enough to touch a sea urchin and an anemone, which lazily wrapped its small tentacles around my finger. Liam came up beside me at the tank and carefully squeezed my hip just once. "Next step: diving," he murmured, his blue eyes trained on me.

I didn't have the heart to tell him there was no way I was capable of diving, so instead I nodded, my nerves humming with the electricity passing between us.

The insistent tug of a student on Liam's t-shirt broke the connection between us, and I spent the rest of the morning watching him explain all about the natural sea life near our city's shores. When the kids finally marched back toward the bus, Liam let out a weary sigh.

"They were energetic," I said.

"They always are." He smiled and took my hand, knitting our fingers together. "Do you have class or can we grab a bit of lunch?"

I checked my watch, surprised to see it was only eleven. "I have an hour and a half."

"Fish and chips?" he offered. It was impossible to resist his imploring eyes.

Outside the air was crisp but still warm enough to not need a jacket. It was an atypically clear day for the rainy Olympic Peninsula without a cloud in the sky. The aquarium was stationed across from the city's main boardwalk, which emptied onto the primary boat dock. We ambled along it toward the walk-up fish and chips counter. Liam ordered for us, and within minutes, I was cradling a newspaper-wrapped order as we found a spot to sit on the pier. I swung my legs over the side, my feet dangling inches from the water.

"I love this place," Liam said as he opened his order with reverence. "They do it right. Like back home."

He bit into a battered plank and moaned.

"You're going to make me jealous," I teased, but I had to admit the greasy food hit the spot.

"Only two things elicit moaning from me." He held up the fish and then leaned in to kiss me. It was an oily kiss and not at all sexy, but butterflies fluttered in my chest anyway.

"What are you going to do when you get back to Scotland?" I asked him. "I mean, when you're done with your degree?"

He stared at the calm water. "I want to get a position on a research ship. There's a lot of interesting work going on in the Arctic right now."

"The Arctic?" I repeated. I couldn't imagine willingly sailing the frigid seas there.

"I'm interested in climate change," he explained. "And that's the best place to start."

"Oh." It was strange to see the serious side of Liam, who made waffles and grimaced at green tea ice cream, and I could almost hear Tara bemoaning my own lack of focus.

"That's months away," he said, pulling me into him, "and who knows what will happen between now and then."

I didn't want to think about that. Of course, he was going back to his home thousands of miles away, but there was no need to talk about it. I wasn't even certain why I had brought it up in the first place. I abandoned my lunch and crushed against him, finding his lips eagerly. His hands fisted into my shirt, drawing me closer as his tongue slipped into my mouth. I let my own hands trail down to the waist of his jeans, hooking my fingers over it.

Liam withdrew first, his eyes glazed over just a little. I knew this look, and it sent a throb pulsing through me.

"You have class," he reminded me.

"Screw class," I said in a low voice, angling my face towards his.

But he didn't budge. "Jills, I was serious about going slow."

I dropped back, turning my attention toward the water rippling under my feet. "I know."

It had seemed like a good idea when he said it. Going slowly meant I wouldn't get in too deep. If I couldn't stay in control of my body, how was I going to keep control of my head?

"Hey." He tucked a finger under my chin and drew my gaze up to meet his. "It took me a while to catch you. I'd like to keep you now."

"I don't do relationships," I said slowly, trying to get the words right. "If anyone fucks this up, it's going to be me."

"That's the nice thing about relationships," Liam said.

"What?"

"There's two people involved. If you fuck up, I'll be around to help you back on your feet."

A smile slid over my face despite the pressure I felt in my chest. I wanted to believe him, but I wasn't sure if that was selfishness or optimism. I was well-acquainted with one, but not so much the other.

"So sea cucumbers," I began as Liam stood and pulled me to my feet. "Have you eaten one?"

"Yes," he admitted.

"Was there ranch dressing?" I asked.

"It was sashimi-style," he said with a laugh. "Although I wouldn't put it past Americans to put ranch dressing on sushi."

"I bet ranch dressing is excellent on sushi."

"I will break up with you if you put ranch dressing on sushi," he warned me.

My iPhone beeped at me and I cursed silently. "I need to use the restroom."

I dashed toward the public restroom, grateful that I didn't have to actually use the toilet. As soon as I was inside I popped my pill and counted to thirty, washing the grease from lunch off my fingers. Liam was lounging against the side of the building when I came out, his body silhouetted by the late afternoon sun. Against the bay's backdrop, the lines of his muscular body were sinuous and inviting. He looked glorious and I had to remind myself that we were taking it slowly and that I would probably get an STD if I jumped him in a public toilet. He held out his hand, and I squinted to see two tiny pills resting in it. My breath hitched at the sight. Had he gone through my bag? Had I left them out?

"Chiclet?" he asked. "I hear it's the greatest gum in the world."

I let out a nervous laugh, thankful that for now my secret was safe, and stole them from his hand. I popped the Chiclets in my mouth and relaxed. He was going back to Scotland in a few months, there was no point in telling him. I'd become adept at hiding the truth, even from myself.

Chapter Seventeen

Interpersonal Communications took on a decidedly more romantic vibe the next day. Now instead of awkward in-class activities, Liam and I spent the time flirting with each other. Even Markson managed to keep his snarky commentary to himself despite catching us holding hands under our desks. I felt a bit like I was back in high school—giddy and wild and hoping Liam would press me against a locker after class. Too bad there were no lockers on campus.

"What are you doing tonight?" he asked me, knitting his fingers through mine as we exited at the end of the hour.

"I received a cryptic text from Cassie directing me to meet her at a tattoo parlor," I told him.

"You should get one right here." He patted me on the butt. "On second thought, don't mar that perfect ass."

"No ink?" I didn't add that there was no way I was subjecting myself to a needle willingly.

"Nope. It's cool," he added. "Vivian begged me to have dinner with her tonight at the house. She wants all the dirty details about this weekend."

"You aren't going to tell her...everything, are you?"

"I'm a gentleman," he said. "I'll tell her we went to the movies and that I kissed you finally."

"Yeah, ya did." I bobbed my head enthusiastically, as memories of the number of kisses we shared this weekend flashed through my mind.

"Of course, she knows I wasn't home all weekend," he said.

"Tell her we kissed a lot."

"I like that, because it's not a lie."

Liam walked me all the way to my next class, stopping at the door. "I have class over in Williams."

"That's on the other side of campus," I pointed out.

"I'll run." He leaned over and kissed me full on the mouth, leaving me too breathless to say anything when he turned and jogged away. I watched as he ran away from me, clutching the doorframe, and wishing for the next kiss.

The tattoo parlor's walls were covered in prospective art ripe for Cassie's choosing. I couldn't help but notice a fair number of "Just Divorced" options, many featuring broken balls and chains. I guess you could celebrate any event in your life with a permanent reminder. Cassie was busy filling out the medical release form, and despite the fact that she was about to willingly let someone drag a needle repeatedly through her flesh, she seemed calm.

"What ya thinking, hon?" The tattoo artist—who introduced himself as Jimmy—asked as he laid a variety of painful-looking instruments onto a stainless steel table.

"I have something with me." She dropped the clipboard onto her lap and rifled through her purse. It was a bit of a surprise. Cassie hadn't struck me as the tattoo type, and when she called to ask me for moral support, I sort of expected her to chicken out. But here she was with art in hand.

"This is nice," he said. "You draw this?"

"No." Cassie's eyes flickered to me. "My boyfriend did."

"Shit, Cass, you aren't getting his name tattooed on your ass, are you?" I couldn't keep the annoyance out of my voice. She had it bad enough for Trevor to do something stupid. I could only hope she wasn't about to do something that she would regret every time she caught her reflection in a mirror for the rest of her life.

"Fuck you, Jills," she said in true Cassie style, which elicited a laugh from Jimmy. She handed me the paper, and I was surprised to see a tastefully drawn image of a sparrow with the words "live free" penned under it.

"This is pretty," I said, giving it to Jimmy.

"Don't sound so surprised." She finished signing the paperwork and left it on the counter.

"No one's drunk, right?" Jimmy asked. "I can't ink you if you've been drinking."

That should have been my first clue that Cassie was serious about getting a tattoo. I'd suggested a round of drinks first, but Cassie had rejected the idea. She had actually done research.

"You sure you want to do this?" I asked her. I had a hard time wrapping my head around getting something permanently etched into my body.

"Fuck yeah." Cassie's enthusiasm spilled out of her and onto me. She was literally bouncing on her heels waiting for Jimmy to call her into the chair.

"You know it's going to hurt like a bitch, right?"

"Jills, you suck at moral support," she said, adding a groan for emphasis.

"Jess would be worse," I pointed out.

"Jess would be checking that everything was properly sterilized."

She had a point. I peeked back into the room where Jimmy was prepping his tools. The artwork was unfolded on the table and he was studying it carefully. I was more than a little amazed that he going to transfer the intricate drawing onto Cassie's skin.

"Looks good to me," I said, like I'd done a brief inspection.

"How thorough," Cassie said. She was biting on her perfectly manicured nails now, and as Jimmy took his time, she began to pace. There were the nerves I was expecting from her.

"What about you?" Jimmy asked when he finally beckoned for us to enter.

I blinked at him. There was no way in hell I was getting a tattoo. "No, thanks. I could never pull one off."

"A lot of girls your age get them here." He pressed a doughy finger to the small of his back.

I stifled a laugh. A tramp stamp? He was definitely barking up the wrong tree.

"I'm on medication," I said in an apologetic voice. There was absolutely nothing about my pills that would interfere with a tattoo, but it seemed like a good excuse to avoid the needle.

Cassie climbed into the chair, and Jimmy began prepping her arm, asking her a variety of questions about color and placement. She wanted it on her wrist. I refrained from telling her that there was no way she could ever hide it there. Jimmy started the outline after a few minutes, and Cassie's eyes rolled up to meet mine as she mouthed "Fuck!"

I clutched her free hand and squeezed it. It oddly reminded me of sitting at someone's sickbed, except Cassie was inflicting this on herself. The world was a strange place.

"Distract me," Cassie ordered me. She squeezed her eyes shut and muttered a string of curse words as he began filling in the tattoo with color.

"Did I mention how much sex I'm getting these days?" I asked her.

"Careful," Jimmy said. "You'll distract me."

Fantastic, a dirty old man was going to listen in, but if any topic could distract Cassie, it would have to be sex.

"Excellent. Details."

I tried to share things that wouldn't cause Jimmy to accidentally tattoo half of her arm. Mostly sweet things, but I ended it on news of Liam's plan to slow things down.

"What the hell does that mean?" she asked me. "He's not one of those secondary virginity types, is he?"

There was no greater offense to Cassie than guys who screwed you and then wanted to pretend like it had never happened. Each of us had experienced a guy like that in our time at Olympic State. Jess tried to tell us it wasn't an insult, but I tended to side with Cassie.

"It's nothing like that," I reassured her. My hand was starting to go numb from how hard she was squeezing it. "But we sort of jumped into bed before we knew each other's last names."

"And what's wrong with that?" Cassie asked through gritted teeth.

"Nothing, but I don't know...he's sensitive."

"Hmmmmpfh." It wasn't even a word, but Cassie made the noise whenever she disapproved of something. It was a distinctly Tara thing to do. "Let me know how long that lasts."

"It's going well," I told her.

"For how long?" It was a pointed question and I knew it, because Cassie had been there when I went on my first date with Liam.

"A few days."

"Yeah, I give you a fucking week," she said.

"Thank you for the vote of confidence." If I was being truthful, I gave us less than that.

"Ok, new distraction," Cassie begged.

I made the mistake of glancing at her wrist in time to see Jimmy wipe away the slight pool of blood forming over the newly inked skin. My stomach turned over a little, but I shot Cassie a brave smile.

"When did Trevor draw that?" I asked her.

"He doodled it in a notebook. I didn't even tell him I was getting this," she confessed. "He doesn't like people to know he's artistic."

Trevor cultivated the image of the up-and-coming young business professional better than anyone I knew. He was always the first to grab for the check, and he drove a Lexus. I couldn't picture him wasting time drawing.

"It's a surprise for him," Cassie said.

I held the groan trying to escape my mouth and nodded. It was totally unfair to judge Cassie for this. It was, after all, not his name on her ass.

"You chose a pretty one," I said.

"I'm trying to loosen up a little."

"Do you think if we dragged Jess up here, she would loosen up?" I suggested.

Cassie didn't need the reminder to live free. She did it better than anyone I had known since my arrival in Washington. She managed to keep a strong GPA while running the Student Publicity Society. Cassie had single-handedly arranged at least ten concerts on campus in the last year. She could throw back a drink and hit the dance floor and still make grades.

"It's worth a shot," Cassie said thoughtfully. "Of course, she'd probably just get an MCAT study guide tattooed on her arm."

"I wonder if that's cheating?" I thought out loud.

"She'd probably have to bubble wrap her arm prior to the test."

And she probably would, knowing Jess. She wasn't the type to look for the easy way out, but if it sounded like a viable method of study, she would try it.

"I saw Brett down near The Jewel Box," Cassie said in a conspiratorial whisper.

"Really?" I couldn't quite figure out why we were speaking in whispers. I doubted that Jimmy had much interest in Jess's boyfriend's shopping trip.

"I almost followed him in, but then I thought that would look crazy."

It would look crazy, but if anyone could spin following her best friend's boyfriend around, it would be Cassie. She'd already found the perfect profession for her. One in which she could display her significant skills.

"It's probably a Christmas present," I told her.

"In October?" Cassie scoffed.

"Brett strikes me as the type that likes to plan ahead."

That was the understatement of the century. Brett was two Volvos away from hitting his mid-life crisis. Of course, Jess had probably mapped out both their five year-plans.

"Jess, too," Cassie said, reading my thoughts. "Do you remember that five-year plan we had to do our freshman year?"

"When Jess lost her mind that we weren't taking serious classes?" How could I forget that? I'd gone along with it to calm her down. Thank god Jess had chilled out since then.

"And your entire plan revolved around turning twenty-one?" Cassie recalled, giggling so hard that Jimmy shot us a warning look.

"You're going to wind up with a crooked bird if you keep up the laughing," he told her.

"Sorry." Cassie's voice was full of sugar, and Jimmy responded with a grudging smile.

"It really has been downhill since twenty-one. I think I was onto something," I said.

"Whatever! You have a boyfriend now." Cassie fluttered her lashes and made a kissy face.

"You look like a fish when you do that."

"A sexy fish." She sucked her cheeks in more and widened her eyes.

"I'm sure you'll catch a fisherman soon," I assured her.

"I don't need to catch anyone. I have Trevor and you have Liam and Jess has Brett. Our boy catching days are behind us!"

I wasn't sure I liked the sound of that. Was Cassie

that in to Trevor? From the sound of it, she might as well have dragged me dress shopping. And Brett and Jess weren't that serious. Jess couldn't actually wind up with Brett. He would bore her to death. As far as Liam and I...

"Why are you frowning?" Cassie asked me. "You don't like Trevor."

It was a fair accusation, but the truth was that I didn't dislike Trevor. I nothinged him, but I couldn't tell Cassie that. "Ohmigod, paranoid much? I was thinking."

"You're done," Jimmy announced.

Saved by the burly tattoo artist.

He launched into the proper care of healing tattoos, and I checked my phone for messages. Liam had texted me, wanting to get together, an hour ago. My thumb hovered over the delete button when Cassie flung her arm out for my approval.

"It looks amazing," I said, admiring the clean black lines of the art. "Does it hurt?"

"Not really. Feels like I scraped my arm repeatedly in the same spot."

"That doesn't sound bad at all," I teased, pushing the sleep button on my phone.

"Come on." Cassie linked her untouched arm through mine. "It's Jillian's turn to do something fun."

"Maybe a nose ring? Or a couple of lip rings?" I suggested.

"I can do those," Jimmy called from the counter.

Cassie barely smothered the smirk that leapt onto

her mouth. "Let's get out of here," she whispered. "Bye Jimmy!"

He grunted a farewell. He didn't look too put out that I wasn't going to be shoving metal rods through my body today. I guess you win some, you lose some. The bell on the door tinkled as it shut behind us.

"That was an adventure," I said to Cassie as we strolled through the hazy twilight in downtown. It was too early in the night for the night owls and bargoers, but long past the dinner hour, so we passed few people. Most of the shops were closed for the night, so we peeked in windows. I preferred being down here at this time of day since I had very little spending money. It was much more fun to look than to constantly go in stores and walk out empty-handed.

"What do you think Trevor is going to say?" she asked as I ogled a pair of knee-heigh suede boots through the glass of Taylor's Shoes.

"About?"

"The tattoo," Cassie said with a sigh.

I turned back to her and shrugged. "I guess I would be flattered, but I'm not sleeping with you. He'll either find it hot or think you've gone all *Fatal Attraction* on him."

"Thanks!" Cassie pressed her lips together into a flat line.

"I'm sure he'll think it's hot."

"I hope so." She dug her phone out of her purse, smiling as she read a message. "Speaking of..."

"The devil?" I offered. She had gotten a booty call from Trevor. I would place money on it.

Cassie winked at me as she typed a quick response. "Something like that. Trevor wants me to come over."

"Okay." I tried to keep my tone even like I was totally cool with this, but my heart sank. I hadn't spent an entire evening with Cassie since she started seeing Trevor last May.

"You should call Liam." Cassie thrust her hips a few times suggestively.

"Maybe," I said, laughing her off. "I have some stuff to do anyway."

"Sure, you don't mind?" Cassie asked, her eyes still glued to her phone.

"Absolutely."

She threw her arms around my neck. "Thanks for coming with me, and wish me luck when I show Trevor."

"He's going to love it," I called after her as she practically skipped down the sidewalk toward Elm Street.

My iPhone stayed in my pocket, even when I felt it vibrate. Did being in a relationship mean constantly bailing on my friends for my boyfriend? Jess wasn't nearly as bad as Cassie, but they'd both done it multiple times in the last few months. It was no big deal if we were somewhere like Garrett's, but Cassie had made a fuss over spending time together tonight only to dash off the second Trevor called her. Love was like a disease creeping into her and slowly brainwashing her. Spending a little time together, then more and more, until she never saw her friends outside of class—but maybe that was bitterness talking. It was Cassie's life and as one of my best friends, I needed to respect that. Besides Trevor wouldn't last forever, regardless of what Cassie thought right now. He had no sticking power, as my MeMa would say. According to MeMa, one person had to have sticking power to make a relationship work, because love wasn't all picnics and blow jobs. Those were her actual words. I loved MeMa, despite her questionable taste in crocheted decor, because her advice was never lofty or condescending.

I wouldn't be like that, I promised myself. If MeMa was right about relationships, that meant there should be some boundaries. Having time with my friends was one thing I wasn't about to give up, not even for Liam or his waffles. I pulled out my iPhone and responded to Liam's message with a quick: "I'm with friends."

His response was lightning quick, and I felt a small pang. Was he sitting around hoping I would call him? I hoped not. But all the message said was "Cool. Maybe tomorrow?"

Tomorrow I could commit to.

Chapter Eighteen

❦

My phone rang as soon as I walked into the apartment. Jess looked up from her textbook and made a kissy face, but when I pulled it from my pocket, the number flashing across the screen wasn't Liam's. I'd spent the day floating on Cloud Nine, so trust Tara to sense that from hundred of miles away and ruin my high. I considered not answering it, but I'd avoided most of her calls the last few weeks, which meant I had to give in eventually or risk her wrath.

"Hi Mom," I said, taking the phone into my room and shutting the door.

"You answered! It's a miracle." The tone of her voice said differently.

"I've been busy with midterms," I explained, which was mostly true. I didn't add that I'd also been caught up in a significant amount of extracurricular activity.

"That's why I called. Your father and I will be

arriving at eleven a.m. sharp on Saturday," she said. "So make sure you're caught up with homework by then."

"Saturday?" I repeated.

There was a long sigh on the other end of the line. "Parents' Weekend."

How could I have forgotten that was coming up? My father insisted on coming into town each year for the football games and other festivities, meant to attract alumni and parental donations to the school. It normally wasn't too bad.

"Bring that boy you're seeing," Tara instructed me.

I froze, grateful we were on the phone and she couldn't see my reaction. "What boy?"

"You know very well what boy," she said. "Jess mentioned him."

"She did, huh?" If I came with a warning indicator, it would be blinking red.

"Remember eleven sharp, and don't dress like a hoochie."

I hung up before I could ask Tara how a hoochie dressed, just so I could get it right to piss her off. Slamming my door behind me, I trudged into the living room. Jess stared up at me.

"Your mom called me," she confessed. "I didn't get a chance to warn you."

"And you told her about Liam?" I asked, planting my fists on my hips to reinforce the glare I leveled at her.

"I accidentally said 'I think she's with Liam.'" Jess chewed on her lip. I knew she was sorry, and I knew it was a mistake, but she certainly hadn't made my life easier.

"Actually I was with Cassie, getting a tattoo," I said. I dropped onto the couch beside her and hugged my knees to my chest.

"Hold it," Jess said. "You got a tattoo?"

"Yeah, I got a huge 'Loose lips sink ships' tat on my ass," I said.

Jess smacked me on the arm. "I'm sorry, okay?"

"Cassie got a tattoo. Some picture Trevor drew."

"Well, there goes their relationship," Jess said, shaking her head.

"Mine will be over this weekend."

"What? Why?"

"Parents' Weekend," I reminded her. Jess's parents never bothered coming in, so last year she'd endured four hours of the Nichols family's two favorite activities: torture and interrogation. Tara should work for a BlackOps devision—she could wear anyone down.

"Oh." Her response was as small as her voice, confirming my suspicion that last year had been as terrible as I remembered.

"And she wants me to bring Liam," I added.

"Maybe he could come down with the Plague or something?" Jess suggested.

"Do you have access to the Plague? He'd probably have to be quarantined to keep Tara away."

"Good point. I do not have access to any pandemics," she said. "Maybe it will be fine."

Jess tacked on the last part for me, because I knew

she didn't believe it. I'd gone to college a thousand miles away to get away from Tara. There was a damn good reason for that.

Ever since Tara called to say she would be coming for Parents' Day, my medications felt like were doing nothing. My hands were weak and I caught myself trembling several times. I'd become practiced enough at calming myself that I could usually handle it, but the thought of Tara sent my nerves into a frenzy. And thanks to Jess, she expected to meet Liam, too. He had been a good sport about the whole thing. He even sounded a little excited, and apparently no amount of forewarning could scare him off from coming along.

If there was one person in the world who would disapprove of me being in a relationship more than myself, it would be my mother. She was such a giver, after all. I'd spent all Friday night cleaning and organizing the apartment. Thanks to Jess's OCD tendencies, it never got that bad, but that didn't mean that I wasn't going to make sure that there was nothing controversial around. I made sure my stash of condoms and my birth control were tucked safely under some papers in my bedside table, knowing Tara would open it the second I wasn't looking. She was a self-proclaimed snoop, a habit she blamed on me. Since I "refused to tell her about my life," she apparently had the right to turn my room into a CSI scene.

In the living room, I caught a *Playgirl*, a birthday gag gift from Cassie, tucked in with our *Cosmos*. I even sprayed down the kitchen counters and rewashed my bed sheets, sure she would be able to smell sex all over the place. I lined up my medications facing out in the bathroom cabinet. Tara would check to make sure I was using them. She'd look for any excuse to pull me out of Olympic State and take me home to California.

Liam stayed away per my instructions, but when I opened the door on Saturday morning, I found him standing there, holding a bouquet of daisies. Tara and Dad would be here any minute, but looking at him in a white button-down shirt with carefully combed hair, I had the strongest urge to throw him on the floor and mess up that neat hair and ironed shirt.

"Thanks," I said, reaching for the flowers and trying to keep myself in check. It took considerably more effort than I expected.

Liam caught me around the waist and kissed me slowly. "They're for your mother, actually."

"My mom hates daisies," I said without thinking.

"Oh." Liam's face fell and he looked down at the flowers.

"She's allergic," I lied. I couldn't stand to see that look on his face. I hated Tara a little for her stupid flower prejudices. *Only accept expensive flowers from men, or they'll think you're cheap, Jillian.* That was her idea of dating advice. "But I love them. Can I put them in water?"

"Of course, chicken." But before I could take them into the kitchen, his mouth found mine again. I ran my fingers down his chest and hooked them over his belt, tugging at it playfully.

"We might have a few minutes," I whispered.

"Don't tempt me," he said with a groan. "I'd like to make a good impression on your parents, and," he added in a low voice, "the next time I get you in to bed, I don't want to rush."

My breath caught in my throat. Liam had been very carefully tiptoeing around sex since we agreed to slow down. "Is it too late to cancel on my parents?"

A knock on the door answered my door. I whimpered a little. On the list of ways I would rather spend a Saturday than going to Parents' Day activities was getting beheaded, walking across coals, and being stung by a thousand bees. I couldn't see a way this wasn't going to be painful.

Liam released me, squeezing my shoulder as I turned to open the door. It swung open to reveal my parents, who both looked like they were in some stage of constipation.

"Ta...Mom," I corrected myself immediately, but the flash of annoyance in her eyes showed she heard me. "Mom, Dad."

There was an awkward hug, full of limp arms and too much space. As soon as they came in, my mother stopped and ran her eyes up and down Liam. He was still holding the inferior daisies, and when neither of my parents spoke, Liam dropped the daisies on the bar and held out his hand.

"Mr. and Mrs. Nichols, it's nice to meet you." My

father shook his hand and muttered something similar, but my mother just stared at him.

"This is Liam, Mom," I said, hoping to break her icy stare.

"He's Scottish," she said. "You didn't tell us he was Scottish."

She might as well have said *He's a leper. You didn't tell us he was a leper*.

"Liam is studying in America this year," I explained.

"And how did you meet?"

Apparently, the interrogation was going to proceed immediately. I had hoped they would wait until we were at the stadium or the club. In other words, until we were somewhere public. I was fairly certain I was less likely to kill them in public.

"In class," Liam said. His lie was smooth. It hadn't even occurred to me that lying was an option, but it was the perfect story. We could have met in class. We would have met in class. There was no reason to mention that we'd actually met the night before at a bar.

"It's nice to meet you, Liam." My mother sounded like it gave her physical pain to utter these words. But now that she'd momentarily paused her interrogations into Liam's life and motives, she turned on me.

"You look tired, and your hair isn't behaving. We should get you an appointment at the salon. Have you thought about cutting it?" She spoke so quickly, bombarding me with so many ideas, that my head was already spinning. I took an unsteady step forward to put the daisies in a vase but stumbled. Liam caught me and steadied me.

"Okay, chicken?" he whispered. I gave him an annoyed look, but the concern didn't vanish from his face.

Tara followed me into the kitchen. "Have you taken your medication?"

"Yes," I hissed. Her eyes flashed to Liam and back to me, narrowing in the process.

Great, now she knew that I hadn't told him anything yet. It would be just like to her let it spill before the weekend was over. I felt the familiar rawness of tears creeping up the back of my throat, but I pushed it back. I wasn't going to let her make me cry. But when I couldn't find a vase for the flowers, I just felt worse.

Liam was talking football with my dad and didn't seem to notice Tara grilling me.

"We need to talk about this boy," she said to me.

"Not now, Tara," I said, shoving the daisies so roughly into an old Quiktrip cup that I broke some of the stems.

"Mom," she corrected me.

"Ladies, we should be going," my father called in to us.

Tara straightened up and ran her hand over her slicked-back hair. It was darker than normal, almost black, so she must have gotten desperate to cover the gray. Despite that, she looked like the essence of the upper-middle-class in her carefully assembled Talbots outfit and pearl earrings. Next to me in my jean skirt and an Olympic State hoodie, she looked like she was going to watch a polo match at the country club. Not that we'd ever belonged to a country club. My mother's sense of style was heavily influenced by what I liked to call wishful thinking. She came from money. Something that stressed my dad out so much that he'd placed most of her money in a living trust and forced her to live a more middle-class existence. I'd never bothered to ask if I was the beneficiary of the will because, other than to pay for school, I didn't want her money.

"We really should do something about your hair," my mother said as Liam held open the door for us.

I turned to lock the door. Liam's hand softly smacked my butt, and he leaned in once she had redirected her nit-picking at my father. "You look so hot, chicken."

I couldn't quite help but smile and since my parents' backs were turned, I kissed him swiftly. For a split second, I considered forcing Liam back into my apartment. I could just lock my parents out. Eventually, they would have to go home. Liam's hand cupped my chin and he raised an eyebrow, trying to guess what I was thinking.

A cough startled us apart, and his hand dropped from my face. My parents were both watching us. Dad looked bemused, but Tara was unreadable.

"Are you coming?" she asked. "We'll never get a parking spot if you two don't stop necking."

I tried so hard to smash a laugh that I snorted instead.

"Coming," I said. I took a step forward, and Liam's hand tangled into mine. His strong warm hand sent a tingle running up my arm, and the familiar pressure in my chest increased.

The car ride was an awkward five minutes of Mom trying to find a "decent" radio station before she gave up and launched into a tirade about the rental car not having satellite radio. Meanwhile, Liam's fingers brushed carefully against my thigh in slow, absent-minded strokes. His touch calmed me enough that I was able to ignore Mom's crazy diatribe.

Because my dad had attended Olympic State, we had access to the alumni parking section as well as a reservation at the Alumni Club where we could watch the game in style. Which meant that at least there would be booze.

My dad had reserved a viewing box. The restaurant was built on one side of the stadium, and the viewing boxes were the best way to watch a football game if you, like me, hated watching football. I could eat and drink. There was alternatively air-conditioning or heat depending on the weather. This would be the first year that I had brought a boy with me though. Cassie and Jess had both done me the honor of attending the most awkward lunch of the year the last two years, but my mother had demanded I bring Liam this year.

Despite her insistence that I bring him, she seemed intent on punishing both of us for his actual presence.

It started with the drinks. As soon as I ordered, she shot me a disapproving look.

"Jillian, darling, you shouldn't be drinking beer. Don't you think that's a bad idea, Liam?" Tara asked him.

"Jillian can make her own decisions." Liam said it with extra charm, almost as if he'd managed to deepen his accent to sound even more Scottish, which I'm sure pissed her off more.

When my beer arrived, I left it on the table. Tara wasn't going to let up on this, and I knew it. It was careless of me to order a drink in front of her.

Our table was arranged so that we could watch the game while eating, but the restaurant was abnormally busy given that it was Parents' Day. Conversation lulled between Tara and I while the guys discussed today's starting line-up, but as soon as salads arrived, Tara dug her claws into Liam.

"What are you studying while you're here?" she asked as he lifted a bite to his mouth.

Liam set down his fork and folded his hands on the table as though he knew he might as well give up on food now. "General studies for the year. Coming to America was more about the experience."

His eyes flickered to mine briefly when he said the word experience.

"That seems like a waste of time, doesn't it?" It wasn't really a question. It was just Tara speaking her mind.

"Mom!"

"No, it's okay." Liam gave me a crooked smile. "The more general the coursework, the greater the chance the credits will transfer back to the University of Edinburgh. I knew I wanted to come over here when I started college, so I did more work in my field of study my first two years at university. I should have no problem graduating in four years."

"And what are you studying, son?" my dad asked.

I relaxed in my chair a little and speared some lettuce onto my fork. My dad was genuinely interested in Liam, unlike Tara.

"I'd like to be an oceanographer. It's one of the reasons I chose Olympic State."

"He volunteers at the aquarium downtown," I jumped in.

"Just for fun. It's not really related to my field of interest," Liam said, looking slightly abashed.

"Which is?" Tara asked. I knew for a fact that my mother cared as little about oceanography as she did sports, but that wasn't going to stop her from trying to pin Liam down.

"Climate change," he said, without skipping a beat.

"Are you one of those Green Peace types?"

"I believe in green and peace," he answered, still smiling. I wondered how long it would be before that smile slid off his face.

"As do you, Mom," I said in a warning tone.

"Well." Tara reached for her wine glass and took a slow sip of it. "At least, *you* have a major. Jillian is totally aimless. You might as well stick her in one of your boats and put her out to sea."

The smile disappeared from Liam's face, and I saw his jaw clench.

I was so embarrassed that I didn't know what to say. "I'm narrowing down a major. I don't want to make a mistake."

"The mistake was sending you to college in the first place, Jillian. For which I take responsibility," Tara pressed her hand to her chest as though this great *responsibility* might be the death of her.

"Mom," I said. "I was going to talk with you about this later. I've had some great classes so far this year."

"She's doing really well in our communications class," Liam spoke up.

"One class isn't a future," Tara said. Beside her, my dad fidgeted with his napkin and turned his attention to the game. I could always count on him to ignore Tara's barbs.

"One class can be enough to show you what you want to do. I took a biology class in secondary school, and we visited an oceanography lab. That's all it took for me." Liam's voice was calm and steady, but his jaw was still tense as he spoke. He wasn't going to allow Tara to belittle me, but, unlike when I defended myself, he was countering her with logic.

"Jillian was never academically-minded and then when she—"

I stood up so quickly that my chair clattered to the floor behind me before she could spill my biggest secret to Liam. "Excuse me," I said, choking back a sob. I darted out of the restaurant and into the lounge, grateful to see that it was empty. Everyone else in the Alumni Club was busy watching the game. They didn't have horrible mothers berating them in front of their boyfriends.

I found a corner near the ladies room and tucked myself into it, letting the tears roll freely. I liked that Liam had a plan. He was amazing at the aquarium. I thought it made him a more interesting boyfriend. But Tara had succeeded in reminding me that I didn't share that same ambition or depth. That was how she operated: suck all joy from Jillian's life.

"Hey." Liam appeared next to me and wrapped an arm around me. I cried into his shoulder, afraid to face him, scared that he saw what my mother had been trying to show him about me. Because part of me knew she was right.

Chapter Nineteen

"I hope you won't be offended by this, but your mother is a bitch."

I nodded, my face still pressed against his shirt.

"It's okay that you don't know what you want to do yet," he whispered. "Three of my older sisters went to university and declared fields because they had to. Not one of them is in a job she likes."

That made me feel better, and then worse at the same time. Apparently I was in a no-win situation. If I chose a major, I could be unhappy, but if I didn't, Tara would drive me crazy about it. Never mind the fact that I wasn't sure what I wanted to do. I pulled back to look at him and saw mascara marks on his shirt.

"Shit," I said. "C'mom, we need to wash that out." I dragged him towards the restroom a few feet away.

"I can take care of this, chicken."

"I can't go back and face her yet," I said in a small

voice. "Let me help you. It will make me feel less useless."

Liam caught my face in his hands. "You are not useless."

The kiss was meant to be sweet, but all the anger and hopelessness rushed away when his lips met mine. His mouth consumed me like a fire growing steadily out of control. I could feel my pain slipping away more and more as we tumbled back against the bathroom door and fell inside. It was mercifully empty.

We kissed like our lives depended on it. Liam's weight pinned me to the wall, but he kept his hands in my hair or my shoulders while I let mine explore the muscles hidden under his shirt.

"Touch me," I whispered.

"Jillian." I could hear the struggle in his voice.

"I need you."

I pushed him into the empty handicapped stall and drew him towards me. Liam unzipped my hoodie between kisses and pulled the top of my tank top down so he could trail his lips over my breasts. But he didn't linger there, instead he brought his mouth back up to mine. He brushed some loose hair from my face and kissed me deeply. I reached for the button on his jeans but he backed up a step.

"I need to feel something else," I told him in a soft voice. "I need to feel wanted."

"Oh, baby, you are so wanted." He didn't need any more encouragement. Liam lifted me in the air, urging my legs around his waist and hiking my denim skirt up around my hips. His rock hard dick strained through his jeans, pressing against the soaked cotton still covering my pussy. It was tricky to maneuver pants and underwear, but then he slipped inside of me, and I gasped at the feeling of wholeness as I stretched over his shaft.

"I missed this," I whispered into his ear as I clung to him. "I missed making love to you.

"Jillian," he breathed as we moved together slowly. "I missed you, too."

"So the whole taking it slowly thing..." My thought trailed off in a breathless gasp.

"Worst idea ever," he whispered.

I tucked my face against his neck and held my breath, focusing on being with him. The feel of his hands clutching my hips and his lips resting on my cheek. I needed Liam. I needed all of him. I couldn't stand to hold myself back when I was with him. My body trembled against his, swelling with anticipated release. It shivered through me as it spread through my limbs and erupted through my veins. I clutched his shoulders, my nails digging through his shirt as I cried out. My name was on his lips moments later, warmth spreading through me.

"We can do this, right?" he said, still pressing me against the wall. "We can make this work?"

"Yes." I crushed my lips to his. I knew then that I was willing to do whatever it took to make it work with him. Not because of this—not because of sex—because of everything else. Everything came naturally with

Liam. For the first time, I had met a man who fit into my life as effortlessly as my best friends.

"We need to go back," he said in a soft voice. "I know you don't want to."

I opened my mouth to tell him that I wanted to go home. I wasn't about to return to let my mother talk down to me, but the sound of the bathroom door swinging open stopped me from speaking, and we both froze. It wouldn't take much for someone to spy his legs under the stall.

"Jillian?" My stomach flipped at the sound of my mother's voice. "Are you in here?"

Liam's wide-eyed panic mirrored my own. We didn't move, but then we heard her try to open the stall door.

"I know you're in there. Stop being a child and come out. Your food is waiting for you," she ordered. I heard her slump against the door.

I untangled my legs from Liam's waist and pushed my skirt back down. He stepped to the side, quietly pulling up his pants. But our movement was enough to alert Tara that she wasn't alone in the bathroom.

"What are you two doing in there?" she hissed.

I took a deep breath and zipped up my hoodie. I turned to check that Liam was decent and he gave me a small, encouraging smile as I went to unlock the door. It looked like he was trying really hard to muster up that smile.

Opening the door, I stepped through and tried to look devil-may-care, but I was pretty sure I failed miserably at looking like I didn't give a shit what Tara thought. Liam followed me out, his hands stuffed into the pockets of his jeans.

Tara's eyes narrowed and then widened in realization. "Were you screwing in the bathroom of the Alumni Club?"

I sincerely doubted that Tara would have cared less if she had walked in on us in my bedroom. Tara had drilled the importance of abstinence into me since I got my first period. It was archaic, but despite knowing that, I felt a flush of shame at being caught by her. Not just because it was embarrassing, but also because this would affect how she saw Liam. She would tell my dad and then there would be awkwardness between all four of us. It was small comfort to consider that Liam would be returning to Scotland by the end of the school year.

"We should get back to the table," Liam suggested. He took my hand gently and pulled me through the bathroom door.

I had no idea how he could be so calm after being walked in on by my mother.

"I'm sorry," I murmured to him as we walked swiftly toward the dining room.

"Not your fault, chicken. It takes two, you know."

"No, for how horrible this is going to be be," I clarified.

"If you're there, it won't be horrible. We can tell our grandkids about our crazy antics someday," he whispered as Tara caught up with us.

I raised an eyebrow to let him know I'd caught the

not-too-subtle reference to a future we both knew we
could never have. But even as I tried to look annoyed,
my heart pounded as though it was more than a mean-
ingless joke.

Don't be stupid, I told myself. Liam was leaving,
and I wasn't going to put anyone through a marriage
with me, let alone put kids through that. And yet, I had
jumped immediately to considering it. This was bad.

We took our places at the table and no one spoke.
My dad looked at each of us, but Tara shook her head
as if to indicate now was not the time. At least she
wasn't going to ruin our meal. Not that I could eat.

My dad caught Liam up on what he had missed in
the game, and they slipped back into easy conversation.
Meanwhile Tara glowered at me from across the table.
It was almost an improvement from her earlier tongue-
lashing. I turned my attention to the field and let my
mind wander to thoughts of Liam. I replayed the last
few times we'd been together. Not just in bed, but at
the aquarium and the exercise we did in Interpersonal
Communications earlier this week.

"I know what you're thinking about," Tara whispered, her words full of admonishment. "You're all
flushed. Stop it."

"What's that, dear?" my dad asked, looking to her.

"Nothing. We'll discuss it later," she replied in a
clipped tone.

I had hoped for a moment that she might be so
shocked by my behavior that she would insist on dropping us off. I could avoid her phone calls for weeks

before she'd sick campus security on the case. She might not even bother. I was clearly a lost cause to her physically and maternally. I not only didn't live up to her expectations, I threw them in her face. Strangely, this didn't make me want to cry. It made me angry.

She was the one who'd pushed me to the breaking point. I wouldn't have left if she hadn't acted like some cracked-out Mommy Dearest. The fury surged inside me, and I clenched my hands into fist, feeling the familiar tingles of stress overtaking my body.

We both stayed silent for the rest of the afternoon. Liam cast worried glances my way, and I did my best to give him reassuring grins, but I knew I wasn't fooling anyone. Least of all the person I was most intimate with. The game ended in defeat, and the men commiserated with a final beer before my dad called for the check. By that point, I could feel my muscles stiffening from the stress of the afternoon. I needed to get home and away from Tara before things got worse.

When we pulled into my apartment complex, I grabbed Liam's hand and hauled him toward the stairs to my floor. He stopped and nodded towards my parents. The last thing I felt like doing was saying goodbye, but my dad stopped the car and I watched in horror as they both got out.

"We need to talk," my mother said in a thin voice.

My heart sank into my stomach. So much for the hope that she would write this off.

They followed us into my apartment. Jess was at the bar studying, and she gave us a huge smile.

"How was the game?" she asked us.

"Great!" my dad said. It was the most enthusiasm he'd shown in the last three years of parents' weekends, and we hadn't even won this time.

"Interesting," I told her in a careful voice. Jess's face stayed placid, even though I could tell she picked up on the tension in the air. I had never known anyone who could remain as emotionless as she could in any situation.

Tara grabbed my elbow and dragged me toward my room. "I need to talk to you."

I wanted to tell her that even if we shut the paper-thin door to my room, everyone in the living room was going to be able to hear what we were saying. But now was not a time to be logical with Tara. We were well past that.

Tara slammed the door behind us and rounded on me.

"What the hell do you have to say for yourself?" she demanded.

I paused for a moment to consider the question, but I couldn't stop myself from saying the first thing that flew into my head. "At least I know why Scottish boys wear kilts."

"Are you joking with me?" she asked, shock written all over her face. "Are you actually making a dirty joke right now?"

That was exactly what I was doing, but I got the impression that Tara didn't want to hear that.

"Our family has a reputation to uphold. Your father

went to school here, and you are fucking some boy in the bathroom?"

This was more serious than I had realized. Tara dropping the f-bomb was equivalent to a nuclear strike by the President.

"No one saw." My argument sounded weak, but I knew it was valid point. Tara had no right to judge what Liam and I did behind closed doors—even bathroom stall doors.

"I saw! Good girls don't act like that, Jillian. Do you think I want to know my sweet baby girl is being screwed by her boyfriend?"

"I'm twenty-one, Mom. I'm hardly your baby girl," I said as I crossed my arms over my chest.

"You will always be my baby girl." The words were soft, and I spotted tears sparkling in her eyes.

Confusion churned inside me. Tara wasn't the sentimental type. She never had been, even when I was a little girl. I has assumed this was about saving face and nothing more.

"Are you even being safe?" she asked. "Never mind the diseases that you probably got from that bathroom stall."

"That would hardly matter now, wouldn't it? My body is already fucked up."

Tara looked like I had slapped in her face. "It does matter. That boy is going back to Scotland, Jillian. *Scotland*. What if you get pregnant?"

"I'm on the pill."

"Do not roll your eyes at me," she said, shaking a

finger in my face. "The pill? You think that's enough? I got pregnant on the pill."

"And we all know what a fucking mistake that was!" I screamed at her. "What a mistake I am!"

"I have never said that to you," she said.

"You think reminding me every time sex has ever come up between us that you got pregnant on the pill isn't a pretty clear way of saying that I was a mistake?" I couldn't believe she didn't see anything wrong with this fucked-up conversation.

"You haven't even told him about your condition," she accused.

"You don't know that."

"Do you really think that boy would stick around if he knew you were going to be dependent on him some day?" she asked me, but then her voice softened to flat horror. "Are you trying to get pregnant? Are you trying to trap him?"

Something snapped inside me. I stormed toward the door and flung it open. "Out! Get out of here!"

She knew nothing about me. No one had better indoctrinated me to the catch and release lifestyle than Tara with her constant reminders that no one would ever want me. The message was clear: I was damaged goods. Slightly irregular. If my own mother couldn't see how anyone could ever want me, what shot did I have at a normal life?

Tara flew through the door after me, and everyone in the living room stilled.

"Ask your daughter—" she spit the word out —"what she was doing in the bathroom!"

My dad shuffled his feet a little and looked over at Liam. "Tara, they're in college."

"I cannot believe you are making excuses for her," she said with an overly dramatic gasp.

"We get it, Mom. I'm a slut." Jess's arm wrapped around my waist, but I pushed her away. I was fully in control of this moment. I lifted my arm to point towards the door before I felt the slowness creeping over my legs, but Jess realized immediately and grabbed me by the shoulders as my muscles locked up.

I could see Liam staring at me, a look of horror moving onto his face.

"Leave. Please leave." I couldn't move, couldn't step forward. If Jess hadn't been holding me, I was pretty sure I would have fallen flat on my face.

Tara appeared with my pills. I wanted to shake my head but I couldn't without risking my balance. Pills weren't going to help me though a freezing episode.

"You need to take them," Jess whispered. "They'll help you after it passes."

Damn Jess and her pseudo-medical student opinions. What I needed was for Liam to leave. I needed my parents to go. Jess and I could get through this on our own. We had before.

"Can you march?" Jess suggested.

"Tell him to go," I told her quietly. "I don't want him to see this."

Jess looked up at Liam. He moved closer to us, but

she shook her head. "She's upset. I need her to calm down if I'm going to help her through this."

Liam didn't understand. "I'll stay. I don't want to leave her like this."

He didn't know what was going on, but something broke inside of me. All of this was inevitable since day one. Maybe if I had told him earlier, we wouldn't be standing here now. Hell, he probably wouldn't have stuck around long enough to witness an episode.

"Please go," I said. I could barely move to look at him, but I saw the pain flash across his face as I spoke.

My dad put a hand on his shoulder and guided him toward the door. Liam glanced my direction, and my heart shattered. They shared a few quiet words, and then Liam walked out the door.

I knew he'd never walk back through it. It wasn't worth it. I wouldn't put him through this again.

My body started to shake, but I knew it wasn't my body unfreezing. I was angry. At Tara. At myself. At Liam for finding out. At Liam for sticking around in the first place.

"Jills," Jess whispered. "There's a line on the floor. Imagine it. Move toward it."

I tried, but I couldn't will my muscles to respond. Furious tears rolled down my cheeks. I was broken. "Stop trying to fix me!"

"I'm not going to fix you," Jess promised me. "We're just going to take a step. Together. Remember how you lift your foot."

I closed my eyes, Jess's hands holding me steady. I

imagined the muscles in my thigh. I visualized lifting them up. My left foot left the ground.

"Good. Now put it back down," Jess coaxed.

I told my leg to step forward. I pictured my legs marching up and down. I counted the beats in my head, and my foot lurched forward. Another step came more naturally. With Jess's help, I made it to the couch. I was scared to sit down. I didn't want to freeze there.

"You can't go this long without medications," Tara said, standing over me. "Did you take any this afternoon?"

There was no point in telling her that I had taken my meds that morning or that the episode was probably brought on by our screaming match. This was one arena where Tara excelled at making me feel totally incapable of taking care of myself.

"Parkinson's episodes can occur when a patient gets upset," Jess lectured her.

"Don't presume to tell me about this disease."

"Then you know Jillian needs to stay calm, so that this can pass." Jess was quiet and removed. Despite the fact that she had been helping me with this for the last two years, this was the first time she had to deal with anyone other than Cassie in the room. I couldn't help being impressed by how smoothly and calmly she dealt with Tara. She was going to be an amazing doctor.

"Let's give Jillian a chance to rest," my dad suggested.

"I'm not leaving my daughter like this!"

"I have everything under control," Jess said. She

knew it was imperative that they leave if I was going to recover from the freezing episode.

"She needs to see a doctor," Tara said. She wouldn't budge, even as my father tugged at her hand.

"I'll make an appointment tomorrow, Mom," I promised her. I would have told her anything to get her to leave, and she probably knew it.

"I will take her, Tara."

Tara hesitated, but she let my dad lead her toward the door.

"Call me."

I managed a nod. There was no way I was calling her. Not after she basically called me a slut in front of Liam. My heart lurched and, for a second, it felt frozen, too. I tried to erase the look on his face, but I couldn't. He knew something was seriously wrong with me now. I wouldn't be able to write this off. He'd ignored it when I tried to hide my pill-popping, but it wouldn't be long until he figured out that I was sick.

As soon as the door shut, the crying restarted.

"It's okay, Jills." Jess laid her head on my shoulder and rubbed my back in slow, reassuring strokes.

"He knows," I croaked over my tears.

"And he'll deal with it. You'll deal with it together," she said.

No, we wouldn't. I didn't tell Jess that though. I'd kept a lot from her about Liam's and my relationship. She might have guessed that I loved him. But somehow the decision to let him go was even more personal. I couldn't share this with her. Right now, it was my own private agony, and soon it would be his, when I could get up the guts to tell him it was over.

Within an hour, my body had relaxed enough for me to stand.

"You want to talk? Watch a movie?"

I shook my head. "I want to go to sleep."

Jess followed me to my bedroom and insisted on helping me into the bed.

"Can you hand me my phone?" I asked her.

Jess gave it to me. "Tara?"

"Yeah," I lied.

As soon as she shut the door, I texted Liam. The message was simple:

SORRY. BYE.

Then I shut off my phone and cried myself to sleep.

Chapter Twenty

Tara showed up on my doorstep on my seventh consecutive day of having my phone shut off. She stood so closely to the door that the only thing I could make out in the peephole were two eyes and an exaggerated nose. The last person I wanted to deal with was Tara, who started this whole mess in the first place. I was in favor of leaving the door bolted and chained, but Jess insisted on letting her in.

She stepped into the apartment and sniffed her nose as though she expected a foul stench to emanate from me. It was probably the stench of my inadequacy, or perhaps her face had merely frozen into a permanent mask of disappointment. She appraised me, her eyes still pinched together and her nose in the air.

"I expected to find a dead body in here," she exclaimed in her most maternal voice—the one she brought out for traumatic occasions.

"That explains your face then," I said before I could stop myself.

Tara shot me a frosty look that couldn't quite break through the shell I'd been building up over the last few days. She was not amused. "Jillian, your phone has been going to voicemail for over a week."

It had only been seven days, but who was counting?

"I probably need to charge it," I said, shrugging my shoulders like this was no-big-deal.

"You promised to call me after your medications set in. It's been over a week!" There was a slight tremor vibrating in her words as she spoke, but I dismissed it as more theatrics.

"I forgot. Things are normal."

"Things are not normal. First, I catch you with *that boy*."

I winced at the pure disgust that coated the words *that boy*.

"Then you yell at me!" she continued. "And it causes an off episode."

As usual, Tara was more upset about my disrespect than my condition. She probably thought my Parkinson's could be cured by good behavior. After all, if I hadn't yelled at her, the episode would never have happened, according to Dr. Tara.

"I think that boy is a bad influence on you," Tara said.

Across the room, Jess froze in her tracks. She'd been tiptoeing around the topic of Liam all week long. She hadn't once asked me if I'd called him, and she knew damn well that I hadn't left the apartment. I was counting on the sympathy card when it came to classes. Not that I cared one way or another. But Tara's insistence on bringing up *that boy* cracked through the careful numb feeling I'd cultivated with a diet of bad take-out and reality television—the two most soul-crushing things in existence. I pushed past her into the kitchen and grabbed a glass of water. I drank it in two long gulps, focusing on the smooth chill as it washed down the tears trying to climb up my throat.

"I have class," I lied to her as I set the glass on the counter. I had no intention of going to class, but she didn't need to know that. Behind her, Jess shook her head at me.

"Nice try, Jillian. It's Sunday."

Shit, this was the danger of watching DVR'ed shows. I no longer knew what day of the week it was.

"And since I suspected that you were too busy applying your butt to the couch instead of going to class or seeing the doctor," she continued, "I'll be sleeping on your couch for the week."

I pinched the skin of my arm hard. It stung so badly that tears pooled in my eyes.

"What are you doing? Are you having an attack?" she asked in a panicked voice.

"I thought maybe I was in a waking nightmare."

Tara glowered at me and held out her palm. "Keys?"

"Keys?" I repeated. "Why?"

"Because I'm going to the car to get my bag, and I

wouldn't put it past you to lock me out and take Jess hostage," she said in an even tone.

She had me there. It would have been an excellent plan if I had thought of it first, and if she hadn't already foiled it. Further proof that Tara was an evil genius intent on my annihilation.

As soon as she was out the door, I rounded on Jess. "Tell her she can't stay."

"She's your mom and besides that..." Jess trailed off.

"Besides that?" I prompted.

"You can't stay on the couch forever."

Jess's betrayal stunned me. She had brought me ice cream and watched at least four hours of *The Vampire Diaries* with me, but now she was going to side with Tara.

"Fine." I stomped off to my bedroom. By the time that I emerged, dressed in jeans and a t-shirt, Tara had laid out her cosmetic and skin care routine on the bathroom counter.

"I'm going out," I called, beelining for the door.

"Hold on, I'll come with you," Tara answered.

I hurried out the door and ran down the stairs before she could catch up with me. Since Tara hadn't attended Olympic State, I took a back way toward campus that she couldn't possibly know about.

Winter had descended on the small town in record time. Whereas last week, the air had a crisp bite to it, today the sun was totally absent in the gray sky. You could feel winter here like the soreness before the bloom of a bruise appeared. It never got horribly cold, but the days grew shorter and the darkness stretched longer, and then there was the near-constant spitting rain. I pulled my hoodie over my head and stuffed my hands into my pockets as the mist hit my skin. I didn't bother to wipe it away; instead it collected in a thin layer of cool wetness.

It was the closest I'd come to crying since the night I broke things off with Liam. Part of me hoped that the moisture clinging to my face would unjam the anger and bitterness that sat like a weight on my chest.

The campus was dead except for a steady trickle of students entering and exiting the library. I decided a cup of coffee was worth the risk of running into a professor, so I followed my backpack-laden peers inside and joined the queue of students waiting for a caffeine fix. The line moved at the speed of smell, and I tapped my foot in a nervous beat on the floor.

How long would Tara be staying? Surely, I could get Dad to call her back to California, but my mother was stubborn. If she had fixed her mind on sticking around, no one was going to talk her out of it.

Her presence meant no late television or outings to Garrett's. She would police what I ate and check my medication bottles constantly. There was a reason I hadn't bothered going home last summer, choosing instead to work at a coffee shop downtown. Being home was like finding myself in a dystopian novel, and I suspected that the end to that story included me setting fire to civilization.

I didn't say it was a happy dystopian novel.

Tara and I needed a couple of hundred miles between us, but she couldn't see that.

"Jillian!"

I looked up to see Trevor cradling two coffees. We stared at each other, both of us trying to figure out what to say to one another without the buffer of Cassie between us.

"Hey!" I tried to sound enthusiastic, but it came out all wrong. Too high-pitched. Too loud. I'd forgotten how to communicate with the rest of my species.

"I was studying," he said. He cast a glance, checking to see who was around him, like this was top-secret information.

"The library is a good place for that." And now I was stating totally obvious facts, although to be fair, Trevor started it.

Also I was apparently twelve years old again.

"Are you with Cassie?" I asked, pointing to the two cups.

Trevor shook his head quickly. "No, um, study group."

I raised my eyebrows at him. He acted like this was the first time he had set foot in this library. "Well, as you were."

Even my joking voice sounded morose.

"I'll see you later?" Somehow he twisted the farewell into a question.

"Sure." I watched as he strode away. Cassie had weird taste—namely she liked guys whose attention came in the form of material affection. Something that had never really suited me. She wasn't a gold-digger. It was more like she needed the promise that they would take care of her, and she found the gifts reassuring. And Trevor had fit that bill so perfectly that she'd gone from vacillating between a small trove of boys she'd collected to his girlfriend almost overnight.

But Trevor wasn't all bad, even if he was acting really oddly. An unpleasant thought clicked in my head, and I immediately jumped out of the line and headed in the direction he had taken. About a dozen small reservation-only study rooms peppered the perimeter of the stacks, and I peeked into each looking for his curly blonde hair. By the time I reached the final room, I sank back against the wall. Apparently, I wasn't just emotionally dead anymore, I was also paranoid.

The library was a large place with two floors that stretched across the quad. He could be anywhere in here. Furthermore, he said study group, not study room. Maybe I was just a horrible person who wanted to ruin other people's happily ever afters.

When I got back to the apartment—because I honestly couldn't think of anywhere else to go—I was coffeeless and cranky. Tara was sitting at the kitchen bar, nursing a generous glass of white wine.

"I'm sorry," I mumbled when her sharp eyes met mine.

"I'm not here to ruin your life," Tara said, taking a sip. "I'm not going to escort you around campus and make sure you get to class."

I eyed her suspiciously, wondering if Jess had

worked some of her parental magic on her. Tara had been singing a different tune a few hours ago. "Then why are you here?"

"Because I was worried about my daughter," Tara admitted in a soft voice. "Ever since you were diagnosed, you've stayed away from me."

My mother had the bedside manner of a *Game of Thrones* character. As a kid, I always went to school when I felt sick because the school nurse would stroke my forehead and give me juice. "I've got this under control."

She looked at me and shook her head. "Maybe you do, and maybe I'm overreacting. Last Sunday was... rough on all of us. But you really scared me."

I'd never heard her admit to being afraid in her life. I had assumed that emotion was beneath her, but as her gaze lingered on me, I could see the terror in her eyes. I'd stayed away from home since my early-onset Parkinson's diagnosis because I didn't want to burden her, but I'd never considered that for Tara I'd merely cut her out of my life.

Honestly, in a way, I had done just that. She'd taught me not to depend on anyone else from a young age, and I'd assumed that I couldn't depend on her.

"It doesn't happen very often," I told her. "I didn't take my pills on time and I was feeling stressed out."

I left out that our fight had brought on my anxiety that night. This was the closest we'd come to talking in as long as I could remember, so I didn't want to jinx it.

"You're distracted by that boy." The disgust was

absent from her voice this time, instead her eyes sparkled a little as she said it, as though she was inviting me to dish on my relationship with Liam.

I swallowed against the lump jammed in my throat. "That won't be a problem anymore."

"It's my fault," Tara said, tapping her wine glass. "He was nice, but I lost it when I found you in that bathroom. I guess sometimes I still see you as my little girl, but regardless, I shouldn't have embarrassed you like that."

"I sort of embarrassed myself," I admitted.

Tara leaned in conspiratorially and whispered, "Your father and I have screwed in bathrooms, too."

I covered my ears and shook my head. "Maybe we should draw the line at our sex lives?" I suggested.

"Fair enough." She swallowed the last bit of her chardonnay. "But love lives are another story."

"I don't have a love life," I said with a shrug. "Never have."

Tara snorted and stood up from the bar stool. "I saw the way he looked at you."

"And how was that?" I asked, not sure I wanted to hear the answer.

"Like you hung the moon."

I rolled my eyes at her, but she simply smiled and headed toward the bathroom to begin her hour-long skin care ritual, leaving me alone with memory of Liam's eyes on mine.

The Communications Department was deserted

on Monday by the time I dragged myself across campus to face Markson. I'd hidden in my room for the better part of a week, but now I had to deal with things. My footsteps echoed in the empty hallway, and for a second, I was sure this was exactly how a death-row inmate felt. Dead man walking indeed. I needed Markson's class to stay at full-time status with the university. But there was no way I could handle working with Liam after what happened last weekend.

Markson's door was open, so I peeked my head in, half of me hoping he wouldn't be there. No such luck. His office, if you could call it that, was a small desk crammed into a room the size of a supplies closet. Check that—supplies closets were probably bigger than this. He beckoned for me to come in, closing his laptop and settling back in his chair expectantly.

The only personal item in the room was a photograph of a large family, each person smiling, on a too-perfect beach. I looked more closely until I spotted him. Each member of the group shared Markson's deep brown eyes and thick, oil-black hair. He was significantly less tanned than most of them though.

"My family," he said.

"That's not Olympic Falls," I noted. "The beaches around here were rugged, full of driftwood and craggy bluffs. The beach in Markson's photo stretched into miles of white sand and clear water.

"They live in Puerto Vallerta," he explained. "My mother's side. My father grew up in Montana."

"That sounds like a story," I said.

"It is." But he didn't offer to tell it. "What can I help you with, Miss Nichols?"

I took a deep breath, ready to launch into a hundred reasons why I needed him to change my class partner. "I have a request."

"I'm listening." Markson folded his hands behind his head and waited.

It was strange to have someone who was only a few years older than me act with such authority. I'd gotten the impression from Jess that he was more laid-back, even funny. But then again, enough bad evaluations could change any professor's approach to their interactions with students.

I needed to spit it out. "I'd like a new class partner."

"Trouble in paradise?" he asked, raising an eyebrow.

Heat flashed onto my cheeks, but I managed a quick bob of my head. "Something like that."

"I'll level with you." Markson leaned forward and looked me in the eye. "I don't have enough students to pair you off with someone else, and what you're asking me to do could significantly damage other students' grades. Do you think it's fair to the other groups to ask them to change at this point in the course?"

A lump was forming in my throat, growing from a tiny pebble into what felt like an Indiana Jones size boulder. I couldn't force any words out past it, but I shook my head. He was absolutely right about asking my classmates to switch this late in the semester.

"Unfortunately," Markson continued, "this is one

of the risks of engaging in romantic relationships with classmates."

I wanted to pretend that it was anger swirling into my blood, but it felt more like shame. I had known it would never work with Liam, and I let him in anyway. Now my GPA was going to pay the price.

"This is why they advise that co-workers don't get involved with one another," he said.

"You pushed me to date him," I accused, before I could stop myself. "You practically assigned us to go on a date."

"A number of students participated in that project. I'm guessing that most of them didn't wind up in bed together."

I gasped at his words, unable to pretend they didn't cut through my carefully constructed apathy. It had been a show for Markson, but now it was painfully obvious that I was hurting. Horror flashed across his face as he realized exactly what he'd said.

So much for cool Professor Markson. I couldn't wait to tell Jess what I thought of her beloved instructor. He had crossed the line, and we both knew it.

"I apologize," he said almost immediately. "That was out of line."

"Then you'll consider my request?" I asked, not above a little emotional blackmail to get what I needed.

"My reasoning still stands. I can't reassign you without affecting other students. I suggest you consider dropping the course." His suggestion sounded weak now, lacking the confidence he'd displayed when

I first came in. He was as shaken by our interaction as I was.

"I can't," I managed to say over my dry tongue. I needed to get out of here, because I could feel the first waves of nausea rolling through my stomach. First, dry mouth. Then watery mouth. And finally, I would spew all over him, which really wouldn't help my case.

"The rest of the coursework will be done in class. I can assure you that I will not allow things to get out of control, and your final will be an independent project. Can you spend a couple of hours a week being civil to your partner?"

It wasn't that I wanted to be Liam's enemy. I didn't want to see him. How many times would I have to relive that humiliating night? I could already see the pity in Liam's eyes when he helped me with class assignments. My mouth began to water.

"Whatever," I said, hoisting my bag over my shoulder and dashing out of his office. I ignored Markson calling after me in favor of making it to the restroom. I barely threw myself at the toilet before the first heaves brought up my small breakfast. I retched four or five times until my body trembled with the aftershocks of vomiting. Clutching the toilet as the stall swam in my vision, I tried not to think about going back to class with Liam. Instead, I focused on other things, like how dirty this bathroom probably was. It was saying something that it was actually an improvement over thinking about going back to Markson's class tomorrow.

But when I finally pulled myself together and managed to get myself out into the cool Pacific Northwest air, the salty scent of the ocean calmed me down enough for me to realize that I didn't have to go back, and I wouldn't.

Chapter Twenty-One

My bedroom looked like a hurricane had hit it. Scarves and shoes littered the bed as Jess rifled through my closet. She and Cassie were both looking for something to wear out to Garrett's as it was our first girls-only night in weeks. Tara had been induced to visit her sister in Spokane, a safe three-plus hours away, so we could count on having freedom from the carbohydrate-tyranny of my mother.

"I told Trevor that he was cut off tonight, and he better not show his fucking face." Only Cassie could make that not only sound threatening but endearing at the same time.

"Brett is studying anyway," Jess assured both of us.

I knew they were trying to be sweet, but the emphasis on their boyfriends just made me feel Liam's absence more acutely. Jess tossed a wispy blue dress at me.

"You look hot in that," she said.

I held it up, frowning at it's spaghetti straps and short hemline. "It's November," I reminded them. "I haven't worn this since the last time I was in California."

Cassie waved off my concern. "These." She held up a pair of brown suede boots.

"Tights," Jess said, handing me a pair.

I stripped out of my yoga pants and started to pull them on, but Cassie grabbed my arm.

"Sexy underwear?" she suggested. Thongs had been part of the required boy catching uniform since our freshman year.

"I'm not bringing anyone home," I said, continuing to get dressed. Tonight was about being with my best friends, not trying to catch a guy. Just the thought made my insides clench.

"It's not about that," Cassie reminded me. "It's about how you feel."

"I want to feel comfortable," I muttered as I slipped into the boots.

Cassie held her hands up in surrender. I tugged the dress over my head and stood for them to inspect me. Cassie wrapped an earthy scarf around my neck and tied it expertly and then she completed the ensemble with a short white leather jacket, courtesy of Jess.

"You look so hot," Jess said as I checked myself out in the mirror. Between the doctor's visits and trying to catch up with coursework, I hadn't bothered to put myself together in weeks. Jess coaxed my hair into a messy twist that tumbled down my back. My hands were still acting up, so Cassie lined my eyes.

An hour later, we were ready to head to Garrett's, but Jess stopped me at the door and handed me a Simenet, one of the many new drugs I'd been prescribed.

She bit her lip, clearly struggling with what to say to me. "Go easy on the drinks tonight, okay?"

"One," I promised her. I wasn't going to ruin girls' night by flushing my meds out of my system—that was a sure way to have an episode.

The night was in full swing at Garrett's by the time we arrived. On the stage someone belted out a twangy melody to the delight of a group of friends cat-calling nearby. I relaxed, immediately comfortable in my second home, which was kinda sad given it was a bar.

"Look, a booth," Cassie said, taking my elbow and steering me toward it. A booth on Friday night at Garrett's was a coup. Most of the time they were occupied by regulars that were too busy shooting nasty looks at the crop of new students who discovered the bar each week.

"We should get a drink first," I suggested. It would take a waitress forever to get to us with this crowd.

"We'll get it," Jess said in an oddly cheerful voice. Were they actually going to be so goddamn happy all night? It was like they were on suicide watch or something. Despite the fact that I was totally fine, they insisted on passing worried glances to each other when they thought I wasn't looking.

Cassie grabbed the seat facing the stage before I could sit down, and Jess pulled me into the other side.

"What do you want for your very special, one-time-only drink?" Jess asked. "Choose wisely."

I knew if I ordered something too strong she'd veto it immediately, so I opted for a beer. I didn't even like beer, so I wouldn't get in trouble with wanting more.

"I need to use the bathroom," I said when Jess stood to head to the bar.

"You haven't had anything to drink yet!"

"That's the funny thing about the human body," I said slowly, "sometimes you have to pee without imbibing alcohol."

"I'll come with you," Cassie offered.

"We'll lose the booth," I said. "Why are you acting so weird?"

"We're not acting fucking weird," Cassie said.

"This is girls' night," Jess said, draping her arm around my shoulder. "We want to spend time with you."

"Well, you can't actually pee for me, so..." I pushed past her and turned toward the bathroom. It was suddenly clear why they were freaking out. Liam stood with a group of guys. Correction: Liam was with some guys, but he was talking to a girl. A really pretty girl in a really short skirt.

Numbness crawled up my chest, freezing my gaze to the spot. The pulse of the music faded into the background as I tried to tear my eyes away, but it was like a car wreck. I didn't want to see, but I couldn't stop watching. The blonde said something, and Liam's head fell back in laughter. He reached out and squeezed her shoulder, gesturing to the empty glasses in front of them.

So what? He was going to buy a girl a drink. I had no claim on him. I didn't want him like that anymore. It was simply a symptom of seeing him for the first time in weeks. It was surprise. But surprise couldn't account for the lump swelling into tears in my throat.

"Let's go," Jess said.

"No, I'm fine." I shook her hand off my arm. "But I still have to go to the bathroom."

"Let me come with you," Cassie begged.

"Oh my god, I can go to the bathroom and come back. I'm not going to get lost." I reached for the stack of coasters on the table and held them up. "I can drop these behind me and find my way back to you."

"We just want you to have a good time," Jess said.

"Then get me a beer already!" I flashed them my widest smile and bounded toward the bathroom before they could stop me.

The tears came as I closed the stall door. Much like puking, this was not a new experience for me at Garrett's. It was the first time I cried alone, however. A phone call from Tara plus a drink was the usual catalyst that set me off, and I shared those moments willingly, because I needed to hear that Tara was being a bitch. I didn't want to hear that Liam was an asshole though, because he wasn't. I couldn't escape the truth: Liam was out there talking to another girl because I pushed him away.

Which was the right thing to do.

A few ruined feet of toilet paper later and my face was dry without too much damage to my eye makeup. Taking a deep breath, I headed back into the swarm. My best bet at surviving the pitying glances of my best friends was a shot of tequila. The no liquor and meds rule didn't apply to extreme circumstances like this. Pushing my way in, I called my order to Frank who slid a shot down with the expertise of a man who had seen enough barroom drama to know when a girl needed a drink.

I tossed it back as the opening beats to a Taylor Swift song echoed through Garrett's. Looking up, I froze. Liam was taking the stage. I'd seen plenty of guys making a fool out of themselves on karaoke night, but this was the pièce de résistance. Across the bar, his eyes met mine as he clutched the mic. I knew then that this was a message to me. I knew this song.

Liam was trying to tell me something, and his message wasn't very nice. Although he had a pretty nice singing voice. My core clenched at the thought of his lips and murmured words shared in the dark. I couldn't believe he was doing this to me. I would have been less embarrassed if he'd Facebooked a pic of my boobs.

He was calling attention to me. To us. The one thing that was unforgivable in my book.

"Is Liam singing a Taylor Swift song?" Jess asked as she plopped onto a bar stool beside me.

"Unfortunately." I leaned back against the bar and watched as Liam wagged a finger at me from the stage.

"Is he singing to you?"

"Yep."

"Ouch," Jess said as she took a sip of her Long Island Iced Tea. She paused a moment to listen to the lyrics and screwed her face up. "That is not the most complimentary song."

"Are any Taylor Swift songs complimentary?" I asked, trying not to show that Liam's performance was hurting my feelings.

"You want to go now?" she offered.

"Absolutely not." The tequila was warm in my belly still, and I shot her a wicked look. A second later, I was pulling her to the dance floor.

If Liam thought he could get a rise out of me, I could play that game, too. Gripping Jess's hands, we started bobbing to the beat of the song. As luck would have it, two hot girls were more than enough to attract a few guys. I dared to look up but Liam was already off the stage. Someone's hands gripped my hips, and my heart hammered fast. I pulled his arms around me and shook my ass against him. I knew I shouldn't, but I couldn't help myself.

I didn't want to stay away from Liam. Not while he was right here with me.

And would it be so wrong to take him home one more time?

The crowd shifted and Liam stood on the other side of it, watching me. I'd let myself believe it was him dancing with me—that somehow he still wanted me despite everything. Even across the room, sadness mingled with fury in his eyes before he tilted his head as if to say *have it your way*. I wrenched myself free from the guy dancing behind me and pushed myself through the crowd.

My lungs had stopped working, turning to lead weights that only allowed for quick desperate pants. I couldn't catch a breath in the crush of people, so I forced myself through them toward the emergency exit. The night air blasted against me and I gulped it down, trying to steady myself. I'd lost control. I couldn't even lie to myself about it anymore. I leaned against the brick facade of Garrett's and counted my breaths. An old physical therapy trick that always worked, even when I was only dealing with an anxiety attack.

I found my phone in my jacket pocket and texted Jess that I was out back. She was right, I had to get out of here. Fast. Liam didn't want me. He sang that song to send me a message.

We were over. He knew I was trouble. The exact thing I'd been trying to tell him for months. I wasn't about to go back in there. It took a few minutes but the exit door swung open and this time I was ready to run into Jess's arms. Pretending that my heart wasn't broken was never going to heal it. I'd gone too far with Liam. There was no way I was coming back from this alone.

But Liam's solid form stood in the shadows cast by Garrett's floodlights. I didn't think, I just started running. I heard him follow me, and I pushed my body harder, willing myself to go faster, but the heel of my boot caught on a hole in the pavement, and I tumbled onto my knees.

"Christ, Jillian," Liam said, reaching me seconds later. He tried to help me up, but I shoved his hands away.

"This is how it's going to be?" he asked me. The blaze in his eyes melted through me as I stood up, ignoring the air stinging my scraped knees. I lounged against a streetlamp, hoping I looked casual despite my humiliating escape attempt.

"I don't want to talk to you," I said. I kept my eyes cast back toward Garrett's. Jess would save me any moment, but the longer I looked at the door, the more I didn't want her to come. Confusion churned like a bad night of drinking in my stomach. I wanted Liam to go. I wanted Liam to stay.

"You've made that clear," Liam said in a wounded voice. "I guess it doesn't matter to you at all what I want."

"It was never going to work." I started into the speech I'd been practicing for this moment. The one where I laughed off his heartbreak and reminded him that we'd started as a fling. I'd said it to myself in the mirror a dozen times, but when I tried to do it now, my words flatlined, drifting into the night surrounding us.

"Why? Give me one reason it won't work."

"You're going back to Scotland," I said. It was as good of a reason as all the others that floated to mind.

"It's the twenty-first fucking century, Jillian." He took a step toward me, and I pressed myself against the cool metal of the pole. "You don't have to take the Titanic to cross the Atlantic anymore."

"I watched Cassie try that with a guy back home. You know what's a helluva lot closer to Washington than Scotland? Texas. You know how long it lasted between them? Two weeks."

"You've seen one failure and that's it?" Liam turned away from me, loosing a hollow laugh. "The thing is I know that's not it. What aren't you telling me?"

"I'm fucked up, Liam. Is that what you want me to say?" I screamed at him, forcing him to face me. "And that's all I know how to do—how to fuck things up."

"You're hiding things from me, Jillian, and that hurts." His voice dropped and he moved closer to me, his body inches from mine. "Because I want all of you. The sexy part and the funny part and especially the fucked-up part."

His body drew me toward him. His pull on me magnetic, unescapable. I clutched the streetlamp behind me to stop myself from folding into him. He gripped the pole, dropping his face close to mine. His breath was hot and laced with whiskey as he hovered there. I took a deep breath and muttered, "That's twisted."

He looked at me like I had slapped him. "That's love."

The swelling in my chest burst with a trembling flood that rushed through my body. My knees buckled, and I clutched the pole to keep myself upright under the weight of his words. He held my gaze, and I couldn't look away from him, our eyes were locked together, each of us unsure what the next move was in this wicked game we were playing.

"You don't know me," I whispered. "You saw though. I'm sick."

"I saw the pills. You can't cover things up with Chiclets, Jillian. I don't care about that." His words were thick on his lips—his perfect, kissable lips.

"You can't fix me, Liam. I have early-onset Parkinson's. In a few more years, it will get worse."

"And you think I'll just walk out?" he asked.

"If you're smart, you'll leave now. The memory will be better than any future we could share together," I said through the haziness caused by his proximity.

"I never promised you forever, Jillian. I'm not asking you to promise me that either. I just want a chance—a real one."

I melted under his eyes, trying to keep my hands from pulling him to me.

"I can't give you that," I whispered.

He dropped back, and I missed the heat of his body, the closeness of him, immediately.

"You want to know the truth? I knew the second I met you that I should walk away. I knew you'd shred me, but I couldn't stay away. But if you can, maybe you're stronger than me." He paused and ran a hand through his hair. A memory of fisting my fingers through his hair flashed through my mind, and I grew warm, praying he would break me. Needing him to hold on.

"I don't think you're strong though. Not anymore," he continued, his voice growing in strength. "I think you're scared, and I deserve more than that and you do, too."

Gravel crunched nearby, and we turned to see Jess approaching us cautiously. She held her phone in her hand and she looked to both of us, waiting for a signal to stop. I ducked away from Liam and ran to her.

"Ask her," Liam called to me. "Ask her what she thinks of you running away from your problems."

Jess caught me and held me close to her.

"Stop it, Liam," she ordered, her eyes fierce. I knew Jess agreed with him, but some bonds couldn't be broken. My best friend would never side with him, even if she knew he was right.

"I want to go home," I told her in a quiet voice. She rubbed my arm and guided me away.

Liam didn't follow us, but he called out as we walked away. "Good-bye, Jillian."

My name died on his lips, and part of me died with it. I wanted a good-bye with Liam. I'd imagined it in the dark of the night. But in those fantasies, we made love and he got on a plane. In those dreams, there were laughter and teasing and kissing. That was how I wanted to remember him, but for the rest of my life all I would hear were those beaten, final words.

Chapter Twenty-Two

❧

The world was gray and it bore down on me, weighting me to the mistakes I'd made. I was bound to an onslaught of memories that I couldn't erase. All the color was sucked from life as I stood in my room trying to sort my feelings into something I could understand. There were no boxes that fit the strange assortment of emotions waging a war in my head. Liam was the worst thing for me, because I didn't want to feel this. Not when life was already too complicated. We were both better off. But even as I thought it, it didn't make sense. I didn't make sense without him. And yet, his life could never make sense with me in it.

That truth left me cold and desolate. At my center, a blackness crept through me, eating away at me and leaving me so hollow that I could barely stand.

My bed was empty and I couldn't force myself into it. It sat staring me down like an abyss that would swallow me whole, as memories of skin and flesh blinked in and out of my mind. If I closed my eyes, I felt his lips on my neck and my stomach and my breasts, but when I opened them, I was alone, stripped to the soul.

I wanted to sleep and forget, hoping that in the morning the sun came out again. But I couldn't count on that any more than I could expect the world to keep spinning. I could see the splinters growing all around me, threatening to collapse the comfortable lie I'd sold myself until they became real, shattering and cracking the walls I'd built to hide behind.

I slapped myself again and again and again, trying to concentrate on the sting left by the palm of my hand. I was stupid. I was worthless. Broken. Feeling the hate coursing through my veins like slow-burning poison was better than the numb chill that threatened to overpower me.

But there were things that I couldn't run away from. I could run from Liam, but my own body was my worst enemy and it turned on me. The tingles started in my hands and stretched into my arms as I ran for the bathroom. I slowed with each step until I fell against the sink, reaching for a medication that could stop the paralysis spreading through my limbs. But I could barely pick them up, let alone open the childproof caps. I screamed and threw them against the wall as the trembling shook my body, and I dropped to the floor. I was an earthquake. Uncontrollable. Unstoppable.

"Jills!" Jess appeared in the door and knelt to hold me.

I heard a litany of curses bursting from me in my voice but I couldn't stop them any more than I could control the episode taking over my body. My fingers hooked and stiffened. I was frozen, my limbs locked and gnarled like the branches of a dead tree. Jess pressed her fingers to my wrist and checked my eyes.

She leapt to her feet and started pulling medicine bottles from the shelf. She tried to force a pill into my mouth but I couldn't swallow. My body was giving up. It was about damn time. I'd given up a long time ago.

"Jills, come on, you have to get this down," she coaxed, but I couldn't relax enough.

"Where's your injectable?"

I answered her but my words were a slur of consonants and vowels.

Jess had been trained to give me a shot when we moved into together. My doctor told us it was only a precaution, but one Tara insisted on. There was no way she would let me live on my own if there wasn't someone there to handle a worst case scenario, so Jess had been tapped. Because she was good and dependable and everything I wasn't.

But she wasn't ever supposed to do this, because twenty-one-year-olds didn't have off episodes like this. It was Tara's paranoia, not my reality. I wished Liam was here so that he could see me like this, because then there would be no chance that he'd promise me anything afterwards. And as my body broke down, it reminded me of one thing, I was saving him from this.

I clung to that as I willed my arms to move. I tried

to remember how to stretch my fingers or push myself onto my feet, but my brain fought against me, pinning me to the ground.

"I'm going to give you a shot, because I can't leave you like this," Jess said in a soft, reassuring tone, but I heard a tremor hiding in her voice. She blinked back a tear as an impassive calm stole over her face. This was Dr. Jess, the girl who had a future I would never have, and she deserved it, because there was no one else that I would trust to see me like this and still love me. It was the blessing of our friendship, and our biggest curse. I wondered for a moment if she would even be studying pre-med if she hadn't been forced into it, but I couldn't feel sorry for her. She was alive and empowered.

When the syringe appeared in her hand, a siren blared in my head. She dropped beside me and tapped the syringe with her finger. Jess blinked back another tear and brought the needle to my arm. Neither my mouth or my body were working, but my mind was, and I knew that Jess had to be seriously worried if she was taking it to this extreme. I tried to push her hand away, but I couldn't force my arms to move. An injection was a last resort, because we both knew it would interact with my current meds. I screamed again as she carefully injected the medication into my vein and then everything went black.

Chapter Twenty-Three

A persistent beep edged into my dreams, awakening me to drab green walls. I blinked as a whiteboard swam into view listing a schedule of care. I tried to sit up, but I found a collection of IVs had me tangled in my bed. It took a second longer than it should have for me to realize I was in a hospital room. Jess was curled into a ball, asleep on the couch next to me. I opened my mouth to discover it was cotton-dry, and that I was too parched to speak. Fumbling, I hit the red call button attached to the side of my bed and waited.

A nurse bustled into the room a few minutes later in Hello Kitty scrubs. She didn't look much older than me, but as she leaned over me to to turn off the call button, I got a whiff of stale coffee and cigarettes that matched the circles under her eyes.

"Miss Nichols, how are you feeling?" She flipped through my chart, casting a few glances toward me.

Jess stirred at her words and sat up, rubbing sleep from her eyes. It only took her a few seconds before she was fully alert and hovering by my bedside.

"Are you okay, Jills?" Jess brushed my hair off my face and peered down at me with concern.

"Water," I mouthed.

"I'll bring in a pitcher," the nurse said absently as she checked off something on my chart.

Jess disappeared and reemerged a second later with a cup. The nurse frowned at her but continued her assessment of my vital signs while Jess held the cup to my lips. The water swept away the dry feeling in my throat.

"Help me sit up?" I asked Jess.

"Of course." She maneuvered an arm under my back and shoved a pillow in the gap she created.

"How long was I out?"

"Only a few hours," Jess reassured me, adding another pillow under my head.

I didn't have to ask why I was here. The events of last night—while hazy as fog on the sound—were clear enough. I remembered the crippling pain spreading throughout my body and locking down my limbs. The lead-up to Jess's injection were vivid, while the most concrete memory I had from the previous evening was the magnetic force between Liam and me when he confronted me. But I couldn't remember anything after the shot Jess administered.

"Please tell me that you didn't call Tara."

"I didn't." Jess paused and bit her lip like she

always did when she was about to spill bad news. "But the hospital called when they were admitting you."

The nurse took the opportunity to slip in her explanation as she handed me a Dixie cup full of pills. There were a lot more in here than normal.

"We need you to take those," the nurse instructed me

"What are they?" I wasn't keen on taking any more pills than I already was, but I also wasn't excited at the idea of staying plugged into a hospital bed.

"The on-call doctor is adding an anxiety medication immediately," the nurse told me.

"Is that safe?" I blurted out. There had been numerous times when I wanted medication to help me deal with the stress of controlling my anxiety levels, a feat which usually ended poorly. I was still an amateur when it came to compartmentalizing emotions, my own and those around me.

"It's safer than another one of these off episodes," the nurse said.

I swallowed the pills one by one with long swigs of water. It had been so long since I drank anything with my meds that I almost spit a couple back up. The nurse, appeased by my willingness to take the medication, disappeared into the hallway, leaving Jess and I alone.

Jess held out my cell phone. "Call him."

I shook my head. I wasn't going to be that girl. The one that called her ex at the first sign of trouble. It was too relationship-y.

"He's going to find out, Jills. He should find out

from you." Jess sat on the edge of my bed, her arm still extending the cell phone to me.

"How would he find out? This is hardly Facebook status news." There was no way I was going to call him, and Jess couldn't make me.

"Because I will tell him if you don't," Jess said in measured tones.

I balked at her. Jess was my best friend. We were practically sisters. "You have no right to tell him."

"Liam is in love with you, and he is scared. You can't keep pretending like he doesn't matter. Look where it's gotten you."

"This didn't happen because of Liam." I knew it was a lie as much as Jess did. "Besides, he's over me."

"I saw you two last night. He's not over you," Jess said. She slid the lock screen off and started paging through my contacts.

"Don't tell him," I said. "Maybe you're right, but I can't face him right now."

"You can't run away from life." Jess's sentiment echoed Liam's argument from last night. Why couldn't they see that I wasn't running, I was protecting myself? I was protecting them.

"I don't want him here." My words were full of fire, sparking Jess to look up at me in surprise.

"Maybe you're right. You clearly don't trust him," Jess said. "Maybe Liam deserves more."

She could have punched me and it would have hurt less. I tried to keep my face impassive, but I knew I was failing. Hot tears were burning at the edge of my eyes, and I blinked against them.

"Not now," I said finally.

"For what it's worth, Cassie agrees with me."

I groaned. "You told Cassie I was here."

"How do you think I got you to the hospital? You were out, Jills."

"By the way, worst girls' night ever," I said, switching the topic before more panic could build in my chest.

"Not by a long shot," Jess disagreed. "Don't you remember the devil tequila?"

We both fell into laughter, remembering the night freshman year when Cassie and I had split an entire bottle of Jose Cuervo. Poor Jess had spent the whole night holding our heads over the toilet and rubbing our backs. For the rest of the year, the bottle sat with "666 DEVIL BOTTLE" scrawled across the label. I was pretty sure I still had it somewhere. It was probably the only night worse than this one in our entire shared history.

"You hungry?" Jess asked me. "You should probably eat something with those meds."

As soon as she said it, I became aware of the gnawing pit where my stomach once was. I nodded emphatically.

"I'll sneak down to the cafeteria and bring you something." Jess leaned over and kissed my forehead.

"Bring pudding. But not the sucky kind."

Jess paused in the doorway. "Oh, and if anyone

asks, we're sisters. That's why they're letting me stay with you. Visiting time was over hours ago."

"Got it." Whoever bought that slender, super-blonde Jess and I were sisters must be blind, but I was grateful. I couldn't think of anyone else I wanted here with me. In fact, there was no one else I'd ever want to see me right now. Jess had seen me in much worse situations.

It seemed like she returned in record time, but when I looked up, Tara was standing there. Her hair was pulled into a tight ponytail and she wore no cosmetics. She looked unusually casual in jeans and sweatshirt, not at all like the Tara that showed up to my apartment ready to stay. But then I realized that my aunt's house in Spokane was over three hours away. She must have jumped in the car immediately. A rush of guilt waved over me. First, Jess had to deal with this, and now my mom. She stopped at the foot of my bed and regarded me with what looked like tears in her eyes, which wasn't possible. Tara was not a cryer. Then she rushed me, pulling at the IVs, as she hugged me.

"Ouch!" I yelped.

Tara pulled back and disentangled herself from the tubes. "I knew I shouldn't have left."

"It's not your job to stick around babysitting me," I said in a sour voice.

"I'm your mother. That's actually exactly what my job is." Tara sat next to me and picked my hand up in hers. "What happened, Jills?"

"Just a bad reaction to some medications." I

purposefully left out the fight with Liam and the tequila shots and the general sense of hopelessness weighting me down even now.

"You should come home. Your father will call the school and set it up. You can transfer to San Diego. It's only ten minutes—"

I held my hand up to stop her. "My life is here."

"What life?" It was a characteristically Tara thing to say, but even she looked abashed at the thoughtless remark. But instead of back-peddling, she kept going. "You have no major. You broke up with that boy. You're barely attending classes. You have no job."

Well, when she put it like that, I did sound aimless, and yet, I didn't feel that way. Being forced to confront reality, I realized I had a life.

"I have friends, Mom," I said. "I like the college even if I've been bad about classes. But once they get my medications figured out, I'll get serious about coursework. I even picked out a major."

Tara raised an eyebrow. "Which is?"

The problem was that this was as much news to me as it was to Tara. "Psychology. I figure I can work with kids coping with a serious illness."

The answer flew out of my mouth, surprising me. Had I really been thinking about that? It was not only a perfect answer, it was actually the perfect major for me. I just wasn't sure when I had come up with the idea.

"That's awesome, honey," Tara said. There was actually something that sounded like pride in her voice, but I couldn't be sure since I'd never heard it before.

Tara hesitated, picking at a piece of string on my hospital gown.

"Spit it out," I urged her.

"And that boy?"

"Liam?" I prompted. "What about him?"

"Where does he fit in this picture?" she asked.

"He doesn't," I said in a firm voice. "You don't have to worry about him."

"Actually, I'm more worried about you. I was really angry over that incident in the bathroom, but your father made me see that he's good for you. Ambitious, polite."

"Two things I am not," I said in a flat voice. First Jess had betrayed me, and now even Tara was siding with Liam.

"I'm not saying that, Jillian," Tara said. "You've gone through boys like tissues since you got to school. It's not healthy."

I stared at my mother. How would she know about my boy catching proclivities?

"You left your Facebook account up at the house last spring. I peeked," she admitted.

I should be mad. In fact, I should be livid. But it was my own damn fault, I'd caught Tara reading my diary when I was eleven. I'd managed to devise a system that included hollowed out books for parental contraband like condoms, and I'd stopped writing things down on paper, favoring an anonymous blog throughout high school. When I set up my account, I'd been so careful to set perimeters as to what my parents could see on Facebook, but she'd been able to see my life for months. I winced, thinking of the things she'd seen over the course of last summer.

"You should really close that account before you look for a job next year," she advised me.

And now my mom was giving me social media advice.

"I'll do that," I promised her. "But I want to stay at Olympic State."

Jess skipped into the room, pudding cups held triumphantly over her head, but she skidded to a stop when she saw Tara.

"We'll talk about it later," Tara said softly.

"Mrs. Nichols, it's good to see you," Jess said. "I can go back for more pudding cups."

"Not necessary." Tara said with a wave of the hand. "Thank you for calling me, Jessica."

I shot Jess a betrayed look and mouthed *what-the-fuck* behind my mom's head. Jess bit her lip and shrugged a shoulder. Apparently, she wasn't going to apologize. She sat the pudding cups on the rolling overbed table next to me.

"I should get home. Class tomorrow," she said, excusing herself from further hospital duty.

"Make sure you update your Facebook status so the whole world knows I'm in here," I said.

"Jills." Jess said my name with a sigh.

I tried to stay angry, but as chocolate pudding cups awaited me and because Jess was the one person I could count on to save me from Tara during my hospital stay, I decided to let it go. "Are you coming back tomorrow?"

"'Course," she said, flipping her hair over her shoulders and grabbing her bag.

"Are you okay to drive, Jessica?" Tara asked her. "You've been here all night."

"I slept on the couch. I got some sleep in exchange for a stiff neck." Jess rubbed it for emphasis.

"Maybe they can pull another bed in here?" Tara said after Jess took off. "It will be like a slumber party!"

"Great!" I tried to sound enthusiastic, and to my surprise, I did. The thought of having Tara around while I was stuck in here wasn't so bad. Maybe Jess was onto something. I could never tell her that though.

Chapter Twenty-Four

T ara insisted I stay hospitalized until a specialist could see me, which meant I spent the next week cooped up in bed watching the small array of channels available on my in-room television and wondering why they couldn't pony up for HBO. I'd seen enough hospital bills to know they could afford it. Ibuprofen at eight bucks a pop? I think that paid for access to *Game of Thrones*. Cassie snuck in lunch and dinner as often as she could so I wasn't stuck eating watery Jell-O and overcooked chicken.

My mother refused to leave the hospital, even to run out for necessities. She'd been in such a hurry to get to me that she'd left without a suitcase, so Jess brought her jeans and t-shirts. It was a sad fact that I'd never seen my mother in a t-shirt except for our one failed trip to Disneyland when I was seven. Tara only left my side to go on brief constitutionals, which made her sound old and British, but gave me a few precious minutes to myself.

Today I watched the clock, waiting for five minutes until two in the afternoon when Tara would stand and stretch and announce her intent to walk around the halls for a few minutes. As soon as she stood, I sat up in bed.

"Going for your walk?" I asked her. I couldn't bring myself to say constitutional.

Tara paused and studied me. "Hot date?"

I winced and shook my head.

A guilty look immediately settled over her face. "I'm going to take that constitutional now."

As soon as she was out the door, I hurried into the bathroom to grab one of the candy bars Cassie had brought me. I'd shoved them in my toiletries bag as Tara saw refined sugar as one of three major threats to the continued sovereignty of America. Apparently, carbs were going to take the country the way of the the Mayans. I had about twenty minutes to eat it, but when I popped back out of the bathroom, I wasn't alone in my room.

Liam was sitting on the edge of my bed, a plate of waffles and a box of Chiclets laid out on the table.

"Waffles for lunch," he offered. He wasn't lounging or relaxed. In fact, he seemed ill at ease here, his hands clutched in his lap.

"Did Jess tell you I was here?" I asked him.

"Does it matter? I'll leave if you want, but..."

I crossed my arms over my chest, aware I was in a

paper thin hospital gown the color of pea soup, and waited for him to find the rest of his sentence.

"But?" I finally prompted.

"But I don't want to go."

"Liam, you're a sweet guy. Believe me, I'm doing you a favor," I said, hoping he couldn't see my lower lip quivering. I needed him to get out of here now before I started to cry. Having Liam here crossed a line I wanted to keep intact. The hospital was where sick people stayed. It was full of death and disease and the horrible acrid scent of bleach. Liam belonged to the world of vanilla and kisses in the rain.

He stood and gestured for me to get back in my bed, but I hesitated, which sent him the wrong message. When I didn't climb back in, he pulled me to him and slid his hand around the back of my neck.

"I don't need any favors," he whispered. "I only need you."

I licked my suddenly dry lips and shook my head. "There's no cure for Parkinson's, and it's only going to get worse. In a few more years—"

"Do you think I haven't read every goddamn book on Parkinson's in the Ellis Library?" he cut me off. "And I talked to Jess."

My eyes narrowed. "It wasn't any of her business."

"Don't be mad at Jess. I confronted her about it after the off episode in your living room."

"You knew?"

Liam nodded. "It took me a while to get my head around it. I wasn't sure I could handle it."

He had known the whole time and he had stayed away. I wasn't sure what hurt worse: Jess's betrayal or that he'd confirmed my biggest fear. "Well, it's only going to get worse, so I hope you have better luck with your future girlfriends."

"I said I wasn't sure. *As in past tense.* You wouldn't talk to me, chicken."

I melted a little when he called me by the nickname. It felt so right after so much wrong.

"But then I realized I didn't need to handle it," he said. "My job is to help you handle it."

"I don't need help," I said, a wave of stubbornness coming over me. I ducked out of his arms and dropped onto my bed, out of his reach. "I don't want pity."

"Good, because I'm not offering any." Liam hovered over me, a variety of emotions flashing across his face. He didn't know what to feel any more than I did.

"Then why are you here?" I asked.

"To fucking bring you waffles and tell you that I love you!"

It was possibly the angriest declaration of love in the history of time, and it didn't matter one bit, because my heart burst at his words and somewhere deep inside me a smug voice said *I told you so.*

But for the life of me, I couldn't say it back to him. Not here. Not like this. We were in a sphere I wanted to keep separate from this fledgling love. Liam waited and I searched for something to say, anything to say that would break the awkward silence in the room.

"You also came to bring me Chiclets," I pointed out.

"I cannot deny you Chiclets." Liam grinned barely before his face grew solemn again. "I understand if you don't want—"

I held up a hand for him to stop. "It's not that. It's this place." I gestured to the anonymous hospital room we were in. "Hospitals are where people come to die. If we're going to have a second chance, it shouldn't be here."

"You forget that hospitals are where people come to be born, chicken. It's where people come to be healed. I know you have a different perspective on them than I do, but hospitals are all about life. You can't only see the scary parts. If you do, you miss all the awesome." He sat on the edge of my bed and gripped one of my ankles, massaging it softly. My skin sang where he touched it, and I realized how much I had missed him.

I wagged my index finger, beckoning him closer. He scooted closer and arranged himself cautiously over me.

"Yes, chicken?" he whispered.

"Thank you for the waffles."

"I will make you waffles anytime," he promised. The vow slid around me like a warm blanket. It was comforting and thrilling at the same time.

"I need to get out of here so that you can make good on that promise." I tousled his hair with my fingers and then brought my hand down to his chin, urging him closer to me. His breath was hot against my skin as he lowered his lips closer to mine. Anticipation surged through my body, lighting up my nerves until every part of me was tingling. When he finally kissed me, it was soft and sweet. His arms held himself suspended over me, but they pressed close to my sides like he was tucking me against him. As he slipped his tongue into my mouth, my back arched up, trying to close the space between us.

"Careful, chicken," he warned me in a low whisper. "I had to sweet-talk a nurse into letting me in here. If we set off your heart rate monitor, they'll kick me out."

"I unhooked it when I went to the bathroom. You are free to pound me."

Liam smirked at my choice of words. "I am, huh?"

"I mean make me pound...err, make my heart pound," I corrected, flushing a little from the heat raging through me. "Although the other stuff sounds good, too."

"When are you getting out of here?" He fingered the tie of my hospital gown.

"Not sure," I said, "but we're alone now."

"I'm not making love to you in a hospital bed," he said, shaking his head. "I need you in a much bigger bed for that. Preferably soon."

The pulsing in my body jumped into a full-blown frenzy, and I pushed up on my elbows so I could press against him as I kissed him again. Through the thin layers of cotton separating us, his heart raced. It was the most precious rhythm in the world—the beat of his heart—and just feeling it made me kiss him with a desperate, hungry passion. How could I have denied this? It was a lost cause to try to stay away from him, and I was no longer interested in trying to escape that fact.

"You should eat," he whispered, barely pulling away from me.

I clutched his neck, drawing him back toward me. "I don't want food."

"Well, pardon me," an annoyed voice said, startling us apart.

Tara stood at the door, her arms crossed so tightly over herself that her fingernails dug into the fleshy skin of her upper arms. Despite how understanding she had been when Liam had come up before in conversation, she looked none too pleased to see him now.

"Mrs. Nichols, it's nice to see you." Liam jumped off the bed, but I caught his hand to keep him from getting too far away.

"Have either of you heard of the expression 'the appropriate time and place?'" she asked us.

My eyes narrowed. "No, but I've heard of 'location, location, location!'"

And right now I was up for kissing Liam anytime, anyplace.

Tara scowled at us until Liam pried my hand from his and moved to sit on the couch. He was trying to please my mother, but the gesture left a cold emptiness in my chest and did nothing to wipe the anger off Tara's face.

"I ran into your nurse in the hallway," she informed

me, not giving Liam a second glance. "She said the specialist will be in to see you this afternoon."

"Finally," I said with a groan, falling back against my bed. "Maybe I can get out of here."

I shot Liam a quick raised eyebrow, but Tara saw it and shook her head.

"Jillian, your priority needs to be on managing this disease. I'm sure Liam has plenty on his plate right now. Maybe it's best if you both focus on your needs separately for the time being," she suggested. She turned toward Liam, as though waiting for his support on the matter.

"I know what Jillian's dealing with—" Liam began.

"You do, do you?" Tara cut him off. "So then you know she's in that hospital bed because of the fight you had, and it took you how long to even visit her? I thought you were good for her, but now..."

"I didn't want him to come," I stopped her. "I made Jess promise to not tell him I was here."

"And now it's time for him to leave," she said. "The doctor is on his way."

"I don't want him to leave." Liam was right. I didn't have to face this disease on my own anymore. Having Tara around wasn't a very comforting thought. She was all business when it came to my Parkinson's. I'd spent the last two years struggling to deal with changes in my body while Tara asked questions about cost, always heavily insinuating that it would be better for me to drop out of school. Her recent interest wasn't more than a fluke to gain my trust.

"I'm here as long as you want me," Liam said in a soft voice. He leaned forward and extended his hand to me.

"Forever," I murmured.

"This is family business," Tara said. She kept her gaze on me, pretending that Liam wasn't here. "Can I have a minute alone with you?"

"Whatever you have to say, you can say it in front of him," I said. A dizzying wave of déjà vu swept over me. I'd heard that line at least one hundred times in my life in movies and TV shows, and now I was saying it. The whole thing was a little absurd.

"You're being dramatic," she warned me.

"You're being a bitch," I said. Liam squeezed my hand, which was either a warning of his own or moral support.

"I am your mother," she said. "And I deserve—"

Her speech was interrupted by the entrance of an older man in a lab coat embroidered with the name Dr. Fales. His name didn't do a lot to inspire confidence in me.

"I apologize. I can return later." He gestured toward the door, but I shook my head. There was no way I was going to wait any longer for information, even if it gave Tara an aneurism.

"Dr. Fales." Tara extended her hand and shook his limply. "I'm Tara Nichols, Jillian's mother and this is Jillian."

"And this is my boyfriend, Liam," I said. "I'd like him to stay."

"That's perfectly fine," Dr. Fales said, and my mother frowned behind him. He smiled warmly at me as he picked up the chart off the end of the bed. "I've been looking over your case, Jillian. It sounds like you've had a rough time of it lately."

"Clearly, her condition is getting worse." Tara tugged at a small pearl pendant as she spoke. It didn't match her casual ensemble.

"Do you feel like you're getting worse?" Dr. Fales asked me.

I hesitated. I wasn't really sure. Things had been strange in general lately.

"I see," Dr. Fales said. He hooked the chart back over the end of my bed. "Early-onset Parkinson's is fairly rare, as I'm sure you know."

He glanced to Tara who was bobbing her head like she was an expert here for a consultation.

"So each case can vary drastically in terms of symptoms and disease progression."

I swallowed hard and risked a glance at Liam. "And my case is bad?"

"Actually, it's not. Based on your tests, I'm surprised that you're having this level of difficulty." He paused to let this sink in.

"Then this is in her head?" Tara asked. I stared at her. I couldn't help being surprised because she'd been the one to see symptoms in everything I did. All roads led to Parkinson's with Tara. For some people that might have given them a free pass, but to Tara, it was just another disappointing fact about my existence. She would be unbearable if she thought I was imagining episodes.

"I'm not saying that. I think we're dealing with a compounding condition. The notes I was given mention that several recent episodes seem to have been brought on by stress. Is that correct?"

The question was meant for me, but Tara answered. To his credit, Dr. Fales ignored her, waiting for my answer.

"Yes," I said. "They were both after fights."

Liam's hand gripped my fingers more tightly. I wished we were alone so I could tell him that this most recent episode was the result of a lot more than our confrontation behind Garrett's, but I didn't want Tara to have any more ammunition for her case against him.

"I assumed as much. College can be a stressful time period and dealing with a life-altering illness makes things even more difficult." The doctor's words were kind, but I balked at what he was saying.

"So college is making my Parkinson's worse?" I asked. Tara was going to have a field day with this revelation. There was no way she'd agree to pay my tuition if the doctor told her I shouldn't be in school.

"Life is," the doctor corrected.

"Would it be best for her to transfer to a smaller school?" Tara asked. "Maybe one closer to home?"

"I don't want to transfer." I glared at her, but she didn't bother to look at me.

"I don't think that's necessary. Jillian is going to

encounter stress every day of her life unless she spends every day eating chocolate in a bubble bath."

"And even then my toes would get all pruney," I pointed out.

Dr. Fales nodded, a grin creeping over his face. "My point exactly. You can't escape life. Jillian needs to learn to cope with stress."

"And how can she do that?" Liam spoke up before my mother could open her mouth.

"Very basic yoga would help. Nothing too trying of her joints and muscles. Very light stretching and relaxation."

I'd tried to get into yoga before but couldn't get past sitting around with my eyes closed. No matter how hard I tried, my mind was never clear. My head was about as organized as my closet, which wasn't saying much.

"You're going to fix her with yoga?" Tara didn't bother to hide her disdain at this prospect.

"Your daughter isn't broken, Mrs. Nichols. I'm only looking for ways to help her live her life more dynamically."

I made a mental note to get Dr. Fales's information before I left the hospital. He was clearly the perfect choice for my care. He listened to me and refused to take any shit from Tara. It was a win-win.

"I can help you with yoga," Liam said. He smiled reassuringly at me, but I had to smother a giggle. He rolled his eyes as if to say *dirty girl*.

"There's no medication that you can give her?"

Tara asked the doctor, turning the conversation back to what my mother saw as practical solutions for my problem.

"I'm getting to that." Dr. Fales kept his voice even, but there was an edge of assertiveness to his words. Yet another reason to take him on for my full-time care: he knew how to handle Tara as well. "This needs to be a holistic program if it's going to benefit your daughter, but I would like to try a new drug. It's still in preliminary trials, so we'll have to apply for it."

"You mean it's untested?" Tara's voice pitched up, showing her disapproval.

"It is, but the results we're seeing are astounding, especially with Jillian's age group. It can slow the disease's progression to under twenty percent of the average rate."

I perked up a little. I wasn't eager to start a new drug, but none of the ones I'd been given held such promise. "I don't mind being a lab rat with stats like that."

"I mind it," Tara said in a firm tone. She planted her hands on her hips, daring me to question her.

But I wasn't about to roll over on this one. "I assume it's my decision if I want to take the drug, Dr. Fales?"

"As an adult in charge of your own medical care, yes."

He just had to add the "in charge of my own care" bit. I wouldn't put it past Tara to get a court order to be my legal guardian. All the times she sent the campus police or called the campus seeking me out would only back up her claims.

"Regardless," he continued. "We'll need to apply for the study. It could take a few weeks. Until then, I'm changing your prescriptions slightly, adding an SSRI, and advising you to seriously consider yoga or meditation."

Liam rubbed my hand, and I looked at him, my eyes met with an encouraging smile.

"I can do that," I said. I could. It would mean less time going out, but I'd already significantly reduced my partying this semester, and going out wasn't going to be any fun if I wound up locked up on a bathroom floor every night.

"Then I suppose my opinion on this doesn't matter?" There was a hint of bitterness in Tara's tone. I couldn't help but think that she was less concerned over the suggestions of Dr. Fales and more upset that she wasn't the one making the decisions.

"It actually doesn't," I said. My hands clenched into fists and I tried to keep myself calm, but anger was rising hot in my chest, and I wasn't going to be able to keep my words from growing fiery if she didn't drop this soon.

"I will not be spoken to like this, Jillian," she warned me.

"And I won't be treated like a child. I've been managing this disease for two years." I was getting louder and I didn't care. If she was going to treat me like I was still ten years old, I would show her I wasn't. "I can make these decisions."

"And what proof do you have of that?" she asked me. "Because you're in the hospital! I don't think you're up to taking care of yourself."

"I just need to be doing more," I argued. "I haven't tried yoga or SSRIs yet."

"I don't think they'll make much of a difference."

Now she was just being petulant. "I'm the one who has to live with this," I yelled at her. "When the doctor talks about disease progression, he's talking about my body!"

Dr. Fales stepped between us. "I understand that this is an emotional decision—"

"Do not condescend to me," Tara snapped.

"Mom, he is a doctor. Maybe you should listen to him."

"Jillian is in here because her stress level exacerbated her condition," Dr. Fales said in a smooth soft voice. "As her physician, I need to manage her care. I will have to ask you to leave if we can't have a calm discussion of her options."

"There's no need to ask me to leave." Tara stooped over the edge of the couch and grabbed her purse. "I can see I'm not needed here."

I didn't make a move to stop her, and even Dr. Fales stepped aside as she stormed out of the room. But even though she'd left, a heaviness settled over my chest, making it hard to breathe. I tried to force the air in and out of my lungs but with each inhale it became harder to exhale.

"Calm down, Jillian," Dr. Fales ordered. He moved to my side and brought an oxygen mask to my face. "This is exactly what we need to avoid."

I nodded, letting the oxygen seep into my lungs. A deep calm settled over me slowly. Liam kept his hand knit through mine tightly, whispering reassurances into my ear.

"Is she..." Dr. Fales hesitated as though he wasn't sure he should ask this question. "Is she the reason you had the episode?"

I shook my head. It would be easy to blame Tara, and she'd certainly contributed a fair amount of crazy to my life, but I would be lying if I laid it all at her feet.

"She doesn't help," Liam said for me. "But Jillian's had some trouble with school, and we had been fighting."

"All couples fight," Dr. Fales said. "You two should take a communications class or talk to a couples counselor. It will help you learn to work through your arguments without it causing too much stress—for either of you."

Liam smirked a little as he nodded. "I know just the person to talk to."

I made a mental note to tell him that there was no way I was going to spill all of this to Markson, especially when I was currently failing his class. But I also knew that Dr. Fales was right. I was going to have to learn to not get so upset or risk hurting everyone around me, even myself.

"I'll leave you two alone," Dr. Fales said. It was well past visiting hours, but he merely smiled at Liam as he made his way toward the door.

"Doctor?" Liam called. "When will Jillian be released?"

Fales stopped at the door and considered the question. "I see no reason we can't let you go in the morning. It will take a while to get approved for the drug trial, but I'll want to see you once a week while we work these new medications into your schedule. I'm sure you have coursework you need to deal with"

I nodded even though just the thought of facing the real world and my professors was enough to set off my stress level again. I pushed the panic down and focused on the fact that I would be home soon. The rest I could deal with later.

"Hear that, chicken?" Liam whispered in my ear. "I'm taking you home."

I liked the sound of that.

Chapter Twenty-Five

L iam treated me like glass when we reached my apartment the following morning. I'd been living with my disease for years, and I was well aware that no one was going to break me. Still this was hardly new. Jess and Cassie had tiptoed around me after the diagnosis. My mother acted like I might shatter at any moment. It was like they thought it was helping me somehow. But all it did was make me feel as though I really was broken. If everyone thought I was weak, was I? I'd answered that question for myself long ago with a resounding *hell no*. But here I was at square one again. This time with Liam.

"Let me," he said, grabbing my purse and juggling it with my hospital discharge paperwork, a pharmacy bag and our take-out order.

"I've got it." I took it back and ran up the stairs before he could offer to carry me, too.

I knew his concern was coming from a good place, which was the only thing keeping me from screaming.

The apartment was quiet. Jess was out, and the place was relatively clean. It looked suspiciously like she cleaned while I was gone.

"Whoa! Is this your place?" Liam said as he dropped various bags and folders on the kitchen bar.

"Apparently when I'm not here, the house elf comes," I said.

My room was another story. It was still a disaster from the night we wrecked it getting ready for girls' night. There was a pile of scarves on the bed. Boots were strewn across the floor along with bras and underwear.

"I don't think the house elf likes you." Liam came up behind me and wrapped his arms around my waist.

"Remind me to give him a sock," I said. I turned in his arms, happy to finally have him alone. The hospital really wasn't the best place to kiss and make up. I brought my lips to his, but I sensed hesitation as I tried to deepen the kiss.

"You need to rest," he said in a soft voice as he withdrew from me.

"I have literally done nothing but sit on my ass for most of the week." I stuck my butt out at him. "It's probably gone flat."

"I assure you that's not the case." Liam bit his lip, but then he shook his head. "Lie down and I'll bring in the food."

"Screw the food," I said. Ever since we'd left the

hospital, I'd felt frenzied, so full of energy that I thought I might explode. "We can eat later."

"It will get cold." Liam backed up and then rushed out of the room.

He wasn't going to give up on this resting thing, which was very bad news. The good news was that I had secret weapons of my own. I pulled off the t-shirt and jeans I was wearing until I was down to boy shorts and a sports bra. Not terribly sexy. Tugging the bra off, I had just enough time to find a thin white tank top. The ensemble had the benefit of making me look innocent, as though maybe I was going to heed his advice and climb into bed. But there was also no way he was going to be able to resist it. I didn't feel bad for my trickery. After all, I'd made Jess haul up a razor, shaving cream and waxing strips just for this homecoming. I wasn't about to let Liam derail that with unnecessary concern.

But when he came in carrying boxes of Chinese with chopsticks sticking out, he barely seemed to notice that I'd changed.

"I told you that I don't eat in my bed," I reminded him, even as I climbed in and propped a pillow behind my back.

"I thought I very successfully broke that rule," Liam said, handing me my order of lo mein.

"I will allow you to make your case one more time," I said in a solemn voice. A small shiver ran up my spine at the thought of ice cream in bed.

"Eat your food," he said with a laugh. "I can't believe you don't have a TV in here."

"Once again, the bed is for sleeping in." I outlined a square in the air with my chopsticks as I spoke. "And for sex."

"And for eating," he added.

I groaned and threw a noodle at him.

He caught it in his mouth, saving my sheets. "No wonder you don't eat in your bed."

I was getting nowhere with him unless frustration was an actual point on a map. It had the unwanted effect of allowing my mind to wander to all of the things I had to deal with starting tomorrow, including begging Professor Markson to let me drop late from Interpersonal Communications.

"I have to talk to Markson tomorrow." It felt better to say it out loud, like I was working through the stages of acceptance. I had to accept it was going to be awkward and embarrassing.

"I'm sure he'll let you make up your work," he said. "He's a cool guy. He asked me about you."

"Oh yeah, what did you say?"

"The usual—you broke my heart, you were amazing in bed, I wanted to make you waffles every morning for the rest of my life."

Professor Markson wasn't even here, and I still wanted to crawl under a pillow and die.

"I'm kidding," Liam said, chuckling at the horrified look frozen on my face. "He asked why you were skipping class."

"And you said?"

"I told him I didn't know." Liam shrugged, but there was a note of apology in his voice.

"It's cool. I have doctor's notes." But that wasn't entirely true. I had doctor's notes that explained my last week of absences, not the ones leading up to it. I wasn't sure if I should lie or just admit to Markson that I was struggling with seeing Liam after my episode. It was all medically related after all, but I knew deep down that I'd been skipping classes for reasons that had nothing to do with my Parkinson's.

"You just need to go in and talk to him," Liam said.

"I will," I said, but I didn't even convince myself. "If he lets me make it up, will you still be my partner or did you find someone else?"

"I'm chuffed that you asked," he said. "There was never anyone else."

His words were husky, and I seized on the moment, spurred not only by what he had said but also the delicious ache spreading through my chest. I wanted to feel it explode through me as I shattered against him. Liam could break me in one way, and he was the only one who could put me back together. I set my noodles on my bedside table. He watched me warily as I climbed onto his lap and pushed his food away.

"I've had enough food for now," I said, drawing his face up to mine.

"You've barely eaten anything." But his eyes closed as he spoke, and I knew I'd won.

Our lips crushed together. His breath was spicy

and mine was hot as our bodies entwined. Liam's hands slid under my shirt, cradling my back. My hands looped around his neck and I clenched my fingers into his hair. I wanted more of him. I wanted all of him. I was hungry for this moment as though it was the first time for us. For me. There was a desperate rawness to our kiss that spoke of discovery.

Even when I was with him before, I was only half in, but all that had changed. There were no secrets left between us now and that liberated us as we clung to one another, exploring each other. Liam tugged my shirt over my head, and I felt vulnerable and safe in the same moment. His eyes stayed on my face as he ran his fingers from my shoulders to my stomach in languorous strokes.

"You're perfect, chicken," he said bringing his mouth to trace whispers over my breasts.

Even though I knew the exact opposite, the truth of it broke over me, and for a split second, I could see myself how Liam saw me.

"Not to argue with you, but you're the perfect one." Liam had told me plenty of times that I was beautiful, but I'd never actually reciprocated. I'd never really admitted to him how much he meant to me.

"Competitive much?" he said with a sigh.

My attempts to give compliments were as clumsy as my ability to accept them.

"Liam." I paused, lowering my eyes as I tried to find the right words. But ultimately they were there all along. My eyes fluttered back up to his. "I love you."

He pulled me to him so that our noses were nearly touching. "I love you, Jillian Nichols."

And then I was on my back as he brought his body over mine. There was a fumble of clothes and kisses and whispered promises until we came together slowly. We lingered in each other, and I was aware of every slight movement. How his breath hitched after a low moan. The soft stubble curving along his jawline. And his hands on my body—safe and steady.

Liam shifted onto his knees and drew my legs around his waist as he pushed deeper into me. The pleasure bordered on pain, but I didn't want him to stop. In this moment, I was certain that we were closer than anyone in history. Splayed across the bed, I stared at him, marveling at the cut of his body, the taut coil of his muscles as he held me firmly against him.

This was the man I loved, a fact that trembled up my limbs and set fire to my skin. The love—the realization of it—shattered across my body in quivers that built into a torrent. His skin on my skin, his hands on my hips, his name on my tongue.

We collapsed together in a heap of slick skin and tangled limbs, but neither of us pulled away. We laid there, entwined with each other. In this moment, I lived a lifetime.

After a few minutes, he pulled away long enough to draw my sheet over us. It was ordinary gesture, but it felt like more. It felt like comfort and home and promises. I turned into him, and we laid, watching each other, not quite touching, without speaking.

A million questions flitted through my head, but I ignored them. I'd spent the last two years of my life trying to escape the future by pretending to live in the moment. I'd been running for so long that I didn't even see it until now. This precise second was the only one that mattered.

"Are you sleepy yet?" Liam murmured against my hair.

I glanced at the small alarm clock on the nightstand behind him. "It's only two o'clock in the afternoon."

"I find myself feeling stuffed and sated." His lips smacked a little on the words as sleep moved over his face.

"That's what she said," we both said at the same time. Liam smiled sleepily, and I wiggled up onto my pillow, pulling his head onto my chest. His arm circled around my back as he nestled against me. I didn't expect to like the feeling of taking care of someone else. I thought it would be a burden, but instead a completeness settled over me.

Questions could wait for the morning, I thought as I stroked his hair. His breathing slowed, matching pace with the beat of my heart. I had a lot to think about, but for the first time, I could see clearly what was right in front of me. I didn't need to be certain of anything more than I was of this. Of him and I. Of us. Love, as it turned out, was liberating. The one thing I ran from turned out to be what finally set me free.

Chapter Twenty-Six

✧❀✧

W e spent the day in bed, finally abandoning it
to throw away our take-out boxes and stretch
our legs. Jess hadn't shown her face in the apartment
yet, and I knew she was giving Liam and I space to talk
about things. She was probably going to be disappointed to hear we spent most of our time doing it
instead. Liam hummed as he deposited forks into the
dishwasher, and I watched him with barely contained
amazement. My first real memories of him were in this
kitchen with MeMa's crocheted dish towels. He turned
and caught me staring at him.

"What wicked things are you devising?" he
asked me.

"I was just appreciating the show," I said. In fact, I
was. Watching Liam bend over in his boxer briefs was
turning me to a puddle on the bar stool.

"I promise I will take you back to bed if—" he

paused and leaned down on the counter to face me
—"you call your mom."

"You know how to kill the mood," I muttered. "I
don't know why you'd want me to talk to her. She was
horrible to you."

Tara hadn't bothered to return after her dramatic
exit from the hospital. There was no apology to me or
Liam. One second, she wanted me to settle down with
Liam, and the next, she was accusing him of causing
my episode. It was enough to give me whiplash. I had
nothing to say to her.

"She was, but she was also upset and worried about
you. That's something I can understand. She's your
mom, chicken."

"When you call me chicken in these situations, it
sounds like you're saying I'm being a coward," I pointed
out.

"You are the bravest person I know," Liam said in a
soft voice. "But you are being a chicken shit about this."

"Chicken shit?" I repeated.

"It's one American phrase I quite like," he said.
Liam pushed my iPhone into my hand.

I threw him a dirty look as I pulled up Tara's contact
and pressed call. I wandered into the bedroom and shut my
door in case things got heated. The phone rang four times,
and I was prepping to leave a message when she picked up.

"Hello." Even her greeting sounded like I was
putting her out.

"Hi, Mom. How are you?" It was possibly the

stupidest way to start a conversation with my own mother, especially given how we left things at the hospital, but I didn't know what else to say.

"I'm fine. Busy." Her tone was clipped and cold, so not much different than usual.

"I thought we should talk," I said. Part of me hoped she would just hang up on me.

"I suppose."

So much for that.

There was a long pause where neither of us spoke. Tara finally broke the silence. "What did you want to say?"

"I know things got out of control at the hospital, but I wanted you to know that Dr. Fales has referred me to a therapist that is covered under our insurance, and I picked up all my new prescriptions." It was all factual information. Safe information. I got the impression that Liam wanted me to apologize to her, but there was no way that was going to happen.

"And school?" she asked.

"I'm talking with my professors tomorrow. I'm sure I can get extensions so I can keep my grades up," I promised her.

Thankfully she refrained from commenting on my past GPAs. "What about next semester?"

"I want to stay in Olympic Falls."

"I don't think that's a good idea. Are you staying for that boy?" she asked.

"He has a name. He's not *that boy*!" I exploded,

kicking my closet door, which actually hurt. I winced and hopped over to the bed.

"It's a simple question, Jillian," Tara said in a steady voice, not matching her volume to mine. "I don't want you throwing your life away on some boy."

"You were the one who told me I was—how did you put it—'Going through boys like tissues?'" I paused and willed myself to calm down. "It would be throwing away my life to move back home and live in my parents' house."

"Do you think we actually want you to move back home? Your father and I enjoy our empty nest."

Of course, they were enjoying it. They'd practically thrown a party when I announced I was moving out of state for college. Tara has already turned my bedroom into a guest suite complete with travel-size toiletries that I was not allowed to use when I visited. "You're sending me mixed signals. One second you want me to move home, but you don't really. You like Liam, but you hate him. Why would I ever want to come home?"

"I don't appreciate being spoken to like this."

"I don't appreciate you trying to control my life."

"Then pay your own bills," Tara suggested.

"I will go to the financial aid office first thing in the morning," I said. I hadn't been forced to take student loans out before this, so it wouldn't kill me to have three semesters of debt when I left school.

"I want you to be serious about something." It was implicit from her tone that she meant serious about anything other than a boy.

This phone call was going about as I expected it to, but I wasn't ready to give up yet. "I know you are worried about Liam, but you shouldn't be. We aren't eloping. I'm not running away to Scotland. He takes care of me without expecting me to be totally dependent on him. He makes me laugh and still forces me to be serious. So you should want him to stick around as long as possible, because he's not just good for me, he's saving me."

Tara sighed into the phone. "I'm glad to hear you say that. I just...he's going back to Scotland, Jillian. It nearly broke you when you two fought. I don't want to keep finding you in the hospital."

"I'm not rearranging my life for him. I'm adding him into it for as long as possible. We could be together for a week or for a year or for the rest of our lives. But no matter what happens, I'm going to be a better person when I come out the other side because I love him."

"And he loves you?" Tara asks softly.

"Yeah, he does." There was a moment of hesitation in my response. Liam loved me, even when he shouldn't. "I tried to keep him away. You know what MeMa always says? Liam has sticking power."

"Good." It sounded like that was really hard for her to say. "If you want to stay at Olympic State, I can support that if..."

"If?" I prompted, more than a little surprised that she'd given in this easily.

"If you pass all of your classes this semester." She stopped and waited for me to respond.

That was going to be a problem. I'd missed enough classes that Markson didn't have to do shit to help me out. I was completely at his mercy, but I wasn't about to tell Tara that. "My grades are fine."

"I hope so, because I can't support you staying there if you aren't going to be serious. Take a page from Jess's book—"

"I have to go, Mom," I cut her off before she could launch into a description of Jess's many redeeming qualities. Ones I didn't share with my best friend.

"Okay. Your father wants me to ask you if you're coming home for Christmas?"

I paused, considering this request. I always went home for Christmas, but this year I had a reason to stay in Olympic Falls. Nothing sounded better than staying in my apartment with Liam over break, but maybe Tara and I needed some healing time. "I will on one condition."

"Which is?" she asked.

"Liam is coming with me. He has no family here."

"That's a pretty big commitment," she said.

Was it? "I know."

"As long as you sleep in separate bedrooms and stay out of the bathroom."

By my count that left at least six other rooms in the house that I could nail him in. "Deal. I'll call you later."

"Good night." There was some hesitation before she added, "I love you."

I was so shocked that I barely managed to respond. Tara was not the type to show her emotions. It was the first time she'd ended a call this way. I shoved my iPhone in my pocket and left my room, feeling triumphant and despondent as the same time.

"How did it go?" Liam asked. He held out a fisted hand.

I opened my palm and he dropped a round of meds into it. "Are you my new medication alarm?"

"I want to be helpful," he said slowly. "If you'd rather—"

"Thank you," I said. It was a sweet gesture, and one I shouldn't take for granted.

"No, thank you," he said, hooking his fingers into my waistband and drawing me close to him. "Thank you for letting me take care of you. I know that's hard for you."

"It's getting easier," I admitted. I couldn't help but like that he cared enough to worry about getting me my medication.

"And as a reward." He held up his other fist. This time he dropped three multi-colored Chiclets into my palm.

"Excellent." I pushed onto my tiptoes and gave him a soft kiss.

"Do you actually like that stuff?" he asked me as I ventured into the kitchen for a glass of water. One of the pills was roughly the size of a horse tranquilizer. It would be a while before I was able to get it down dry.

"Not in the beginning," I admitted. "I didn't want people to know I was taking pills. If someone asked, I offered them a Chiclet. But I'm now genuinely addicted."

"I was thinking I could help you with a new addiction." Liam leaned against the kitchen wall and beckoned me with his finger. Standing there in his form-fitting boxers and thin t-shirt, he looked more like a Calvin Klein ad than anyone had a right to in real life.

"I like my addiction. Maybe you should get your own."

"I will gladly steal those Chiclets from your mouth," he offered. A thrill shivered through my body at the memory. I sauntered toward him, trying my best to pout but failing miserably.

"You look constipated," Liam told me with a laugh.

"I'm being sexy," I said.

"You don't need to try. You are sexy no matter what you're doing."

"Unless I'm trying to be sexy."

"The world might collapse into the whole of space and time if you actually managed to act sexy at your current hotness level," he said. He reached forward and grabbed my shirt, forcing me to come closer to him.

"Global warming?"

"I think that's safe to say," he said. His hands slid across my waist and under my shirt as I sighed in anticipation.

"You promised to take me to a very big bed," I reminded him.

"Didn't I do that already?" he asked, even as crooked grin stole across his face.

"I can't remember, but I'm game for another try."

Liam reached behind me and caught me up in his arms like a baby. "So you want to go back for seconds?"

I nodded, wetting my lips with my tongue. Tomorrow I would deal with classes and Markson, but tonight I was all Liam's, and I wouldn't have it any other way.

Liam carried me into my room and laid me gently on the bed, but he didn't climb in beside me.

"Promise you'll tell me if it's too much," he asked.

I could tell from his wide thoughtful eyes that he was serious, but instead of answering, I grabbed the pillow from under me and swung it into the side of his head. "I...am...not...going...to...break!"

Liam caught the pillow and held it for a split second before he lobbed it at my head. I screamed and grabbed for another pillow, getting one just in time to ward off a second strike by him. Liam bounced onto the bed and knocked me over with a hefty swing of the pillow. I collapsed onto the bed, feeling lighter and happier than I had in a long time.

"What did your mom say?" he asked me, dropping down to my side.

"The usual. I'm a disappointment, but she did agree to let me stay here if I pass my classes next semester," I said. I didn't want to talk about this. I was already working hard enough to keep the nagging concerns over my grades at bay.

"What about Markson's class?" he asked, his

eyebrows knit together. "You're way past the drop date."

"I'll have to talk to him. Maybe he'll understand." Jess had stressed to me the extent of Markson's coolness when she took the class last year. I hoped she was right.

"What about an incomplete?" Liam suggested.

"Maybe." I hesitated and wiggled down flat on the bed. "I don't want to talk about it right now."

"Is there something else you'd rather do?" he asked.

"I have three or four things in mind," I said, tracing the outline of his abs through his t-shirt.

"That sounds challenging, but I can be persuaded to try." He rolled carefully over and hovered over me.

"I am excellent at persuasion." My hand snaked around his neck and brought his mouth to mine. He met my lips greedily, pressing his weight into me as I wrapped my legs around his waist. I sighed, content and complete, as he kissed along my collarbone. Sliding his hands under my shirt, he pulled it off and laid his head over my chest. We lay like that for a long time, his breath tickling across my breasts as he listened to my heartbeat, my fingers raking lazily through his hair.

There was nothing that needed to be said. This moment said everything.

Chapter Twenty-Seven

There was a note on my counter the next morning from Liam, asking me to meet him at the aquarium before eleven. Next to it, he'd laid out my medications. I glanced at the clock, pleased to see that I had an hour and half, which meant I could actually take a shower and get dressed before he was done with his shift.

I dutifully took my meds as I started the shower. I almost didn't want to wash last night off my skin. My only saving grace was that I was sure there was more—much more—where that came from. As the warm water flowed over my body, I remembered Liam's lips and his hands and the promises we whispered in the dark until my whole body throbbed with energy. I shut off the shower and threw a towel around my hair. I couldn't wait to see him.

But as I dabbed a little concealer over my under-eye circles, I thought of the other things I had to see to today. I couldn't avoid talking to Markson any longer. Most of my other classes were large lectures where my absence probably went unnoticed, but Markson would know I hadn't been there, especially since I had drawn attention to it by visiting him before. I hadn't been to class since that day, which meant I had missed over three weeks. As far as excuses went, mine was pretty solid, but that didn't mean he had to help me out.

So when I went to get dressed, I opted for a loose blue sweater and yoga pants. I wanted to look nice for Liam, but I figured it was best to look a little less put together for Markson. I'd wasted an hour already, so I didn't have time to obsess any more over the ensemble and its subliminal messages. But as I darted out the apartment, Cassie caught me at the door.

"Hey, I was coming to check on you. Jess said you were released, but..."

"But?" I raised an eyebrow.

"She said Liam brought you home. I thought I should give you two some space." Cassie puckered up her lips suggestively at me, and I smacked her arm.

"That was very considerate," I said. "I'm actually on my way to see him at work now."

"Where does he work?" she asked me.

I couldn't believe I hadn't told her, but then I realized that Cassie had barely even met Liam yet. In fact, I hadn't seen much of her lately either, except for her brief visits at the hospital.

"He does programs at the aquarium," I told her. "Can you walk with me?"

I wanted to catch up with her. I didn't want to become one of those girls that I'd promised myself I would never become.

"Yeah, I can do that," she said. "So did you have a nice homecoming?"

"There was definitely coming," I said, shooting her a wink.

"Jealous," Cassie pouted. "Trevor's been so caught up in his finals and study groups, I've barely seen him."

So that's why I had seen him at the library. Of course, I'd jumped to the wrong conclusion then. He was nervous over his upcoming exams. "Only two more weeks and then you'll have Winter Break together."

"Maybe." Cassie paused and bit her lip. "We haven't even talked about it yet. For all I know, he's going back to Chicago."

"Go with him," I encouraged him. "You can stay with your sister."

"It would be nice to see Meghan," she said. "Do you think he'll get annoyed if I invite myself to Chicago for the holidays?"

"Why would he get annoyed? I bet he misses you, too."

Uncertainty flickered through Cassie's eyes. "I hope so."

I looped my arm through hers and pressed my head to her shoulder. "Of course, he does. It could be worse. You see how much Jess studies, right?"

"Maybe I can call Brett and commiserate with him," she said, but then we both laughed. Brett had spoken less than fifty words to each of us since we first met him. In all fairness to him, he probably couldn't get a word in between the three of us.

"What are you doing for Christmas?" she asked me.

I took a deep breath. "I'm taking Liam to my parents' house."

"So I'm guessing your Christmas list this year is basically booze and more booze?"

"Pretty much."

We rounded the corner, and my heart jumped when the aquarium came into view. Cassie pulled her arm from mine, and I stopped to find her smiling at me. "You're glowing."

I tried to shrug it off like it was nothing, but I couldn't wipe the goofy grin from my face. "I think this what they call lovesick."

"Whatever it is, it looks good on you," she told me. "I should get back to campus. I have an eleven-thirty class."

"See you later!" I called after her.

"Next week at Garrett's!"

"Next week at Garrett's," I repeated. It was a tradition for us to meet up on the last day of finals for drinks. This year Liam would be there with me, and as giddy as that made me, it also reminded me that I probably wouldn't be celebrating next Friday. At least I could drown my sorrows with all my favorite people in the world.

The aquarium's parking lot was empty and no one was at the desk when I entered. I called out, not wanting to scare anyone, and Liam peeked out from a back office.

"I didn't think you were going to make it," he said, beckoning for me to join him.

"Sorry, I ran into Cassie on the way here," I told him as he pulled me down onto his lap.

"Ah, the lovely Cassie. How is she?" he asked.

"Good." I paused, biting my lip. "I haven't seen much of her lately. She visited me at the hospital a few times, but we haven't spent much time one on one."

"You should make a date with her," Liam suggested.

"I will after finals. I think we're all just stressed out right now."

"Speaking of finals," Liam said carefully, "I went and talked to Markson."

Jumping off his lap, I turned to face him. "You did what?"

"I wanted to talk to him about the final," he said.

"Your final?" I asked hopefully.

"Kind of. I was never reassigned a partner, chicken, and I'd feel like I failed that class if I let my partner fail."

I crossed my arms over my chest and glared at him. "Your partner is doing just fine failing that class on her own."

"I know it might seem out of line, but you need to work on your stress level, right? I could tell Markson's class was bothering you. I just wanted to be helpful," he said, holding his hands out to me.

I softened a little at his honesty. Of course, Liam was trying to be helpful and he knew me well enough to know that I would reject his help if he'd offered it directly to me. "I suppose I need to get used to letting people help me."

"Yes, you do, chicken," he said. "Do you want to know what he said?"

"I don't know, do I?"

"He's going to let you do the final without docking any points, but there's a catch," Liam said, eyeing me nervously.

"What kind of catch?" I was beginning to hate that word.

"We already proposed our final topics, but I knew you hadn't turned one in. So I sold Markson on one for you."

"You what?" I couldn't control the volume of my voice. What had he gotten me into?

Liam held up his hands in surrender. "I know, I know. But he wasn't sure if he should let you do it, so I gave him a good reason that you should."

"What did you tell him I would do?" I asked slowly.

"I suggested you talk to the class about your Parkinson's," Liam admitted. He shifted in his chair, bracing his hands on its arms, like he was preparing for a death blow.

"I don't talk about my Parkinson's."

"That's exactly why he accepted the idea," Liam

said. "I know it seems scary, but no one is going to judge you."

I couldn't form complete thoughts anymore. I couldn't explain to him that talking about my Parkinson's like that, in front of the entire class, wasn't about what the other students would think. It was about how I would feel. "I don't talk about my Parkinson's, because...then it will be real."

"It is real, chicken," Liam said in a soft voice. He stood and moved cautiously toward me, wrapping an arm around my waist and drawing me toward him. "It's part of you."

"You're asking me to go and share the most personal part of my life with a bunch of people I don't know?" I shook my head. I couldn't do it, not even if my grade depended on it.

"There's a lot more to you than your disease, Jillian." Liam took my face in his hands and forced my eyes to meet his. "Your disease is only a small part of you."

Rawness crawled up my throat, and I fought back tears as love and fear mingled into a potent cocktail of nerves in my stomach. "I can't do it."

"I will be with you the whole time," he promised me. "I don't want you to fail that class."

"I think I'd rather do nude modeling in the center of campus," I said, but even as I said it, I knew there was no way out of it. I needed to pass Markson's class and now I had a chance to do it. Staying in Olympic Falls would be worth ten minutes of embarrassment.

"You can model nude for me later," Liam whispered in my ear. His lips trailed along my jawline, his touch searing across my skin and distracting me from the fear I felt. With each moment he lingered there, the love pulsing through me expanded until it swallowed my fear entirely.

"When do I have to do this?" I asked him.

Liam dropped back, victory glinting his blue eyes. "Next Friday," he said. "I'll help you prepare."

"I'd rather wing it," I said. The more I worried about getting up in front of the class, the more likely I was to chicken out.

"Remember, lots of 'I' statements," Liam said.

"'I' statements. Bare my soul. Hell, why don't I do it in the nude?" I laughed nervously, almost maniacally.

"It would probably ensure an A," Liam said, grabbing my hips roughly and pulling me to him.

"Can you imagine Markson's face? It would almost be worth it."

"Sorry, I can't. You've given me much more inspiring images to picture at the moment." Liam cupped my face and drew my mouth to his. I crumbled into him, dissolving against his body like ice meeting with fire. The kiss grew more urgent as our tongues tangled together. I shoved him into the wall and pressed against him, needing to feel his body on mine like I needed to breathe. But before I could slip my hands over his shirt, the aquarium's door buzzed, reminding us that we weren't in the comfort of my bedroom. We leapt apart, straightening clothing and fixing mussed hair.

"I'll see you later?" Liam asked, his breathing still heavy from our make-out session.

"Yes." I gave him a quick peck and darted out the door past a young mother showing her two toddlers the jellyfish tank. I heard Liam greet them as I exited. He was still panting.

As I headed back toward campus, I tried not to think about Markson's final, even as pressure mounted in my chest, but with each step, it felt like brick after brick was being laid on top of me until I finally had to stop and practice one of the breathing exercises Dr. Fales showed me at the hospital. After a few minutes, I felt calm enough to head toward the library.

I had less than a week before finals started, and if I was going to stay in Olympic Falls, I needed every minute of them.

Chapter Twenty-Eight

Ｔhe day of my final presentation in Markson's class, I woke up at six in the morning. Trying to fall back asleep proved futile, so I stole from the bed as not to wake Liam. He shifted in his sleep, and for a moment, I stood and watched him, wondering if when he woke up, he would be as nervous as I was.

The apartment was quiet, the barest hint of dawn peeking through the blinds in the living room as I made coffee. Despite being unable to go back to bed, exhaustion crept through my bones. I dragged my body around the kitchen, contemplating making breakfast for Jess and Liam before I remembered that Pop-Tarts were my idea of haute cuisine. But not doing anything left my brain too much space to think about what lay ahead of me today, so I cleaned instead. I scrubbed the counters and the sink, reorganized the dishes in the cabinets, and swept the tile floor. As I hung a fresh

MeMa-made dishtowel, Liam stumbled in and pointed to the coffee pot.

"Why are you up?" he asked me, rubbing sleep from his eyes. "We have hours until class."

"I couldn't sleep," I admitted as I poured him a mug. Settling onto the stool beside him, we both sipped cautiously and didn't speak again. There was a heavy tension in the air, both of us worried about things outside our immediate control.

"Let me make you breakfast," Liam said, but I shook my head. It would be impossible to eat right now, because my stomach was already churning.

"I just want it to be over," I admitted.

Liam draped an arm over my shoulder and pulled me close to him, kissing my forehead. "There's no reason to be nervous, chicken. Markson won't be hard on you."

I refrained from pointing out that asking me to get up in front of twenty of my peers and spill my guts wasn't exactly the definition of going soft on me. But I couldn't expect Liam, who was always so at ease in front of others, to understand that.

"Do you want to practice?" he offered.

Even though I knew he was trying to be helpful, my response came out harsh and cold. "No, I don't want to think about it."

Liam's shoulders slumped, and he leaned forward, bracing himself against the counter. He had gone out of his way to set this up for me, and I was being horrible to him.

"I'm going to lie back down," I told him. If I could fall back asleep, I wouldn't have to spend the next few hours torturing myself—or Liam.

"Okay," Liam said. "I have a final in an hour, but I'll head straight to class after that."

"Cool," I said lamely.

As I stood, he grabbed my waist and drew me into him. "You are going to be spectacular, Jillian."

I managed to nod before I fled back to my room and climbed under the covers, pulling them over my head and willing my body to fall asleep. But my mind was on turned on already, firing questions at me rapidly. What if I had gone to class instead of hiding from it? How would the other students respond to my condition? Was I ready to share something this personal with an entire room of my peers? Would I be "that girl with Parkinson's" after today?

It was clear that sleep was a lost cause, so I got up and searched for the perfect outfit, momentarily contemplating arriving to class naked to throw attention away from what I had to say. No one would give a damn about my sad story if they were looking at my boobs, but there were probably rules against giving presentations in the nude.

By the time I finished coaxing my hair into a manageable ponytail, Jess was up and moving around the apartment. She tapped lightly on the bathroom door, and I opened it for her to join me. I tried to look calm, but my hands shook as I smeared foundation over my forehead.

"I'm going to come, Jills," Jess announced as she brushed her teeth. She had finished all of her finals the day before but was waiting to celebrate the end of another semester with me this evening. We were meeting at Garrett's when it was all over, even though part of me feared it might be my last post-semester happy hour.

"You don't have to," I told her, wiggling past her.

"No, I want to." She turned to me and gave me an encouraging smile. "I'm really proud of you for doing this."

Pride had nothing to do with this. If I was proud, I wouldn't air all my dirty laundry to pass this class. I wasn't above making a fool out of myself to stay at Olympic State, which I guessed was an improvement over the girl I was two years ago. She would have turned tail and ran away from confronting this side of herself. I still wasn't sure if that meant I had grown as a person or if it just meant I was desperate.

Only half the class was in attendance that afternoon. Everyone else had presented already, and I was surprised to feel relief that I didn't have to speak solely to Markson. I hadn't been back to his class since I visited him in his office and that was weeks ago. I wasn't sure I could face him if it came down to him and me.

Jess was already there, surreptitiously chatting with Markson, and I couldn't but notice how she angled her body toward him like he was a magnet drawing her

closer, proving my suspicions that Jess's devoted attitude toward him had a lot less to do with the subject
and a lot more to do with his slightly geeky sex appeal. I
suppose if any of us were going to get hot for teacher, it
would be Jess—the studious one.

She saw me and waved, but I hung back by the
door, hoping Liam would arrive. A hand came to rest
on the small of my back, and I immediately felt calmer.
Liam had seen my Parkinson's at its worst, and he was
still here by my side. One more hour and my fate would
be decided. It all felt very end of the world at the
moment.

"Miss Nichols," Markson called to me, and Liam
gently pushed me toward him.

"Come on, chicken," he whispered.

"Not a good nickname at the moment," I said as I
made my way to our professor.

"How do you want to do this?" Markson asked
when I got closer.

I hesitated, not ready to admit that I'd avoided
thinking about this for the last week and a half. My
most well-conceived plan was basically to vomit out as
much as I could to fill the ten to fifteen minute presentation window.

"Jess and I are going to help here," Liam spoke up. I
stared at him, unsure if he was my white knight or the
face of death itself.

"Interesting. Why?" Markson asked.

"Well, this is an Interpersonal Communications
class," Jess said, still leaning in close to Markson. "We

thought it would be more interesting to show us communicating about Jillian's condition. I've been around since she was diagnosed, but Liam only found out a few weeks ago, so we both have completely different perspectives about it."

"And sometimes I get the impression that we don't know what's going on inside her head," Liam added. "We're all working on communicating our needs and concerns more to each other."

This caught me off-guard. Although I knew Jess and Liam had spoken about me after my off episode in the apartment, I didn't know they talked about it in more depth than that. Now it was obvious that they'd spent considerably more time discussing me than I thought. After all, they were planning to be part of my presentation. I was simultaneously relieved to know I didn't have to do this alone and a little hurt by their secretiveness.

"I like the sound of it," Markson said, and I felt Liam relax a little behind me. I hadn't even realized he was stressed out. I'd been too caught up in how I felt.

We arranged a cluster of chairs at the front of the room, talk show style, and took our seats. If I was lucky, this was the closest I'd ever come to appearing on the *Jerry Springer Show*. Although this could still easily devolve into name-calling and screaming, and there would be no one to drag me offstage if that happened.

Markson stood and addressed the class, congratulating them on a great semester before he turned to the subject of my final presentation. "We have two students giving their presentations today. I'm sure we're all pleased to see Miss Nichols back and healthy. She's been on excused medical status for the last few weeks and today she's going to talk about why she's been absent. I'll let Jillian and her friends explain what they hope to communicate to you today."

I took a long, steadying breath as somewhere in the back of my mind a tiny voice said, "Imagine them in their underwear." If that advice had ever worked, I wanted to see the case study.

"Thank you, Professor Markson, for being so understanding about the last few weeks. It's been very stressful for me," I said. It never hurt to butter up the teacher a little.

He nodded and gestured for me to continue. We only had fifteen minutes to prove I deserved to pass the class, and I was already stalling.

"A couple of weeks ago, I had what's called an off episode. It was brought on by stress and eventually it led to me being hospitalized," I began. I wasn't actually sure where to start. This had started much earlier than that, if I was being honest. It had started with waffles in the kitchen after a one-night stand. It started with a mother who wanted to coddle me and push me away at the same time, unsure how to have a relationship with me. It had started with a surprise diagnosis two years ago that had rocked my world and left me unsteady and unsure of my future.

"Why did you have an off episode?" Jess jumped in, helping me out. I shot her a grateful look.

"I was diagnosed with early-onset Parkinson's Disease two years ago," I explained. "It's pretty rare to find out before twenty, but basically I have issues with my nervous system. An off episode is when the condition flares up."

Liam cleared his throat like he wanted permission to speak, and I looked to him expectantly. "I've read a lot about Parkinson's in the last few weeks, and I feel like I understand what happens, but I don't know how you feel when you have an episode."

"I feel like I'm losing control." Plus one for using an "I" statement. I hoped Markson was taking notes. "It starts out like dizziness or weakness and sometimes that's all it is, but other times, it takes over my body. I feel embarrassed about it, so I try to hide it and hope I don't lock up in front of anyone."

"But you told Jess about it?" Liam prompted, a slight hint of accusation in his words. Markson tutted at him. Apparently, that was a poor interpersonal question. "I noticed that you are open with Jess about it, but you weren't willing to talk with me about it."

"I didn't want you to know," I answered. "Truthfully, I didn't want you to see me as broken. I don't want anyone to see me as broken because that will mean that the disease is in control."

"Over the last two years..." Jess hesitated, and I braced myself for what she was about to say to me. "I've worried that you'd given up a little. I want you to act like Parkinson's isn't controlling you life, but sometimes it feels like it is."

I had to hand it to Jess, she had really internalized what she'd learned from Markson last semester.

"I guess I have. Knowing that you're living with something that will eventually take over your life is hard," I admitted.

"Or it could give you perspective," Liam noted.

"In a lot of ways, I've been avoiding it. I've hidden it from a lot of people, because I didn't want it to define me. But the whole time I've let it define myself." I felt raw and vulnerable saying this out loud, as though I was stepping out of the carefully constructed shell I'd built for myself. Seeing things from this perspective made me realize that I'd never considered how Jess had felt for the last two years. I'd thought a lot about how Liam would feel about my disease, but even then it had been in a purely selfish way.

"How did you feel when I was diagnosed?" I asked Jess.

"I felt helpless. You were my best friend. My wild friend," she added. "I thought you were the strong one, and I didn't feel like I could do anything for you."

And yet, Jess had stuck around. She'd learned how to give me shots and handle episodes. She'd run interference with Tara when I felt overwhelmed. "You might have felt that way," I told her, "but you've always known exactly what I needed."

I looked to Liam, unsure how to ask him what was on my mind. If I had thought talking about my condition in front of the class was difficult, bringing up our fledgling relationship felt too personal. But he was sitting next to me, sharing his thoughts and concerns, and I owed it to him to be honest.

"I feel like you've treated me differently since you found out, like I am going to break." Our recent experiences in the bedroom sprang to mind, but I left that out.

"I think that has a lot more to do with how you reacted when I saw you during that episode. I wanted to talk to you." He was choosing his words carefully, struggling not to say the wrong thing, so I put a hand on his arm to reassure him. "I don't know how I would have felt if you had told me from day one. I like to think that it wouldn't have been a big deal, but I was hurt when you pushed me away after that night. If I hadn't already been in love with you that might have been the end."

Our audience murmured to one another at his declaration, clearly impressed by Liam's honesty, and I felt a swell of pride in my chest. Somehow, we'd made it through this to sit here today. That might have been due to Liam, but I finally understood that it took both of us to get here.

"What do you wish people knew about Parkinson's?" Jess asked me, and I wondered how much time she and Liam had spent preparing for this. The question sounded well-rehearsed.

"I guess that it doesn't make me all that different. If people knew that—" I immediately thought of Tara "—I think I would spend less time hiding it."

"Okay, last question," Liam said. "Do you really like Chiclets?"

"I can unequivocally say that I love them," I said with a laugh. It was over. I had gotten through it and come out on the other side.

There was brief applause from our small audience, but no one spoke until Markson stood and addressed everyone. "Thank you to those of you who showed up. I'm sure we can find the rest of the class on Pine Street, and thank you to Miss Nichols for being brave today. I hope that this wasn't too painful for you."

I glanced around, momentarily confused. Markson had said there were two finals left today, but he didn't stop anyone as the other students gathered their things and exited. A few stopped to share their own secrets with me, and one girl threw her arms around me. That had never happened after a final before.

When it was only the four of us left in the room, Markson handed Liam and me a sheet of paper. "Your presentation was excellent, but remember to watch those 'I' statements Liam."

Liam bowed his head to him. "Will do."

"But there were supposed to be two final presentations today," I pointed out.

"There were," Markson said. "Yours and Mr. McAvoy's."

"You told me you already presented." I turned on Liam.

"'I' statements," Markson said behind me.

"I didn't want to stress you out any more," Liam confessed. "So I fibbed."

"I feel like that wasn't very good communication."

But even as I said it, I took his hand to let him know I was grateful. He was thinking of me, like always.

"So what did you get?" Liam asked, pointing to my sheet of paper.

My heart froze when I realized what Markson had handed to us. He'd graded the presentation in class and given us our final scores.

"What did you get?" I asked, wanting to avoid the moment of truth.

"I got a B," he said, "with a note to work on my 'I' statements."

If Liam got a B after attending every class and doing all the work, I was going to be lucky to skate by with a D. Tara wouldn't be pleased, but it was technically a passing grade. I turned the paper over and read through it. I'd missed enough classes to drop my participation score to an F, but it was only a small percentage of my grade. The midterm project and final presentation accounted for well over eighty percent of the points. I held up the paper to show Liam a clear C written at the bottom.

"I'll take it," I told him as he leaned down and gave me a swift kiss. When our lips met, it felt victorious, as though we'd overcome something huge together. Suddenly, all the things that had stood in our way vanished, leaving only the two of us for that brief second.

"Save it for the bedroom," Jess said, and Markson looked at his feet.

She grabbed my paper and raised an eyebrow.

"I know, I know. You got an A," I said.

"That's a passing grade, Jills. You know what that means! First round is on me tonight." She wrapped me into a tight hug.

But I knew that it meant a lot more than meeting Tara's ultimatum. It meant I was staying at Olympic State, and that I'd finally faced the one thing I'd been hiding from for two years. It meant I'd finally realized I wasn't broken.

Chapter Twenty-Nine

When we arrived at Garrett's, the party had already started. The bar was packed with students drinking to their successes or drowning their sorrows, and we had to fight our way through the crowd. We finally spotted Jess and Brett in a booth, waving us down. Liam and I slid into the seat across from them while Jess poured two beers from a pitcher.

"Sorry," she called over the din surrounding us. "I figured a pitcher was our best shot at getting drinks tonight."

"It's cool. Where's Cassie?" I asked.

"She stepped outside to call Trevor. He's MIA." Jess raised her glass to us. "To being done with our fifth semester."

"It's all downhill from here," I said as we tapped our plastic cups in a toast.

Liam's arm snaked around my shoulder, bringing me close to him. I cuddled against him, dropping a kiss on his neck. Across from us, Jess and Brett didn't touch, although Brett shifted a little closer to her.

Cassie plopped into the booth beside me, still holding her phone.

"Any luck?" Jess asked.

"No. He was supposed to be here by now." Cassie frowned, trying to look pissed, but her eyes glinted with something else: fear. She checked her phone again and sent a text.

"Let's dance," I suggested, eager to get her mind off Trevor for a second.

Pulling her arm, I dragged her out to the dance floor. Jess followed close behind us, and we began to dip and move spastically to the latest Billboard hit. This is what I loved about Olympic State: my best friends and me. Despite being independent women and set on very different paths, we always came back together in the end.

Two familiar hands grabbed my hips, drawing me against the firm body I knew so well. I gyrated close to him as his hands held me tightly. It was the perfect end to the semester. Laughing, dancing, being together. The deejay called out for karaoke participants and we took the cue to flee the dance floor, heading back to our booth.

Brett sat, guarding our pitcher and jackets, and looking mildly put out that we'd left him there alone.

"I tried to get him to come out there, but he said he doesn't dance," Liam whispered against my hair.

That hardly mattered. None of us could dance, but

I resolved to stay in the booth for the rest of the evening anyway. We managed to procure another pitcher while Cassie checked her phone again.

"I'm going to head over there," she told us after another hour. Poor thing. She couldn't be having too much fun hanging out with her best friends and their boyfriends. I'd been in that situation myself these last few months, so I gave her a hug and watched as she pushed her way through the crowd to the exit.

"When do you leave?" I asked Jess.

She shrugged, casting a sideways glance at Brett. "I haven't decided yet. Things are kinda up in the air."

It occurred to me then that a single word hadn't passed between the two of them all night. Later—in the morning maybe—I'd ask her about what was going on. Brett wasn't much of a partier, but this was morose, even for him. For now though, I downed the remnants of my beer and turned to Liam.

"I'm exhausted. Take me home?" I asked him.

Something wicked gleamed in his eyes as he nodded at my request. "I've been waiting all night for you to say that."

"I'll see you both in the morning," Jess said as we stood to leave.

"I'll make waffles," Liam promised her.

Jess winked at me, and I realized I was going home with him tonight because of her. She had guided me to Markson's class and nagged me to give Liam a second chance. Tomorrow, I would give her a giant hug and thank her.

As we made our way past the bar, Liam grabbed my hand and motioned for me to stop. He disappeared past the crush of bodies and returned a few moments later with a bottle of water.

"You should drink this," he suggested as he handed it me.

"Worried about my hydration?" I asked, twisting off the cap.

"A couple of beers and your meds are not a great combination." But before I could be annoyed, he added, "And I want to make sure you stay alert. I have plans for you."

A shiver ran through me, raising bumps on my skin. I liked the sound of that. The thought of taking Liam home for the night made my knees feel weak. Of course, he usually had that effect on me, but tonight there would be nothing hanging over our heads. My new medications were working wonders, I was through finals, and I'd managed to pass all my classes per Tara's orders. Best of all, I was staying in Olympic Falls.

Who needed Garrett's? The party was at home tonight. In my bed. With Liam.

He hooked a finger in the back pocket of my jeans as I led the way out of the bar. Night had fallen while we were inside, and the world was painted in shades of deep blue. A chill cut through the air, so I tugged my jacket together and pressed against him. There was no rush as we walked toward my apartment under the star-speckled sky. When we reached my complex though, it was a different story, Liam took the stairs two at a time, bouncing on his heels as I struggled to unlock the door.

As soon as were inside, he lifted me off my feet, cupping my ass and pressing me against the door, pushing it shut behind us. His lips moved slowly against mine, soft and certain, but I felt greedy, hungry for more after weeks of stress and distraction. I clutched his neck and slipped my tongue into his mouth, licking against the back of his teeth, biting gently on his lower lip. Liam groaned and carried me into the bedroom.

He laid me on the bed softly, but it wasn't an act of caution. He watched me with reverence as I unbuttoned my shirt in slow, precise movements, letting it fall open to reveal a lacy bra I'd worn just for him.

"I want to stare at you all night," he murmured as he stripped off his shirt to reveal his chiseled chest and carved abdomen. I could same the same thing to him. Except for the fact that his jeans hung low on his hips, showcasing the deep V cutting down past the waistline of his pants.

"This is a hands-on exhibit," I told him, wiggling off my shirt and tossing it to the floor.

"In that case." Liam bent forward and tugged off my pants in a swift, urgent motion as he dropped to his knees, positioning himself between my dangling legs. He hooked his arms around my thighs, kissing along them until his lips brushed against me, sending a tremor of anticipation through my body. Blowing softly against my sensitive skin, he trailed up to kiss along my pelvis. "I want to worship you."

"I won't stop you." My words came out as moans as he bit down on the elastic edge of my thong, drawing it slowly off me until his hands removed it completely. He stayed there, nestled between my legs, dropping kisses along my skin as my core coiled and tightened, ready for him. Instead, he gripped my left leg and urged me on to my stomach, pushing me further up on the bed and spreading my legs apart. My hands clutched the sheets and he continued his exploration along the curves of my back down to my ass. His fingers traced its outline, their marks scorching into me, leaving a trail of fire and longing in their wake until they tracked down between my legs. He lingered there, massaging long caresses across the sensitive area as my muscles tensed and pleasure mounted in my body.

"I need you," I whispered. "I need to feel you."

He wrenched my hips up to him. My chest remained flat against the mattress as he slid inside me agonizingly slowly. I was full of him, stretched to the line between pain and pleasure as he slipped in and out of me in hard deep strokes.

"I could do this all day," he said, and I could feel his gaze on me.

"Promise?" I flipped my head to the side to watch him as he moved against me, our eyes meeting as I moaned his name, and he met my call by plunging faster and farther, his hard abdomen smacking against the soft flesh of my ass. He stopped, leaving me empty and swollen, but only to flip me over so that our eyes could meet.

"I want to see you, Jillian," he murmured, his words half whispered, half growled.

As he reached for my thighs, something animal took over in me, and I pushed him onto his back, settling in on top of him with the sort of graceful expertise that would have been a little embarrassing with anyone else but him. Liam and I fit together so smoothly, so easily, that I allowed my body to make the decisions for me.

"Even better," he said, staring at me in wonder as I took charge. Our eyes stay locked together as he grasped my hips, urging me to slow down, and when I did, he reached for my shoulders and drew me down for a gentle kiss. He released me immediately, and I sat up, reveling in having control of him for the moment. Seeing Liam pinned beneath me gave me a wild thrill that sent my head flying back, loosening my hair to fall over my shoulders.

His hands gripped me tighter at the exact moment that my body tightened, and my orgasm burst through me, splintering through every piece of me in glorious surges of pleasure. My name was a whisper on his lips. A promise that in this moment we were whole and infinite.

Liam wrapped his arms around my waist and drew me to the bed without leaving me. We lay in near-silence, the only noise our quick shallow breath. Although I was sure the rapid beat of my heart vibrated in the air around us.

The stillness of the dark left room for thoughts of tomorrow and the months ahead. I tried to push them away, to ignore the burning ache that consumed me at the thought of the end of next semester. There would be no celebrating for me then, but, I argued to myself, that was months away. I was sure to fuck things up before then.

"What's wrong, chicken?" Liam asked in a whisper. I realized then that my entire body was tense, rigid with self-doubt and fear.

"I was thinking about next semester," I said in a quiet voice.

"You were thinking about me leaving?" he guessed. He brought his hand to rest over my heart, and I thought it might collapse under the weight of our uncertain future. I would always love Liam, but I couldn't bring myself to believe the old platitude that it was better to have loved and lost. Still, I would never ask for a do-over. He was a permanent piece of my life, etched irrevocably into my heart. From now on, there would be a Before Liam and someday there might be an After Liam, but I realized then that I hoped there wouldn't be.

"How do you feel about Scotland?" he asked me.

I laughed joylessly at the suggestion. "I barely convinced Tara to let me stay at Olympic State. It might kill her if I cross the Atlantic Ocean."

"I think you would like Scotland," he continued,

ignoring my response. "We have months left before we have to make a decision."

My breath hitched at his last statement. "Before *we* have to make a decision?"

"*We. As in you and I. Together.* I know you want this to work as much as I do, and the only way it will is if we discuss things. My student visa says I'm going back to Scotland in May, but that's a piece of paper, chicken." His arms tightened around my waist as he spoke, as though he was waiting for someone to try to rip us apart.

"The U.S. government might think differently," I said, but even though I knew there were complicated decisions ahead of us, I felt safe and reassured in his embrace.

"People have fallen in love on different continents before," he said in a soft voice. "That's how we became a global community."

"But —"

"We have time to figure things out, and I promise we will. You aren't getting rid of me so easily, Jillian Nichols," he promised and I relaxed into his arms. "Not when I finally caught you."

It was silly to be worrying about this now when we were together, so I rolled over to face him. Minutes—maybe hours—passed as we looked into each other's eyes. We didn't need to speak to understand how far we'd come over the last few months. The "we" he spoke of was a fixed point in time that would define us both for as far ahead as

I could see. And while part of me wanted to reject that and spare myself the chance of future heartache, I knew I was as much a part of him as he was of me.

Liam's brought his lips to mine to seal the unspoken vow flickering between us. Our limbs tangling together, our breathing slowed until we were dependent on each other for the air we needed to survive. No matter what happened in the coming months, it was worth it for this one moment. His kiss ravaged me, rendering me incapable of any thought, except one.

He had finally caught me indeed.

TEACHING ROMAN, the long-awaited next book in the Good Girls Don't Series arrives on bookshelves November 7, 2017!

The Good Girls are back! Jessica Stone has her future figured out until life throws her for a loop. When she's dragged against her will on a vacation to Mexico, she runs into the last person she expects: her hot, former professor Roman Markson. As sparks fly the pair decide to break the rules for one week. But can what happened in Mexico stay there when something fun turns into something more?

Acknowledgments

A number of people offered encouragement, advice and enthusiasm while I was working on this project. I am blessed to be surrounded by an incredible team. Thank you to Elise Lee and Joshua Albin for the many hours they've spent with my words. A big thanks to Stephanie Sanders for enthusiasm and support.

I'm fortunate to be represented by the formidable Louise Fury, who is the best agent a girl could ask for, and her excellent team at The Bent Agency.

Lastly, thank you for reading this book, for taking a chance. You make writing through the long hours worth the stress and weight gain and craziness. I can't wait to share more stories with you. Our adventures are only beginning.

About The Author

Geneva Lee is the *New York Times*, *USA Today*, and internationally best-selling author of over a dozen novels. Her best-selling Royals Saga has sold over one million copies worldwide. She travels frequently with her husband and two children but calls Washington state home.

Learn more at:
www.GenevaLee.com

Lightning Source UK Ltd.
Milton Keynes UK
UKHW040929290819
348779UK00001B/94/P